Copyright © 2019 by C. M. Kent

For more information,
Email: c.m.kent.publishing@gmail.com

First Paperback Edition February 2019
First E-Book Edition February 2019

Book design by C. M. Kent

ISBN 9798849478050 (Paperback)

Miami Connections: Secrets and Lies

Part Two

By

C. M. Kent

Also by C. M. Kent

Miami Connections Novel Series

Miami Connections: Secrets and Lies. Part One
Miami Connections: Secrets and Lies. Part Two
Miami Connections: The Domino Effect. Part One
Miami Connections: The Domino Effect. Part Two
Miami Connections: Redemption. Part One
Miami Connections: Redemption. Part Two
Miami Connections: Liberation. Part One
Miami Connections: Liberation. Part Two
Miami Connections: Peace, Love, & Retribution. Part
One
Miami Connections: Peace, Love, & Retribution. Part
Two

Love Novel Series

Love & Destiny
Falling
Truly, Madly, Deeply
Heavenly
Love & Heartbreak
Bound 2 Love
Crazy in Love
Just Us

Playlists relating to all books available on Spotify
C. M. Kent (Author)

Dedicated to
The Magic City

Chapter 11

The sound of a phone ringing snaps Enrique out of the daze he's been in for the last hour or so. What the fuck? Where am I? Looking down at the GPS, he realizes he's just off Alice Island's coast in Bimini! Fuck, this is not good! Pulling back on the throttle, he takes the flip phone from his pocket and opens it to find a missed call from Ziv.

Why can't this guy just leave me the hell alone?

Before he gets the chance to flip the phone shut, it rings again; this time, it's Gutiérrez, the only other contact on the phone. He sets the boat into idle, allowing the waves and current to take control. "What? What do you want?" Enrique snaps down the phone.

"We now have the information we need to get your father back," Gutiérrez says, trying to stay calm. As much as he understands why Enrique is behaving the way he is, he can't help but be angry with the entire situation himself. He can't believe José has even let this happen. He's way too clever for this.

"Tell me then... tell me everything," Enrique demands.

"Not now. Not over the phone. Come back to us, and we will explain everything." Gutiérrez hangs up the phone, not giving Enrique a chance to respond or reject the idea. He needs him to come back to the dock.

Slamming the phone shut, Enrique throws it across the deck, and it lands on the floor at the back of the boat. "UUUGGGHHH!" He growls before turning and lashing out at the seating area. "MOTHERFUCKER!!! FOR FUCK'S SAKE!!!" He yells, punching the chairs as his frustration radiates out of him. He's being pushed so far beyond his limits; he doesn't know what to do with himself. "FUCK!!"

With rage pulsating through his veins, he runs both hands through his jet-black hair; he needs to focus and calm the fuck down. Taking a deep breath, he sits down on one of the chairs. Leaning forward, he rests his elbows on his knees and runs his hands through his hair once more. With his hands resting on the back of his neck, he closes his eyes and tries to regain some kind of equilibrium; he needs to figure out his next move. What do I do? Do I go back? Can I even face it? Do I even want to know what's happened?

Lifting his head slowly, he takes in his surroundings in a desperate attempt to disburse some of his anger. As he sits quietly on the boat, he glances around the warm turquoise waters, feeling the sun on his face with only the sound of the gentle current lapping against the hull. He's nearly in the Bahamas. Apparently, this is where his father's being held, and right now, he could be so close to where he is. For a second, he allows a fantasy to flow through his mind; he could find out where his father is and simply go and get him. But he knows that isn't a possibility, plus he would be putting himself in so much danger. He can't do this alone, and as much as he hates to admit it, he needs their help. He knows he doesn't have a choice. He has to turn back.

A sense of resentment is beginning to hang around every thought of his father. This feeling of resentment as well as frustration is becoming an all too regular occurrence at the moment. He's not used to feeling this way about José. He's always been the perfect father; his rock. It feels so unnatural to him, but how can he feel anything else right now?

He resigns himself to the fact that he has to see this story through to the bitter end. What other option does he have? He prays that this isn't going to affect his relationship and the trust he's beginning to build back up with Kristie. Can he even tell her what's going on right now? Will she even understand? He doubts it. Who would?

In his mind, he can hear her telling him that he needs to call the police, and this is something he would completely understand. That would be the advice he would give anybody else. Hell, it's the advice he keeps giving himself; but it's not that simple. Calling the cops could be a matter of life and death for José, and right now, he simply can't take the risk.

All he can do at this moment is give Gutiérrez and Ziv the benefit of the doubt. After all, according to them, they have answers to what's happening, and by the sounds of things, they have a plan.

With his decision made, he heads back to the helm and starts up the engine. He takes a look at Bimini in the distance and contemplates asking Kristie if she would like to run away with him to his Caribbean hideaway. They could live happily ever after in the tropical oasis that would become their home for the rest of their lives. For a second, he visualizes them living a happy yet simple life, full of love and joy with their baby without a care in the world. But he knows that is simply nothing but a fantasy. He has no other option; he has to go back and play the game. He can't run from this. He has to face the music.

He looks at the clock on the console; it's 9:30am. It will take at least two hours to get back to Stiltsville, depending on the weather and the seas, but at least it will give him a little time to contemplate what the best course of action will be. Pushing the throttle forward, he turns the boat and points it back toward Miami; back into the storm that is his life.

During the trip back to Miami, the wind had picked up, making the sea choppier than he would have liked, causing the journey to take longer than usual to reach his destination. It's now midday, and the sun is hiding behind the building clouds; he expects it to be raining within the next hour.

As he sees Stiltsville in the distance, he pulls back on the throttle and slows to a crawl. He's close enough to be seen if people are looking out for him, which knowing Ziv and Gutiérrez, they probably have the entire bay on watch. They always seem to be ten steps ahead.

Drifting in the current, he confirms with himself if this is what he really wants to do. Is he just getting himself deeper and deeper into this mess? He's so full of mixed emotions he doesn't know how he feels from one minute to the next. And right now, he's asking himself why he's even bothering. He can't help but feel like he's just along for the ride and has little or no choice other than just to accept it.
Shaking his head after the final check-in with himself, he pushes the throttle forward and heads back to the Stiltsville dock, and whatever craziness is about to happen.

As he closes in on the jetty, he can see Ziv standing on the wooden platform with someone else. Probably one of their goons, Enrique thinks to himself. Slowing down, Enrique pulls up alongside the jetty of the yellow wooden stilt house. Ziv jumps down onto the rear of the boat, the goon jumps down onto the front, and they both quickly tie her up. Ziv heads toward the helm where Enrique is standing. He has a stern look on his face, or is it just his standard look? Enrique can't tell. Before he has a chance to speak, Ziv places a hand on each of his shoulders, and grips them tightly, then he gives Enrique a firm shake.

"We have good news!" Ziv almost seems excited to be telling Enrique this. This is a surprise to Enrique, as he doesn't think that Ziv is even capable of any kind of emotion. "Come with me, and Gutiérrez will explain everything that we have learned."

Taking a deep breath, Enrique nods his head and gestures for them both to get off the boat. Following Ziv, he climbs up onto the dock, and the men move quickly toward the doorway. Suddenly, Enrique hears the engine to the boat startup. "What the Fuck? Why the fuck is he taking the boat?!!" Enrique exclaims.

"It's OK. You know we aren't supposed to be here. He's just going to circle around until we need him to come back. We can't be attracting the wrong type of attention out here." Ziv's response is matter of fact but also logical.

"You'd better not be fucking with me!" Enrique replies sternly as he watches on nervously. His gut is telling him to tell Ziv to stop the man from taking it, but as he thinks about it, it does make sense, but he doesn't have to be happy about it. He just wants to find out where his father is, and according to them, they have the answers, and at the moment, he is willing to do anything to get to the bottom of this.

Stepping through the doorway, it takes his eyes a moment to adjust to the dim light inside. There's no light in the wooden house, except for what's coming through the cracks between the boards covering up the windows.

As he looks around, he can see an old tatty sofa that looks like it has been there since the '60s, and the remains of a bar is against the far wall. Gutiérrez is standing by the bar, wiping his hands with a towel that's covered in what looks like blood.

As Enrique's eyes study the space, he sees only one other person standing back in the shadows. It is then that he notices a lone chair by one of the boarded-up windows with a dark stain underneath it. It's difficult to see what it is in the poor light, but he's safe in the knowledge he really doesn't want to know either. The optimism he felt when he arrived at the dock is starting to fade. This is again, way more than he really cares to be involved in; he's made a huge mistake.

"Just tell me what's going on so that I can get the fuck out of here." Enrique's had enough. He just wants to get this over with, so he can go back home, and right now, he doesn't give a fuck if he has to swim back to his building; he has to get the fuck out of there.

Gutiérrez answers without turning to face him. "I have questioned Manolo. He now understands the importance of us getting your father back."

As he listens to Gutiérrez, Enrique starts to smell urine. He looks at the floor, and with his eyes now adjusted to the light, it's apparent that Manolo had been tied to the chair and must've pissed himself during Gutiérrez's "questioning." The extent of the questioning obviously extended to torturing the guy, and Enrique can't help but feel sorry for him. But at the same time, by the sound of things, Manolo is involved in his father's disappearance and is the only link to finding José.

Gutiérrez continues talking as Enrique looks around the room.

"Manolo is going back to his boss. He's going to broker a deal for the release of your father. He wasn't easily convinced that it was the right thing to do. But we came to an understanding, shall we say." A dark, sinister grin spreads across Gutiérrez's face. The shadows in the room make him look every bit of the gangster he so obviously is; he's in his zone.

"How do we know that we can trust him? It seems like we're placing a lot of faith in a man whom you have just beaten the shit out of! What's to stop him taking his revenge out on my father?" Enrique asks.

"Oh, don't you worry. He won't be doing anything that we don't want him to do!"

The evil glint in Gutiérrez's eyes sends shivers down Enrique's spine. He doesn't want to ask the question, but his curiosity gets the better of him. "What do you mean? How can you be so sure?" Enrique stills himself, waiting for the inevitable response that he knows he's going to hate.

"We have his family, Enrique. He's going to do everything we want... he's not going to give us any trouble at all," Gutiérrez says, way too calmly for Enrique's liking, as he walks across to Ziv and pats him on the back.

"What the FUCK! You can't go kidnapping people to justify getting my father back. This is insanity! What the fuck is wrong with you all?" Enrique fails to contain his rage and disgust. "You're all fucking crazy! Surely we could have just paid him to help us?"

"You're delusional, Enrique. This isn't how our world works. It isn't a boardroom negotiation where an extra couple of hundred thousand is going to swing the deal. This is about leverage. They had it when they took your father... and we've taken some of it back by taking Manolo's family. He now has a vested interest in getting your father back to us alive. This is how this works." Gutiérrez states in a low, matter-of-fact tone. "And honestly, I don't give a fuck if you like my methods or not."

Enrique knows he's brought this on himself. He invited this man into the situation when he contacted him, rather than the police. But he still doesn't have to like the situation or accept it, and he has every right to voice his disgust at these monsters' methods.

"Fine! Whatever you say! I'm leaving!" He snipes. "Are you gonna get me the boat, or shall I fucking swim back?! I really don't give a fuck either way! You've obviously got this under control, and you don't need me anymore," Enrique says sarcastically. He can't believe these morons. How can they think this was a good idea?

Gutiérrez nods to the man behind him. Without saying a word, he walks out of the room to the dock. "Enrique, this is how this has to be. You understand the boardroom... I understand the streets. Like I keep telling you, this is my world, and this is how I do business. You can go, and I will be in touch." Gutiérrez says. He turns to Ziv. "Go with him. Keep eyes on him at all times. I will contact you both when I have more information."

Gutiérrez turns and walks into the far room. Enrique knows that there's no point arguing with him, so he stays quiet. Looking into the room, the darkness makes it difficult for Enrique to see where Gutiérrez has gone until he sees a small flickering flame in the far corner. He has just lit a cigarette, and the slight glow of the embers is the only thing that gives away his position in the room. As he turns back to face Ziv, Enrique's face and body language have given him away.

"Trust us! I know this isn't how you want it to be. But I promise you; this is the best way. We have dealt with these situations before… many times." Ziv's confidence improves Enrique's mood but only slightly.

"How am I supposed to trust you? You said you had information about where my father is. You have clearly lied to me. Let's just go. I've had enough of this shit today," Enrique says with irritation.

"We have set things up so we can get the information. Plus, we had to get you to come back somehow. We will get your father home… don't you worry," Ziv tries to reassure Enrique but doesn't succeed.

"That's not having the information, though, is it?" Enrique snipes. "This whole situation is crazy. It's like I'm stuck in a perpetual nightmare." He shakes his head with disbelief. "Ugh… I just want to get the fuck home!" Enrique can't deal with it anymore. He needs to get away from all this. He absolutely detests the way they have dealt with the situation.

Enrique heads out onto the dock with Ziv. The bright sunshine forces Enrique to squint his eyes while he adjusts to the brightness. Another thing he forgot this morning; his shades. Apparently, his prediction of it raining is wrong. Typical Miami weather, you never know what it will do from one minute to the next, even a Miami native like Enrique sometimes struggles to read the skies.

As they head down the sun-bleached wooden jetty, he sees the boat closing in on the dock. Thank God, Enrique thinks. As it pulls alongside, he jumps down onto the stern as Ziv holds it in place. Gutiérrez's man leaves the helm and passes Enrique without a word. As he climbs off the boat, Ziv pushes off and steps down onto the stern as well.

Feeling relieved to be heading home, Enrique pushes the throttle forward and heads back to the marina. Ziv stands alongside him as they head back along the coast; the awkwardness and tension crackles in the air like a lightning storm.

Looking to his right, he can see families walking along the ocean wall at Cape Florida. Key Biscayne is popular on the weekends with fishermen as well. Enrique can see children looking into buckets the fishermen have next to them on the ground. He can just about see the excitement on their faces as they find the catch of the day in the containers. This reminds him of when he used to do the same thing with his parents. The memory catches in his throat; it's both special and painful all at the same time. He's lost in the moment until Ziv taps him on the shoulder. "Where did you go?" Ziv asks.

"What do you mean? Where did I go? When?" Enrique asks with confusion.

"Earlier when you left me on the dock?"

Ziv almost sounds upset that Enrique had left him there. Maybe this guy does have feelings, Enrique thinks to himself. He takes a few moments to try to put the words of his answer into order. "What happened at the marine stadium was horrific enough... and I couldn't see or be a part of whatever you were gonna do to Manolo. It's not who I am... it's not the way I handle things," Enrique says with disgust in his voice. "I didn't plan on where I was going... but I ended up in Bimini."

"That would explain why I couldn't get hold of you on the cell for a couple of hours. Look, I get your struggles. This isn't your life; how can you understand this? But I must say, you've done better than I had expected you to. But as the Americans say, 'we are in the home stretch.' Your father will be back home soon." Ziv sounds so sure of what he is saying.

"Let's hope you're right!"

"I am right!"

A little further along the coastline, Enrique remembers he still has Ziv's gun in the back of his jeans. "Here!" Enrique hands Ziv his gun. "I won't be needing this anymore," He's glad he remembered. He should give it to him now, away from prying eyes, as opposed to in the parking lot of the marina. You never know who might be watching. It's a bit different in the early hours of the morning when it's still dark.

Ziv takes the weapon and slides it in the back of his jeans. "Don't forget the vest too." Enrique looks at Ziv with confusion. "The vest I gave you for protection earlier?"

"Oh yeah," Enrique replies as he remembers. Still controlling the boat, he quickly removes his hoodie, unfastens the vest, hands it to Ziv, and puts his top back on. With that, he pushes the throttle forward. The quicker he gets back to the marina, the quicker he can get away from this shit. All he wants to do is get back into the safety of his apartment.

Suddenly, he feels a desperate need to talk to Kristie; he needs something positive in his life right now. When he gets back to the penthouse, he's going to text her and then have a workout, he decides. He needs to get his routine and life back on track, plus he needs to release some of this frustration and anger. A workout is the best solution for this. It will help him get his head straight. After all, it isn't like he can sit down and talk to anyone about all of this.

Returning back to the marina, Enrique slows the boat down, turns it around, and slowly reverses it back into the slip it was docked before this godforsaken journey. Ziv is already out and tying her up to the dock as Enrique shuts off the engines.

As Enrique steps onto the dock, Ziv asks. "The penthouse under yours is empty? Yes?" This is a statement as much as a question. It's apparent that Ziv already knows the answer.

"It is. Why?" Enrique asks, but he guesses what Ziv is about to say.

"I need to set up in there. Update your security and keep you safe," Ziv tells him.

"Not a good idea," Enrique replies firmly. "Absolutely not. I'm not bringing this shit to my building… to my home! No way!"

"It's not like that. I will be discreet. We just need you to be safe. We can't have you being snatched as well. They obviously know who you are now, too. Plus, I will arrange the best security for all your family, Kristie and her family too. They will also be discreet. They won't even know they are there." Ziv's voice has a hint of concern.

Enrique thinks for a second. "Fine," he snaps. "Like I've got any real choice in the matter... after what you've done today, I'm probably more at risk now than ever." He pauses for a second before continuing. "I want the best of the best security... better than the Presidents... and I'm not fucking around here." He points. "Nothing... and I mean nothing will happen to anyone else in my family, to Kristie, to me, or Kristie's family! Do I make myself clear?" His tone is one of warning.

"You got it. You have my word. Nothing will happen to any of you," Ziv replies with firm confidence.

"I must be out of my fucking mind trusting you with this... but how the fuck am I supposed to explain any of this to my security company?" Enrique feels like he needs his head looking at for this. But what else was he supposed to do? He has some of the best security in the world, but right now, he doesn't feel he can involve them in this.

"Trust me, Enrique. They are the best."

"Good! Let's go." Enrique heads along the dock back toward the SUVs. Turning back to Ziv, he says, "Whatever you need to bring into the building... do it via the service entrance. I don't need you and your thugs scaring the residents, do you understand?" Enrique is in no mood.

"OK. You got it. I will contact you later so you can allow me access to the service area. I will leave you now. I have things to arrange. We will speak soon." Ziv slaps Enrique hard on the back and walks away toward his SUV.

Enrique calls after Ziv and runs back toward him. "Once the security detail is in place. Text me the infomation."

"Of course. You carry on your life as normal. These guys will know where you are at all times and follow you. You won't see them. They are the best covert security in the business. Trust me," Ziv reassures Enrique.

"My whole family, Kristie, and her family... plus our friends! Not just me!" He warns. "And you better make sure that you're right. I don't want to cause alarm to any of my family, especially Kristie. Nobody can know they are there. Do you hear me? Nobody!" Enrique says, almost threatening Ziv.

"Don't worry. I will have everything covered," Ziv says with a smile.

"You better had."

Climbing into his SUV, Enrique pauses for a moment to take stock of the ever-escalating situation. How have we gone from my father's kidnapping to murder, torture, and more kidnapping? He dreads to think that this situation could get any worse, but he also fears that it will get worse before it gets any better!

Taking a deep, steadying breath, he starts the engine and heads back to Alta Vita. He needs to get back to his sanctuary.

Chapter 12

As he arrives at Alta Vita, Enrique opens the glove compartment, reaches in, and takes out his cell. He exits the SUV and lightly throws the keys to Jorge. "Park her up, please, Jorge," he says.

"Sure thing Sir," Jorge replies.

In a world of his own, he heads through the lobby and checks his cell for calls or messages relating to his father; there's nothing. He would have taken his phone with him in case somebody were to contact him, but he didn't want to risk being tracked in any way; good job too!

Reaching the elevator, he checks the time on his cell screen; it's 3pm already. It's been a long shitty day! A flashback of the bloodbath he witnessed being played out only a few hours ago tries to consume his entire being, but he refuses to entertain it for a second. He rapidly diverts his thoughts to something way more positive.

With his shaking hands, he types a message to Kristie.

Hey Sweetheart,
How are you today?
How are you feeling?
When can I see you again?
I don't want to rush things, but I miss you.
I love you.

E
xxxxx

As he hits send, he hopes that what he's just text her makes sense. He wishes he could have checked in with her sooner, but it's been impossible to do so. He puts his phone back into his pocket and waits for the elevator to reach the top floor. Exiting it, he makes his way to his front door, opens it, and walks straight through to the kitchen.

Through the adrenalin that's screaming through his veins, he begins to grow anxious about somebody finding the bloodbath left at the marine stadium. As he reaches the kitchen, he finds the remote and turns on the TV, which is mounted on the kitchen wall. As he switches to the news channel, he prepares himself for the impending report of the bodies being discovered at the marine stadium.

With his eyes glued to the TV, as he stands in front of it, he sees nothing relating to the stadium. After about fifteen minutes, he changes to another news channel and watches for a while longer; nothing! Ziv did say that it would all be cleaned up, but Enrique can't help but worry that somebody may have seen something or perhaps some kind of trace would be left behind; but it would appear that they really did clear everything away. How? It doesn't even bear thinking about.

Placing the remote down on the kitchen counter, he decides he can't be dealing with Ziv anymore today. Thinking it's best to get it over with now, so he could forget about him for the rest of the day, he picks up his phone and calls Armando to arrange access to the service area for Ziv and his crew. Without mentioning any names, of course, he explains that they're coming in to do some work on Penthouse B for him.

Taking the burner phone out of his pocket, he types a message to Ziv.

Access to Penthouse B and service area approved.
Your company is Z.E.C. Securities.
You're doing an estimate for upgrading the security features.

Putting the phone down on the side, he takes a bottle of water from the refrigerator and drinks it down in one. He hasn't had a drop of anything to drink all day. Then suddenly, the flip phone buzzes on the side.

Very good.
All security in place.
Carry on as usual.
No need to notify what you are doing.
You are all covered discreetly by the best.

Enrique replies.

OK.

Thank you.

That was quick. At least it's dealt with the best way it can be right now. What else am I supposed to do, Enrique asks himself. The irony of the situation is, he has offered his father, Penthouse B, as a gift, but he refuses to take it. Enrique thought it would be a good base for him when he attends functions and gala's Downtown, but José won't accept it; he says he's happy traveling back to his home on Star Island. For a second, Enrique wonders if there's more to José's refusal of the penthouse; now he knows what he knows about his supposed secret life. There probably is, he tells himself. There's probably way more to it than I will ever know; nothing surprises me anymore.

He knows he needs to get in the gym now and work this anger and frustration out of his body before it eats him alive.

He's about to become a father, which is supposed to be such a happy time in his life, yet it's being shot to shit by his father's lies and greed. But he's had enough of it; he's not going to allow this situation to dampen the happiness and joy becoming a father brings.

It's a fact, that a part of him still wonders if this is actually true, but the more time that passes and the more he sees; he's starting to believe it is. But he's going to push against the darkness that José's disgusting secret life is trying to impose on him.

26

And the first step to pushing back is to get into some workout clothes and beat the shit out of his punch bag.

He climbs upstairs and heads to his closet. As he passes through the bedroom, he notices his bed is up against the wall, with pillows and bed linen everywhere. One of the nightstands has been knocked over too. What the fuck? He's confused. Then, through his fogginess, he remembers his early morning fit of rage. Thank God Gabriela is off this weekend, he thinks to himself. He would hate for her to find this.

He walks over to the mess, moves the super king-sized bed back into place, and rearranges the luxurious white bed linen; the bed is now made neatly just like it usually is. He picks up the nightstand and shifts it back into place before picking up the lamp and placing it on top. To his surprise, it's not damaged. Enrique has great respect for his possessions; this is so out of character for him. But it's not every day you find out your father is head of a drug cartel, and your whole life is now in tatters as a result of it.

Once the bedroom is rearranged to his satisfaction, he heads to his closet. Getting changed into a pair of sweatpants and sneakers, he heads to the gym, which is on the rooftop overlooking the pool.

He walks into his gym and looks through his music library on his phone. He selects his hip-hop playlist, consisting of Rick Ross, Meek Mill, Lil Wayne, Drake, and many more. "Ima Boss" by Meek Mill starts to play loudly through the speakers.

He moves over to the cabinet that stores towels and all his workout accessories like chalk, talc, and boxing tape. He reaches for the tape and starts to wrap his hands for protection. He's so ramped up he doesn't know what he's capable of right now. He can't ever remember feeling this way in his entire life. He needs to get rid of this feeling before it takes him over.

He opens the door to the refrigerator, which is next to the cabinet, and gets out a bottle of Fiji. He needs to remember to stay hydrated. He walks over to the punch bag and places the water on the floor close by. With the hip-hop music blaring, he bounces from side to side, clenching his fists at the same time. Then he starts to punch the bag, one fist at a time, hitting it so hard, like his life depends on it.

Going crazy, he kicks as well as punches it, over and over again. In no time, sweat is pouring down his face and naked torso. He doesn't give a fuck. He continues punching and kicking harder and faster. His breathing grows more rapid with every blow to the punch bag, which is swinging back and forth rapidly, every time he assaults it.

This continues for well over an hour. Enrique has lost track of time. He has so much built-up aggression he doesn't stop. He can't stop. It's like he's a caged animal that's fought his way out to freedom. It's so liberating for him to release everything he's been suppressing, not just over the last few days but for all the years since his mom passed. It's all coming out at this very moment.

As he pours every ounce of pent-up anger into the punch bag, his mind floods with so many questions about José. Did you have something to do with mom's death? What really happened to her? Was it you… something you did? Fuck!!! Now he's wondering if his father's secret life has something to with his mother's death. He wants to ask him so many questions. It's like everything he's believed about his life was all a lie. His whole life hasn't been real.

All he wants now is to start a new life with Kristie and their baby. No more fucking around. Yes, he's worried about his father, so, so worried. But his dad has not just put himself in this situation, he's forced Enrique into it too, and he doesn't know if he can ever forgive him for this. José has put the whole family in danger, the business, everything, and he's been doing this throughout Enrique's entire life. This is something he wonders if he will ever get over. How can he ever trust him again? He thought he was everything to his dad. He was his protector, but he was wrong. All his father has done is put him at risk by being involved in this line of business and so much more. It isn't even like he needs the money. They have both become billionaires through hard work and dedication. Why on earth does he need to get involved in a world that's so dangerous and, in Enrique's opinion, disgusting.

Enrique hates drugs. Yes, it's true; he dabbled a little as a teen but not anymore. It was pure adolescent curiosity, nothing more. But this world couldn't be further from who Enrique is or what he stands for, and his father knows that. He knows that because that's how he brought Enrique up. This is one of the reasons why this is so hard to believe.

And these people, Gutiérrez and Ziv? What kind of people are they? He can't believe his father, the gentleman he knows, is involved with murderers and drug barons. Is his father a murderer too? Most probably. Right now, nothing would surprise him. Enrique has so many questions to ask José, but he feels if he saw him now, he'd kill him himself; he's that furious with him.

Enrique continues punching the shit out of the punch bag until he finally collapses on the floor in front of it. His body has been pushed as far as it can go. The punch bag is swinging above him and then slowly comes to a standstill. He's soaked with sweat and can't move. His body is heavy. Every muscle and limb feels like lead, and his heart is beating out of his chest. The hip-hop music is still blaring through the speakers as Enrique lays on the floor in a heap panting, with sweat rolling off his body onto the floor.

After what seems like an eternity, he manages to pick himself up into the sitting position with his legs stretched out in front of him. As he tries to recover his equilibrium, he places his hands on the floor and hangs his head. Eventually, he picks up the bottle of water from the floor beside him and drinks it down before managing to stand. His sweatpants are saturated and stuck to his legs. Uneasy on his feet, he stumbles over to the refrigerator and retrieves another bottle of water, opens it, and takes a slow sip as he leans back on the cabinet.

With his breathing calm and back to a steady rhythm, he turns and leans on the cabinet with his hands, and with his head hanging, he takes deep, steadying breaths. I need to take better care of myself, Enrique tells himself silently. Not eating properly, drinking way more than he cares to admit, not sleeping, smoking too many cigars, and lack of working out is taking its toll on his body and mind. This is something that is alien to him. Working out is one of the things that helps keep his mind straight. Apart from alcohol and the occasional cigar, Enrique has a strict health and fitness regime. This is something he needs to get back on track. To him, this means he is losing control; not a feeling he tolerates well.

Eventually, he picks up his phone and unlocks it. He checks his notifications. Work has left him alone again today, which pleases him. The fact that it's a Saturday generally means nothing; his cell doesn't usually stop.

Then he notices something that stirs a familiar warmth in his heart; he has a text from Kristie. This makes him smile from ear to ear, yet it's making him nervous, too. She has taken a few hours to get back to him. This is unusual, but he knows he has to give her space. He has to give her time. It's still very soon.

Then fear tries to take over. Has he overstepped the mark by asking when he can see her again? Should he have let her come to him? He's also worried she might change her mind, even after what he promised her last night. He knows, in the past, he has made promises to her and not kept them. This was never deliberate; he tried his absolute best, but he simply wasn't capable at the time, but now is different.

He's scared that she might feel that this is just him making false promises again, which couldn't be further from the truth. He feels like something has shifted within him, and he finally has the courage to face his demons; he's never been more serious about anything in his life. Taking a deep breath, he slides his finger from the top and down the screen of his iPhone to pause the music and then selects Kristie's text.

Hey babe,
I'm great, thank you.
I feel good.
Hope you are OK, too?
Fancy brunch at Zuma tomorrow?
I love you, too.
K
xxxxx

"Thank you, God," Enrique says out loud, looking up to the ceiling.

Of course, Enrique wants to do brunch with her. And at Zuma? For sure! They love brunch at Zuma. It's incredible. Over the years, they have spent many Sunday mornings until mid-afternoon at Zuma, having the best time. He replies straight back.

Hey Beautiful!
So glad you're well.
I'm good, thank you.
Of course. I would love that.
What time?
Shall I pick you up from your place?
E
xxxxx

Within minutes she texts back.

Perfect!
Pick me up at my place.

11am?
K
xxxxx

Great!
I'll make the reservation.
I can't wait to see you, babe.
E
xxxxx

OK. Thanks, babe.
I'm looking forward to seeing you, too.
K
xxxxx

No. Thank you.
I'm so grateful you want to see me again.
Did I mention I love you?
E
xxxxx

Of course, I do.
And yes, you did. LOL.
K
xxxxx

xoxoxo
E

Enrique smiles so widely it can be seen from
space. He can't believe his luck. He's elated that his
fears were just that: fear. He's going to see the love
of his life again tomorrow, and he's so excited.

Things are heading in the right direction, although he's not entirely out of the woods yet. When he last saw Kristie, he agreed to go to therapy, and just thinking about this makes him shudder. Suddenly, he's overwhelmed with dread. But what else is he supposed to do? He has to push through it. He has to do this for both of them and their little baby. He promised Kristie he would go, and he will. She's worth going through intense therapy sessions for, as being without her is a pain he simply cannot bear; a pain a lot worse than going to therapy.

Once he's made the reservation for brunch and has a shower, Enrique lays on his super king-sized bed and looks out of the sliding glass doors. The sun is setting, painting the sky every shade of pink and orange. He's exhausted. Not sleeping properly for months and hardly at all since his father's disappearance will explain that. Plus, he's just spent however long beating the shit out of his punch bag. He needed it, though. It's helped to vent a lot of his frustration, and he's feeling slightly more centered as a result of it.

He lays on the bed alone with his thoughts; thoughts he cannot bear, but for some reason, he allows himself to dwell on them anyway. Where the fuck are you, dad? Is this really happening? Did I really watch seven people get their brains blown out right in front of me, plus a kidnapping today? What the hell is going on? Am I ever going to wake up from this nightmare?

Finally, he forces himself to snap out of the negative mindset. Gutiérrez and Ziv are on the case. They will find him. It's their world, not his. He needs to trust them to deal with it; there's no other option.

Taking a deep breath, he picks up his phone from the nightstand, selects the photo gallery icon, and browses through photos of Kristie. Over the years, he's created a collection of folders filled with perfect memories of their time together. There are many photos of Kristie, but also of them as a couple. Some from their trip to Europe last year, plus their many other vacations, also there are pictures of their nights out or days out on one of the boats. They have so many amazing memories.

Kristie is absolutely breathtaking. He's so blessed to have her in his life and so lucky that she's going to be the mother of his child. Kristie will be the best mother in the world; there's no doubt about that. She's so kind and caring and always helping people, just like she tried to help him.

Shaking off his feelings of disappointment in himself for not allowing her to help him, he tries to imagine what their future will be like together and how wonderful it will be. For a moment, Enrique wonders if the baby will be a boy or a girl, but he's happy either way.

As his eyes study Kristie's beauty on the screen of his cell, he thinks about how he simply can't wait to meet their little baby and start their journey of bringing up their child together. These thoughts help Enrique feel calm, at peace and excited for the future.

With his heart full of hope and unconditional love for Kristie and their baby, he begins to drift off to a peaceful sleep.

Chapter 13

Enrique wakes feeling disoriented. Lifting his head from the pillow, he looks around the room, trying to figure out where he is. As he realizes he's in his bedroom, he relaxes and lays his head back down for a few seconds.

Glancing over at the clock on his nightstand, he notices it's 8am. He must have slept over twelve hours. That's a first. He can't remember the last time he's slept for this long. After the previous days' events, it's a miracle, but he's been so exhausted; his body must have just shut down.

As he shifts slightly, he feels something resting on his chest. Looking down, he figures he must've fallen asleep looking at his phone, as it is sitting on his firm pecs. He hasn't moved all night. Picking up his phone, he checks it. On the lock screen, he has messages from Sánchez and García. As he unlocks his cellphone, a photo of Kristie and him on his boat just off of Key West appears. It reminds him of the feelings of peace and happiness he felt while going through photos of the two of them before he floated away into a sea of dreams, with only the love of his life, and their unborn child on his mind. He smiles at the memory. Then suddenly, out of nowhere, he feels an extreme surge of excitement rush through his entire body, forcing him to dart straight out of bed. His brain has just woken up and reminds him that he is going to brunch with Kristie, and he can't wait to see her.

As he heads to the bathroom, he plans what he's going to do with his morning. With two and a half hours before he has to leave to pick her up, he decides on a workout, the best way to start his day, plus he wants to look his best for her. But first: cafécito.

Enrique heads into his closet and quickly puts on some black sweatpants and a black t-shirt with "Fania" written across it in multi-colored letters, paying homage to some of his favorite salsa artists. Finally, he puts on his black Yeezy sneakers before running downstairs like an overexcited child and almost skipping into the kitchen.

He's so energetic this morning, he probably doesn't need the coffee, but he still goes ahead and makes some anyway; cafécito is always a good idea. Once the coffee is made, just the way he likes it, he pours some into an espresso cup. Then he opens the stainless-steel refrigerator, takes out a bottle of Smart Water, and closes the door slowly with his foot, sipping his coffee at the same time. He heads back upstairs and toward his gym on the rooftop, carrying his coffee and water.

As he enters the gym, he finishes the last of his coffee and puts the cup and water down on the cabinet. He feels a world away from how he felt when he was in here yesterday. He actually feels hope, hope for a brighter future; hope for his relationship with Kristie, and the possibility of them becoming a family together.

Putting on his reggaetón playlist, he starts up the treadmill and begins to run, picking up his pace moments later. Nicky Jam, Daddy Yankee, Wisin y Yandel, Maluma, Gente de Zona, and all his other favorite reggaetón artists blast through the speakers as he sprints. He thinks of nothing. He just runs and runs as fast as he can for about thirty minutes; sweat is pouring off him.

He slows his speed down as "El Pardon" by Nicky Jam and Enrique Iglesias finishes and "Como Soy" by Pacho, Daddy Yankee, and Bad Bunny starts pounding through the speakers. After another ten minutes of jogging, he slows to a walk, wiping his face and neck with the towel, which is hanging over the bar on the side of the treadmill.

Once he's finished on the treadmill, he starts to do some weights and abdominal work. This is much needed in his eyes, as he hasn't done a proper full workout in nearly a week; this is unheard of. In between exercises, he changes the music. He wants something light, so he chooses his '80s playlist. This consists of Phil Collins, Huey Lewis, and The News, Billy Ocean, Prince, and many others. Right now, Steve Winwood's "Higher Love" is playing. Enrique is a massive fan of the '80s. He has started to collect and restore a few original collectibles from that era, including a Wellcraft Scarab 38' KV and a white Ferrari Testarossa.

He also has an extensive original vinyl collection, which seems to be increasing on a weekly basis. Miami Vice is one of his favorite shows, not that he gets much time to watch TV, but when he does, he loves to watch a few episodes during those rare moments of downtime.

Not only does he love the show, but he also loves seeing Miami in the '80s. He always finds himself appreciating how well preserved so much of Miami is, especially the Art Deco architecture. Miami was beautiful in the '80s, but he also loves Miami now. Enrique loves his city, Miami has been through so much over the years, but that only adds to her charm.

As he finished his stretches, "Land of Confusion" by Genesis is playing. Ummm… the title to this song is very apt, Enrique thinks for a second. Then he dismisses the thought as quickly as it came. He feels so good to be back in his gym and working out; taking control of his life again. In fact, despite all the shit that's going on around him, he feels on top of the world. As strange as it seems to Enrique that he feels this way, he's going to enjoy it. He needs a break from all the bullshit that has gone on relating to his father. He's going to see the love of his life and the mother of his baby, and he simply can't wait.

Back inside the penthouse, his Marc Anthony playlist plays through his sound system. He has the speakers inbuilt into the ceilings of every room throughout the penthouse. Enrique sings along to the songs as he takes a shower and gets ready for his very special date.

He can't help but dance to the salsa music. Enrique loves to dance. It's in his blood. He walks into the closet to decides on what to wear to meet Kristie. He opts for a beige Armani suit with a light blue shirt and pocket square, which he prepares into a peaked fold. For shoes, he chooses his dark tan Guccis.

Opening his watch drawer, he decides on his gold Audemars Piguet, the same one he wore the other night, as it complements his look superbly. With his hair styled to perfection, and his face clean-shaven, he sprays on a little of his Chanel cologne, and with his body pumped up from his workout; he's good to go. Enrique feels so good, better than he has in, well, forever. Thoughts of the shit storm that is his father try to put a black cloud on his blissful feeling of contentment, but he pushes them straight out of his mind. He's had enough of his father's bullshit trying to ruin his life. No more!

Enrique calls down to the valet and asks for his black Range Rover to be brought around. He feels it's still sensible to blend in, although he's really feeling his Rolls Royce. He loves his Range Rover, but he likes to change it up when it comes to the car he drives.

He heads out of the penthouse, picking up his blue mirrored Aviator sunglasses on the way, and calls the elevator. For a moment, he shudders at the thought of Ziv being camped out in penthouse B but takes a deep breath and tries to justify it as him having no choice right now. What else can he do? He hates it. He despises the whole godforsaken situation, but he has absolutely no choice right now.

In the elevator, he sends a group message to his friends Sánchez and García.

Hey!
Sorry for just getting back.
Been super busy with work.
Will update you soon.
E.

Vague and to the point. Aside from updates about Leon, they don't need to know anything right now. Plus, this is nothing unusual. He would do this often due to work commitments. Running a multibillion-dollar company is a lot of work, and they understand this; they have their own businesses to run. They know how it is. They won't think anything is out of the ordinary; he just needs to check in with them. He doesn't want them to worry, as he hasn't got back to their first lot of texts.

Once in the car, his phone links to the sound system and continues to play Marc Anthony. "Vivir

Mi Vida" starts to play as he pulls onto Brickell. He turns it up and sings along, dancing in his seat and tapping his hands on the steering wheel to the beat. The words mean more to him now than ever. The song is all about how you only have one life, and you should live it, and this is what he is going to do. Thoughts of his father's kidnap, the clandestine meets with various cartel members, murders, another kidnap, and José's sickening lifestyle, are trying to force their way to the surface, but he is shooting them down before they get a chance to take over. He has to focus on one thing at a time, and right now, he will focus on Kristie and their baby. As far as he's concerned, his father can go to hell right now.

There's a buildup of traffic as he gets further down Brickell, but it doesn't bother him. He has left plenty of time to get to South Beach, and nothing is going to ruin his day. As he turns right off Biscayne Boulevard, he accelerates up the ramp and joins the MacArthur Causeway. The bridge is clear, which pleases Enrique even more. As he picks up speed, he checks in his rearview to see if he can see anybody following him; he can't see anything out of the ordinary. Ziv's right; whoever his security is, they're very discreet, and it better stay that way, he thinks to himself.

Once over the bridge, he slows and makes a right onto Alton Road and heads toward South Pointe Drive, where Kristie's apartment is located. He actually has butterflies in his stomach; he's that excited. He pulls into the entrance of the parking lot. The gate has license plate recognition, and he's thankful Kristie still at least has the Range Rover as an authorized car. As the gate lifts, he drives in and finds a space, then heads to the elevator and calls it. He types in her security code, and the elevator whisks him up to her apartment. Once the elevator doors sweep open, he walks the short distance to her apartment, rings the doorbell, and waits.

Kristie opens the door, and smiles sweetly as she greets him. She looks absolutely stunning. She's wearing a light pink fitted dress, which hangs just above the knee, and black four-and-a-half-inch Jimmy Choo sandals. Her dark hair is lightly curled, and her make-up is perfectly applied, not too much, but just enough, just like always. Her look is accessorized with simple diamond earrings, a platinum Cartier Love Bracelet, and a black Hermès Birkin bag. Kristie is holding her black oversized Wayfarer sunglasses in her hand, ready for the Miami morning sunlight.

"Wow!" Enrique gasps. "Wow!" he says again. "You look sensational. So beautiful." He reaches his hand to her face and brushes the back of his fingers down her left cheek before leaning in for a tender kiss. They both close their eyes, savoring the moment. As they open their eyes slowly, they smile against each other's lips. Enrique kisses Kristie once more before looking at her with a huge smile and says. "Are you ready to go, or would you like me to come in and wait?" His eyes are giving him away. He's looking at her like he wants to stay with her in her apartment and make love all day long. Forget about brunch, he thinks to himself. We can order take out and lose ourselves in each other like we used to. But no, he has to take things slowly as she asked, but as always, he finds her completely irresistible. He kisses her again, putting his arms around her waist.

"I'm ready." She smiles. Kristie knows how Enrique feels, and she feels the same way too, but they both need time. "And thank you, babe. You look gorgeous." She kisses him once more. "Shall we go?"

"Sure," he says, taking her hand. He can't help but feel disappointed, but he knows it's the right thing to do. He calls the elevator, and it's still on her floor. The doors open, and they step in.

"How are you feeling today, mi amor?" Enrique asks, standing opposite Kristie, brushing her cheek with the back of his fingers once more, then kissing it tenderly.

"I'm great, thanks," she replies with a smile, looking deeply into his eyes.

As they hold their gaze, the sexual tension between them is palpable. They're standing so close to each other; close enough for Kristie to know what Enrique wants, and she wants it too.

Enrique reaches both hands to her face, cups it gently, and rests his forehead on hers. As they close their eyes, they can feel the undeniable connection between them; it's just as strong as before, if not stronger.

Suddenly, the elevator arrives at the parking lot of the condominium, snapping them out of their intimate moment. They quickly realize where they are, as they had forgotten for a moment. They have a habit of getting lost in each other, to the point where it feels like they are the only two people in the world.

Stepping out of the elevator, they walk to the SUV. The car unlocks automatically, and Enrique opens the passenger door for Kristie. He holds her hand as she steps up into the car and sits down. He pulls the seatbelt out for her, and she clicks it into place. He leans in for another kiss before closing the door, and walks around to the driver's side, climbs in, and his phone links up to the cars' sound system. He selects "Nos Fuimos Lejos" by December Bueno and Enrique Iglesias, one of their favorite songs; he can't think of a song that's more fitting. It reminds him of his feelings for Kristie; it always has, and she knows it.

As he reverses out of the space and heads out of the parking lot onto the street, the Latin urban beat is playing through the speakers. Enrique turns to Kristie and smiles. Smiling back, she knows what he's thinking, and she feels the same way.

As they drive onto the bridge, they have a view of the Port of Miami and Downtown on the left, and on the right, they have Star Island and other islands like Palm Island. It's such a beautiful drive, but Enrique can't help but think of his missing father as they drive past the bridge for Star Island.

Unbeknown to Enrique, as the involuntary thoughts enter his mind, his grip on Kristie's hand gets tighter. She looks at him and grips his hand back. Luckily, she doesn't say anything. In fairness, he's surprised with how well he's handled himself in front of Kristie. He knows he's a pro at burying his problems, but this is way beyond anything he could ever imagine, and she has a way of knowing when something's wrong with him.

He prays that he can continue to protect Kristie from all the worry and anxiety he's going through. He would never want her to be burdened with any of this horror. Enrique's been subjected to some of the most horrific situations over these past few days, and right now, it would appear that he's in complete shock and denial. But if that's what's going to hold him together, for now, he will take it any day over losing control and blowing everything with Kristie.

Today is another day in paradise. The climate is typical Miami weather: ninety degrees already at

11:30am. Summer is approaching, and it's about to get hotter but also wetter. But as they say: "If you don't like the weather in Miami, wait five minutes, and it will change." This is a very true statement, especially during the summer months.

As they turn into the Epic Hotel, where Zuma is located inside, the valet comes to open their doors. Enrique hands the valet driver his keys and takes the ticket from him. Enrique reaches for Kristie's hand and holds it as they walk into the stylish, air-cooled lobby of the hotel. As they walk toward Zuma, they always stop and look at the various art pieces on display. They are so incredible, and today is no different. Kristie and Enrique love art.

After admiring the art pieces, they walk into the restaurant, which is decorated in beiges and creams with an oriental feel to it. There is a square bar in the middle, and they have a beautiful shaded terrace outside overlooking the river. It's already starting to get busy. The brunch is truly magnificent. The Japanese cuisine is beautifully presented, and the choice is incredible. They love brunch here, as it allows them to have a little of everything. This restaurant is very special to them, as this is where they had their first date, and during their relationship, Kristie and Enrique would spend hours here, either just the two of them together or with friends and family. They love this restaurant.

"Good morning, Mr. Cruz. I have your reservation. Please follow me," the maître'd says as they arrive at the reservation desk. "Miss Carrington, it's so nice to see you. How are you both?"

"Fantastic," Enrique replies.

"I'm great, thanks," Kristie says. "Looking forward to brunch. How are you, Cynthia? Your hair is beautiful today."

"I'm great, thanks. And thank you so much. I decided to get braids. I wanted a change. You look beautiful as always. Your skin is glowing. I must come to your spa and get a facial," Cynthia says.

"Awww, thanks, babe. I love the braids... and you have my number... call me anytime... I'll fit you in." Kristie smiles and hugs Cynthia before she pulls the chair out for her to sit down.

"Would you like the champagne brunch or regular?" Cynthia asks.

"Regular, please," Enrique replies, looking at Kristie with a smile.

Kristie smiles and nods back at him.

"Sure," Cynthia says, not picking up on the private meaning behind their looks. "A waiter will be right over to take your drinks order. Enjoy."

Enrique reaches for Kristie's hand over the table, lifts it to his lips, and kisses it, looking deeply into Kristie's eyes full of love. She reciprocates his look. This makes Enrique's heart burst with joy. He can't believe he's here, at Zuma, with the love of his life, after everything they've been through.

They are finally here, and he is going to make this work, and nothing is going to stand in his way. He's going to be a father, and he's going to be the best father to their little baby, and he knows for certain that Kristie is going to be the best mom. He can't believe his luck after everything. After all the pain, after everything he has put Kristie through, she wants to be here, with him. It may be early days, but the fact that she even wants to see him makes him feel so incredibly blessed.

Suddenly, he feels so hungry. Walking in and seeing all that glorious food has made him realize that he didn't eat a single bite yesterday, and he is ravenous.

They order their drinks and get up and choose some of the delicious fare. Kristie remembers that she can't eat certain things now that she's pregnant, but she doesn't mind, as there's such an array of food to choose from, she definitely won't feel like she's missing out. After selecting various items from the buffet, they sit back down at their table.

As they begin their meal, they start to reminisce about their past travels and talk about where else in the world they would like to go, the Maldives being somewhere Kristie would like to visit. Enrique agrees. Then they start to talk about their trip to Maui. Enrique leans over and whispers in Kristie's ear. "I have very, very fond memories of Maui." Then, he kisses her just below her ear.

"Do you?" she teases, acting like she doesn't have a clue what he's talking about. But of course, she knows exactly what he's referring to.

"Oh yes, I do, Miss Carrington. And you know exactly what I'm talking about," he says, leaning back slightly to read the expression on Kristie's face. Their eyes lock as they give each other a flirtatious smile.

When they vacationed in Maui, they rented out a yacht for the day. But first, they went to a grocery store and bought food for a barbeque, champagne, and other refreshments. Enrique sailed the boat offshore, and they took lots of gorgeous photos of the island from the ocean. Once they had stopped the boat and anchored it, they enjoyed spotting the fish in the sea beneath them and swam in the warm tropical waters. Then they cooked the food they'd brought and drank some champagne. It was such a special day. There was nobody around, so they both took off their swimwear, sunbathed together naked, and made love in the sunshine, over and over again.

It's such a wonderful memory, and Enrique knows Kristie is teasing him. She knows exactly what he's talking about, and the fact that she's behaving this way only makes him want her even more. Right now, he wants her so badly it's insane, but he's desperately trying to respect what she asked him for when they last saw each other. He has to take things slowly, he can't rush this, but she drives him absolutely crazy with how sexy she is.

She's flirting back with him, and she knows what she's doing. Kristie knows how to drive Enrique wild. The fact that they're in a public place only makes it even more intense. This is how Kristie and Enrique are. They tease and torment each other to the point where they feel like they can't take anymore, and not being able to actually touch each other the way they want, as they're in public, is all part of the fun. It's like foreplay to them, and when they finally get home, or sometimes before, they would have explosive sex all night long. Enrique can't help but hope this is what Kristie's leading him to today, but he doesn't want to build his hopes up. As much as she drives him to the point of insanity, with her seductive beauty, he can't ruin the chance of them reuniting by rushing things.

They talk about the many trips they have made to his houses in Beverly Hills, Bimini, Aspen, and his apartment in New York overlooking Central Park. They would often hop on his jet and go wherever their hearts' desired on the weekends. They made so many special memories together.

Since he and Kristie broke up, Enrique hasn't been able to bring himself to go back to any of his houses, or should we say, their houses, as he always likes to call them. It's just too painful for him. He had to take a business trip to New York a couple of weeks ago. Instead of staying at his apartment, he flew there and back the same day. He always hoped that one day they would visit the houses together again.

He misses their trips away together. Traveling with Kristie was always so much fun; even the journey was unforgettable. They would fly all over in Enrique's Gulfstream G650ER, which has a private bedroom, and of course, they would make very good use of it. Enrique misses how free he feels with Kristie and how she brightens up every day when he's with her. She's like a dream, and he was such a fool for letting her go.

They also reminisce about their European vacation last year. Kristie and Enrique have traveled together to Europe a few times, and both love Italy. During last year's trip, they went to the Amalfi Coast and Milan, and they also went to Paris, Saint Tropez, and London. They loved the history, the food, and the wine; also, the scenery was breathtaking. They were away for three weeks in total and were so relaxed. It was really romantic, walking through the beautiful ancient streets of Italy and enjoying the authentic Italian cuisine in tiny restaurants away from tourists.

When on vacation, they always liked to explore places away from where the tourists go; they want to experience the real country they're visiting. This meant they found some tiny hole in the walls that served some of the most authentic, delicious food. They had both put on ten pounds by the time they got home, but they didn't mind; the experience was more than worth it.

They also found some fantastic pieces of art on their travels. Wandering around tiny towns and villages, they discovered some exquisite art created by unknown artists. Flying private meant that there was no trouble getting the artwork home in the same perfect condition they bought it in. This was something they were both glad about as they treasure their art collection, especially the pieces that have more meaning to them, like the ones by unknown artists or ones they found traveling the world. Although Enrique is a billionaire and can buy anything he wants, he has huge respect for art, expensive or not.

"Hey, my darling. My beautiful friend! How are you?"

They're both forced to break their gaze and look up at the overexcited, as always, Mario. Mario is Kristie's friend. He's Italian, full of life, always permanently tanned and dressed sharply. Today he's wearing navy slim-fit chinos, which turn up at the ankle, white loafers, and a fitted white shirt with a few buttons undone. He's mostly dressed in Gucci, his favorite designer, and his hair isn't dissimilar to Enrique's and is perfectly styled with a beard that's trimmed and shaped with precision. Mario is married to his husband Gustavo, and they live in Bal Harbour.

"Hey, babe!" Kristie says, standing to receive the hug Mario has his arms out, ready to give her. "It's so nice to see you. How are you? How's Gustavo?"

"I'm super fabulous, my darling!" Mario says enthusiastically, taking off his tortoiseshell-colored Gucci round Havana sunglasses. "He is beautiful. Beautiful as always. And Enrique, my darling. How are you?" Mario asks, moving around the table to hug Enrique. He's so happy to see the couple together but doesn't make it obvious, as he doesn't want them to feel awkward.

"I'm great, thanks, man. Brunch has been amazing as always," Enrique responds, sitting back down.

"Isn't it fabulous, darling? I am here with my brother Antonio." Mario waves his hand in Antonio's direction. Not wanting to intrude, he says. "I have an appointment for a facial and Botox next week. I can't wait, my darling. Enjoy your brunch. I will see you then, but we will text before then, I'm sure, my darling. Ciao bella!" Mario says, kissing them both on their cheeks as he goes to sit with his brother.

They both wave him off and wish him a great day.

Once they have finished brunch, Enrique asks Kristie what she would like to do afterward. "Would you like me to take you back home, baby?" he asks with great reluctance, signaling the waiter for the check. "Or we can go for a walk along the bay?" He smiles sweetly, hoping she will want to spend more time with him. Secretly he would love nothing more than Kristie to come back to his penthouse, but he's so scared to suggest it.

"I fancy some Cuban coffee," she says with a glint in her eye.

"Oh, OK, babe. Shall we go to La Carreta or if you want something a little closer, we can stop at la ventanita on West Flagler?" he asks, trying not to read into the look she's giving him. He knows her well enough to know what that look means, but he tries to downplay it. He's scared he will blow things.

"No. I was thinking more about your place," she says quietly as she leans in closer to him, brushing her hand over his thigh. "You make the best cafécito, babe... the best in Miami," Kristie leans in and kisses him, and her hand travels up his thigh.

They always pull their chairs close together when at a restaurant, as they always like to be close to each other, and today is no exception. Sitting apart doesn't feel natural to them, not to mention the fact that they can't keep their hands off each other. Today it feels like they're back to being Krissy and Enrique, and it feels so good. But Enrique has to keep reminding himself it's still early days.

"Really? Do I?" he smiles; kissing her some more, he puts his arm around her and caresses her arm. "Well, I guess I will be taking you to my place and making you some coffee." His smile widens as his body responds to Kristie as she runs her fingers dangerously close to his crotch. It feels so good to be back in their bubble, and he never wants it to end. He kisses her and says, "Let's go. I'll pay the check on the way out."

Chapter 14

After brunch, they arrive back at Enrique's building. As excited as he feels to have Kristie back here after all this time, he can't help but feel the anxiety that is blooming in his chest.

He feels incredibly nervous. Firstly, because he has to tread very carefully with Kristie; he can't blow this, and secondly, because of everything that's happening with his father. The situation with José is making him so worried for Kristie and the baby's safety; God only knows who might be out there looking for him or her. The thought alone is harrowing to him and not one he's going to dwell on.

In some ways, he feels that she's safer with him than she is alone. His building is extremely secure, and not that he's overly keen on his decision; he knows he has the security Ziv has arranged. As discreet as they are, Enrique saw them following him in his rearview earlier.

As they enter the apartment, he can feel the strong pull between them. They are finally alone, for the first time in what seems like an eternity. Is she feeling the same way, too? She was flirting with him in the restaurant, but he worries that now they're back in his apartment, she might feel differently. Was she just swept away in the moment? He's so unsure of everything right now.

Standing facing each other, holding hands, Enrique looks into her dark brown eyes. She's looking back at him in a way he knows extremely well. At this point, he knows what she wants, but he has to respect her wishes. She told him she wants to take things slowly, and he's worried that if anything happens between them, she will regret it and run; the mere thought is intolerable to Enrique.

It's so important to him that she doesn't feel like he's taking advantage of the situation: taking advantage of her vulnerability. He knows their break up has been super difficult for her, and he is more than aware of how much he hurt her by the way he has treated her over the past few months. He also worries that now she's pregnant, her emotions are most probably running high as well, and he doesn't want to do anything that would make her feel anything other than loved and special; because that's what she is.

Putting that all aside, he wants her more than anything; why wouldn't he? And he loves her more than anything in the world, he always has, and Christ, she looks so damn hot; smoldering even. She seems to have that glow already, and she is so, so beautiful.

Still holding their gaze, Enrique smiles at her. "You are so beautiful."

Before he can say or do anything else, she steps toward him, holds his face in her hands, and kisses him so hard she pushes him against the wall of the living area. Enrique reciprocates. He can't resist her; he never can. He kisses her back passionately and wraps his arms around her curvaceous body, pulling her closer to him. He loses himself in her; they lose themselves in each other. Moaning into each other's mouths, their hearts race as their kiss deepens. They're both desperate to feel as close to each other as they possibly can; they've missed this so, so much.

Enrique reminds himself to take a breath. "Are you sure about this, baby? I... I don't want you to do something you'll regret later."

Kristie looks at him with eyes blazing with salacious desire for this handsome man, and she kisses him again. Her hands travel down his rippling torso, feeling his defined muscles through his shirt as she does. "Yes, babe." She whispers. "I've missed you... I've missed you so, so much."

"I've missed you too, baby... more than you'll ever know." He whispers back, holding her cheek in his hand and looking into her eyes with concern. "But... I... I just worry... worry about you... after what you said... I...."

"It's OK, babe. Don't worry. I want this... I want you." She kisses him tenderly. "I need you."

With that, she kisses him deeply once more, pinning him up against the wall again. Enrique surrenders; what else can he do? The love of his life, the lady of his dreams, is making herself so hard to resist, and he has dreamt of this moment for weeks, now she's finally here; he can't help himself.

Kristie urgently pulls off his blazer jacket, and drops it to the floor, then makes quick work of unbuttoning his shirt, rips it out of his pants, and pushes it off of him. She looks down for a second, drinking him in. He is the hottest man she has ever seen, and she has missed seeing his perfect body.

She trails her kisses down to his chest and glides her hands down over his sculpted torso until she finds the waistband of his pants. She unfastens his belt and pants, and they fall to the floor, pooling at his feet. He kicks off his shoes and socks as well as his pants, and now he's standing in front of her wearing just his black Tom Ford boxer briefs; he looks insanely hot and handsome.

Kissing back up to his lips, she kisses him with fervor, holding his face in her hands as she does. Enrique needs this more than anything right now. He's so hard, he feels like he's about to explode, but as always, it's so much more than that with Kristie. They always have a way of perfectly combining love and lust, and it's the most intoxicating feeling in the world; she is intoxicating.

Sweeping his hands from Kristie's waist and up her back, he stops at the zipper of her dress and waits for a second, checking in with her. Looking into his eyes, she smiles and nods; she knows he's waiting for her confirmation that she really does want this.

He starts to unzip Kristie's dress slowly. As the dress falls open, he gently runs his hand down over her soft skin; he is in heaven. Her skin is like silk. Once unzipped, he glides his hands up her back and gently brushes the dress off of her shoulders. Kristie stands back slightly, allowing the dress to fall to the floor, revealing her beautiful tanned figure.

She's wearing a white silk and lace La Perla bra and thong. Enrique loves white lingerie against her sun-kissed skin, and she knows it. She is so perfect, and she's carrying his baby; this makes her look even more beautiful to him. His eyes follow his hands as they glide down her body and caress her curves as she stands in front of him wearing just her lingerie and heels. Enrique finds this sexy as hell; he always has. He can't believe how lucky he is to have her there, and after everything that's happened to him over the past few days, this is exactly what he needs. She is his remedy.

Their eyes meet as Enrique holds Kristie's hands as she steps out of her dress. As he looks deeply into her espresso-colored eyes, he can see into her soul, and at this point, there is no denying that she still loves him just as much as she did when they were together, which makes Enrique feel on top of the world.

They begin to kiss first tenderly before giving in to the scorching passion that's charging through them. Enrique's kisses travel down her neck and back up to her mouth again. Plunging his right hand into her hair, he pulls her closer to him, kissing her deeper and deeper.

Kristie jumps up to him with her arms around his broad shoulders and wraps her legs around his waist. Holding his head in place with one hand, she grips onto his back with the other, digging her nails in as she does. He lets out a loud groan of pleasure as he relishes in the feel of her nails scraping over his bare skin.

Kristie kisses down his neck and bites his shoulder as she rubs herself on his erection, which is pressing into her as he holds her up to him.

"Make love to me." She whispers breathlessly. "Please, Enrique... make love to me."

With that, Enrique slowly walks toward the stairs, kissing her at the same time. He carefully climbs the stairs, and heads toward the bedroom, still kissing her as he holds her up to him.

Once in the bedroom, Kristie glides down his body and finds her feet. Her lips kiss from his mouth, down his neck, over his firm pecs, and down his muscular torso. Kneeling in front of him, she hooks her fingers into the waistband of his boxer briefs and pulls them down.

Looking up at him, with dark eyes full of wanton need, she takes him into her mouth... all the way down. Enrique's head tilts back as he lets out a long, breathy groan, trying to absorb the overwhelming charge of extreme ecstasy as it forces its way through his veins. Fuck he's needed this for so long; he's needed her for so long.

He places one hand on the side of her head, guiding her as she takes him deeper and deeper. He looks down and watches as he disappears into her mouth. Fuck, this is so sexy; she is so sexy. Kristie looks up at him again, and their eyes meet; it's too much to bear.

"FFFUUUUCCCCKKKK!" He hisses through gritted teeth, throwing his head back as he explodes in her mouth.

Once his orgasm subsides, Kristie kisses him all the way back up to his lips and kisses him hard. He picks her up and lays her down on the bed. Hovering over her glorious figure, he kisses down over her full pert breasts and over the white lace of her bra. He looks up at her, checking on her once more. She smiles and brushes her hand over his hair. He smiles back at her and continues down over her stomach. Every touch and kiss have so much more meaning to it now she's pregnant with their baby.

He feels his eyes sting with tears as he becomes overwhelmed by this beautiful moment. To be here, with Kristie, being this intimate with her, being this close to their little baby, floods Enrique's heart with a love he has never felt before. He has always loved Kristie in a way he never knew existed until he met her, but now, this is different; this is more profound than he has ever experienced.

Enrique's lips move further down Kristie's body until they reach her thong. He kneels before her, and slowly, he pulls it down. She shifts her body so he can remove it entirely before he places it on the floor beside him.

Still kneeling in front of her, he gazes at his brunette beauty wearing just her white bra and heels; she looks absolutely incredible. After a few moments, he starts to kiss up each leg; kissing, teasing, and licking her soft silky skin. Taking his time, he enjoys every second of watching her body react to his touch. Enrique loves watching her; he loves the way her body shimmers and moves, with every kiss, every bite, and every touch of his fingertips. She truly is a sight to behold, and he has always been so captivated by her beauty.

As he kisses up the inside of her thighs, his lips moisten with her arousal. "Hmmmm...." He moans as he tastes her before he has even reached her sweet spot.

Licking up to her clitoris, he begins to lick and suck gently, and Kristie's hands pull him closer to her as her breathing accelerates and her soft moans fill the room. As a wave of carnal pleasure crashes through her, she wraps her legs around his neck and pulls him even closer, gripping the sheets with her hands.

Enrique's eyes are blazing with desire as he watches Kristie's body move like quicksilver as he teases and torments her with his tongue; she tastes and smells so good, and he can't get enough of her.

Her moans are getting louder, and her breathing is more rapid. "Ahhh… Enrique! Please… ahhh!" She comes over and over again, screaming out his name as she does.

As her body calms, Enrique slowly kisses back up to her mouth and kisses her deeply; tasting each other's arousals on their tongues. They roll onto their sides and press their bodies into each other, moaning into their mouths as they do.

Kristie rolls onto her back and shifts her body so Enrique can enter her. He slows for a second, opens his eyes, and looks into hers. Knowing what he is doing and loving him even more for doing it, she smiles and whispers. "Make love to me…."

Holding her face with one hand, he glides his other hand through her hair and gazes into her eyes full of love. "I love you." He whispers against her lips.

"I love you, too." She whispers back.

Before the tears come, he closes his eyes and slowly enters her.

"Ahhhh...." He moans as he feels her wrap around him. The intimacy he feels with her takes him to paradise, just like always, but this is way more intense than ever before. He feels like he's living in a dream. He cannot believe Kristie is here with him, in his apartment, making love to him. This is a moment he has longed for, ever since the day she left, and now it's happening; it just doesn't seem real.

As their bodies move as one, they reconnect with each other, and it feels so good. They are meant to be, and now they have a baby on the way, they have even more to look forward to.

With all the craziness going on in his life right now, this is his calm, his peace. He can really feel himself opening up to her on a much deeper level, and he feels so much closer to her. He starts to become overwhelmed again and tears well up in his eyes. He buries his face in Kristie's neck and breathes in her delicious scent, trying to distract himself from his tears.

As they move as one, their bodies start to tense, and their breathing becomes more and more rapid. Kristie wraps her legs around Enrique's, pulling him deeper inside of her, arching her back at the same time. Kristie's grip tightens on Enrique's back, and she bites into his shoulder as she tries to absorb the extreme painful pleasure of her impending orgasm. Then suddenly, she cries out as she comes, pulling Enrique with her.

As they find their equilibrium, Enrique helps Kristie onto her side and cradles her in his arms.

"You OK, baby?" Enrique asks, concern is etched across his face. This is new territory for him, and he's worried he may have hurt her in some way.

"I'm absolutely fine, babe," she smiles. "There's no need to worry... people make love all the time when they're pregnant." She knows why he's worrying.

"It's not just the baby I'm worried about... I'm worried about you too. I'm scared...."

"Baby, please... don't be scared... I'm OK...." She kisses his lips softly. "I wanted this... I wanted to make love to you... I've missed you... I've missed us."

"Really?" Enrique says, full of hope.

"Yes, really. You know I have…." She kisses him softly.

"I know you've said things… on the phone… and the other night… but I just worry, that's all." He tucks a loose strand of hair behind her ear. "I just don't want to rush you… I was so awful to you… I treated you terribly… shutting you out the way I did… and I know how much I hurt you." He shakes his head, disappointed with himself. "I will never forgive myself for the way I behaved… all you were trying to do was help me, but I… I shut you out… pushed you away… and for that, I am so, so sorry."

"I know, babe." She kisses him again. She can see how hard he's trying and how regretful he is. "But I can see how serious you are about changing that and getting the help you need to guide you through this. It means the world to me that you're ready to face it all now."

"I should have been ready when we were together… I should have found a way… we should never have broken up…."

"Well, you're ready now." She smiles, trying to reassure him. Kristie knows this is very different now. Enrique has always rejected the idea of therapy, he could never face it, but she can see he's opening up to the idea, and she's willing to embark on the journey with him. She loves him so much and always has.

"I am." He replies. "I just wish I had found a way to face it all before... before I hurt you the way I did... before you left... I just wish...."

Kristie places her forefinger on his lips and stops him from saying any more. He looks at her expectantly. She smiles sweetly, removes her finger, and kisses his lips. "You're ready now." She whispers. "You're willing to make the change now... and that's all that matters. I love you... and I am so proud of you for having the courage to do this... to face this... to go to therapy... I know how hard this is for you... but you're taking the first step...."

"I will do anything for us." He says quickly.

"I know you will, babe. I always have." She smiles. "I just knew you needed time... time to figure it out for yourself."

Enrique nods. She's right. But he still wishes he had felt this way sooner instead of being caught up in his own anger and frustration.

"I know you're in pain... you always have been... and I know how much you have wanted to release some of that pain... to be free of it... but you could never find a way... I have always known that right from the start." She looks down with sadness before looking back up at him. "I always hoped that I would be the one to help you with it, but unfortunately, I couldn't...."

"Baby, you helped me more than you'll ever know." He says, holding her beautiful face in his hands.

"I tried... but...."

"You did everything in your power to help me... I just didn't know how to let you. But now I feel I'm ready to face therapy... to do whatever it takes to fix the mess I've created... to be a better man for you... for our little baby." He places one of his hands on her tummy and holds it there.

They look down together and smile.

"Our little baby." Kristie whispers.

"Our little baby."

They kiss tenderly and hold each other close. Kristie shifts her body and moves on top of Enrique, sitting astride him. His body responds instantly. They have missed each other so much, and it's very obvious with the passion they pour into their kiss.

Enrique runs his hands up her back, into her hair, and pulls it slightly, kissing her hard. He feels so grateful to share this moment with Kristie, and to hear her say the things she just has, fills him with hope.

Rubbing herself on him, Kristie moves her body upward and eases herself down onto him. As she starts to move, Enrique sits up and begins to move in time with her, still kissing her. She grips onto his perfectly toned back, and her nails dig in. Enrique moans at the contact. He loves it when she does this.

Enrique unfastens her bra and brushes the straps off of her shoulders. Removing her bra, he places it on the bed beside them before cupping both her breasts with his hands and tugging both nipples at the same time. Kristie cries out, throwing her head back, allowing Enrique to kiss and gently bite her neck before he kisses down to her full, pert breasts. Taking the nipple of her left breast into his mouth, he first sucks and then gently bites it while pulling and tugging at the other with his thumb and forefinger.

"Ahhh!" Kristie cries through her orgasm, digging her nails harder into his back as she does.

Once her climax has subsided, she pushes him back on the bed and starts to move back and forth. Enrique looks up at her with eyes full of carnal passion and the purest of love.

"I've missed this so much, baby... I've missed us... I've missed you," Enrique says as he pulls Kristie down to him and kisses her with fervor.

He holds her hips as she moves up and down on him, keeping in perfect rhythm with him. Their tongues are teasing each other as they kiss deeper and deeper as their bodies move in unison.

Kristie's moans get louder through her breathlessness; she's close, and Enrique can feel it. This only pulls him closer, and before he knows it, she's taking him with her, and they both come violently together.

Laying together, floating back down to earth, Enrique holds her tightly as the afternoon sun tries to shine through the tinted windows of the bedroom.

"I love you," He whispers as he runs his fingers through her glossy brunette hair.

Kristie lifts her head and looks at Enrique with a smile. "I love you, too."

After a few moments, he kisses the top of her head and whispers. "I will book an appointment with the best therapist there is in Miami tomorrow morning."

Kristie looks at him, smiling widely. "It means the world to me, babe; it really does." She kisses his chest as they hold each other. "It's the first step to you healing... healing the pain you've been carrying inside for so long."

Enrique nods nervously. He knows he has to do this, and he will, but it still scares him to death. "I know, baby." Gazing into her eyes, he continues to play with her hair. "It's been affecting our life together... my life... for way too long now. I've just been ignoring it and trying to bury it. It's all I've known... but I want to heal... I want to learn...." He swallows as a wave of dread crashes through him.

Kristie can see how scared he is. She rests her head on his chest and whispers. "I will be with you every step of the way."

They hold each other even closer. Enrique kisses the top of her head once more and says. "You will never know how much that means to me... to hear you say that... after everything... I'm so lucky to have you."

"And I'm lucky to have you." She whispers back.

Chapter 15
Kristie

As she lays in Enrique's arms, Kristie feels elated that Enrique has opened up to healing himself. He deserves to feel at peace. Enrique's a very kind and caring man who gave Kristie everything during their relationship. He made her feel so loved and the most special person in the world. But during the last few months, the pain he's been suppressing since he was a child was trying to burst out of him and made living with him unbearable.

She wants nothing more than to move on with him and start their family together. She never wanted to leave, but he gave her no choice. He was drinking heavily and used to get so contentious with her and pick arguments. He was in so much pain with grief, which would sometimes turn into anger.

For the most part, their relationship was so loving and brimming with happiness, but of course, there were times when things didn't go so well. Most of the time, this was down to Enrique struggling with his grief and frustration at himself for not being able to open up to Kristie, or anyone else for that matter. He knew that if he could just talk about it, he would feel better, but the words just wouldn't come out. It was impossible for him.

When the grief gets too much for Enrique, he drinks to excess, and things always end badly. It's almost like because he's trying so hard to push down his feelings about his mother, the slightest thing will set him off at times. To Enrique, drinking alcohol is a stress reliever, an escape, but Kristie feels differently. When he's struggling to deal with his emotions, she thinks it's the worst thing he can do, and Kristie simply couldn't live like that anymore.

Leaving Enrique was the hardest thing she has ever had to do. The love she has for him is so pure, and their connection is so strong and powerful, it's undeniable; she has never felt the way she feels about Enrique ever before. Kristie fell in love with him the moment they met, it was love at first sight for both of them, and she's never loved or been loved the way they love each other.

Enrique's such a true gentleman and is quite old-fashioned in the way he treats a lady. With his elegant sense of style, impeccable manners, and a strong sense of respect toward people, especially women, he really is part of a dying breed. He works super hard, and his priority with the company has always been to make his father proud, but most of all, his mom. And there's no doubt about it, especially with his extreme sense of kindness and generosity when it comes to his philanthropy work.

Kristie loves Enrique so deeply, and it tortured her to have to end their relationship, but she had to do it not just for her but for him too. He had to see things for himself, as it seemed there was no way of her making any difference.

When Kristie left, she stayed strong and didn't see Enrique for the entirety of the separation. She needed space from him, and he needed his own space to figure out his head. The truth of the matter was, Kristie wanted nothing more than to see him, but she knew it wasn't a good idea, so they kept in touch on the phone.

During these conversations, he would generally be at work or in his office in the penthouse working. Although he would always deny it, she knew he would be out on weekends getting totally wasted; Miami is surprisingly small, and things would get back to her. She knew he was still running from his pain, and the sad thing was, she couldn't do anything about it. She had to let him do his own thing and hope that one day he would finally realize what he needed to do.

Staying strong, they continued to have their chats on the phone, and things were mostly calm and friendly between them. At times, they would get upset, more Kristie than Enrique, but she knew in her heart that was a different story in private. Kristie knew that Enrique was suffering because of their break up, and in a lot of respects, she felt responsible, but she couldn't carry on with the way things were until she found out about the baby. There was no way she was going to keep something so important from him, so she had to make an exception on this occasion.

Kristie casts her mind back to Thursday when she found out about the baby.

Lisa, Kristie's friend, had convinced her to take the test, as she had missed her period. Kristie had put it down to the stress of her break up with Enrique, but when she actually sat down and looked at her diary, she worked out that she had missed two in a row. This was so unlike her, but who could blame her for being so disorganized with everything she was going through. Not only was she distraught and heartbroken, but she was also so worried about Enrique.

She was so scared of the outcome due to their situation, and because of that, she had put it off for more than a week. She couldn't face it. She was devastated over their break up but was staying strong, but if she was pregnant, she didn't know what she would do. She didn't feel ready to have a child, especially now that she and Enrique had parted, plus she also knew Enrique was definitely not ready.

When she finally took the test with Lisa, she couldn't believe what she was seeing. She stared in disbelief as the word "pregnant" appeared on the stick. She took another. She thought it must be faulty or something. She couldn't be pregnant. The second said exactly the same. She gave the test to Lisa. "You look. Please tell me I'm seeing things."

"It says you're pregnant, babe," Lisa said with a screech. She was over the top excited. "You're going to be a mom! Awww, I'm so happy for you!" She threw her arms around Kristie, hugging her tightly.

"No! No! No! No! No!" Kristie pleaded. "This can't be true. I can't be pregnant. Not now. Enrique and I aren't even together, and I'm not ready to have a baby. There's so much more I want to do with my life." She started to cry as she clutched onto her friend.

"It will be OK, babe... I think you need to talk to Enrique. This changes everything. He will be so happy. I know he will." Lisa is always so optimistic and a born romantic. She loved Kristie and Enrique but understood why Kristie left, although she was desperate for them to sort things out. "It will make him sort his shit out once and for all. I know you guys are made for each other. The pair of you have been so miserable since you split. You belong together," Lisa reassured Kristie. "You need to tell him, babe... it will be OK. I promise."

"Oh God, Lis, I just can't even think straight at the moment. I need to get my head around this first. It's all such a shock... I mean, I would like to think this would help Enrique find the courage to face his problems… his pain… and get the help he needs to heal, but life doesn't always work like that."

She admired Lisa's optimism, but Enrique had issues that Kristie wasn't willing to overlook. If there were any chance of reconciliation, she would need to see progress and change; there's a baby now.

As she considers what lies ahead, she wonders how Enrique would cope with a child messing up his all-so-perfect penthouse and custom-made suits. He's never been a huge fan of kids in general, but deep down, she knows he will be a great father, as she has seen him with the children in his family. This may be a shock to Enrique, but it's just as much of a shock to her, too. She most definitely didn't see herself getting pregnant at this stage in her life, especially when she isn't even together with her child's father. What on earth was she going to do?

Kristie pulled herself together and looked at Lisa. Taking a deep breath, she said. "Well, it's happening, and I'm just going to have to deal with it, with or without Enrique… we'll have to figure out a way of co-parenting."

"I'm telling you, babe; he'll be over the moon. I don't believe this act that he's not keen on kids… he plays with the kids in his family all the time… he loves it… and has even looked after them, too. It's just his insecurities… you know what he's like... because of his issues. You will both make great parents. I'm super excited," Lisa said with conviction.

"Thanks, Lis... it's nice to hear. I'm just so scared... this was the last thing on my mind. I can't believe I was so careless. With everything that's been going on over the last few months, I've missed two periods and didn't even realize. I feel so stupid... I'm usually so good with all this. My pill must have stopped working or something?" Kristie replied.

"Everything happens for a reason. I think this has happened to help make Enrique realize he needs to find a way to deal with his problems, so you can both move on with your lives together. I understand why you left him, but you really are made for each other, and I think this baby is God's way of bringing you back together. This will make your relationship flourish, and you will be stronger than ever before."

"I hope so, babe," Kristie said with worry etched on her beautiful face. "I really hope so. But if not, I will do this on my own. Plenty of other women do... I will do the same."

"You won't have to... I'm tellin' ya. Now, shall I make us some coffee? Or do you want something stronger? I know you shouldn't drink in your condition, but one won't hurt. It'll calm your nerves," Lisa smiled.

"No, I hadn't better. I'd never forgive myself if anything happened to the baby because I had a drink," Kristie said, rubbing her hand across her stomach, not believing the words that she was saying. She was going to have a baby.

Lisa got the coffee pot ready in the kitchen of Kristie's apartment. Then the phone rang. Kristie answered.

"Ma'am. There's a delivery for you. Would you like me to get someone to bring it up for you?" the doorman asked.

"Yes, please... thank you, Anthony," Kristie said.

"Who was that, babe?" Lisa asked, looking at her friend curiously, as Kristie was looking a little strange.

"That was the doorman... I have a delivery. But I'm not expecting anything. I'm just wondering what it is? He's getting someone to bring it up now."

"I wonder what it could be?" Lisa replied curiously as she poured the coffee into cups on the kitchen counter.

Then the doorbell rang, and Kristie answered it. The porter carried a massive bouquet of white roses into the apartment.

"Where would you like them, Miss Carrington?" the porter asked with a smile.

"On the kitchen island, please," Kristie replied, trying to contain the surprise she was feeling, tipping the porter as he left. "I know who these are from already," Kristie said, admiring what looked like ten dozen roses and recognizing the name of the florist on the card. "They're from Enrique." She smiled as she reached for the card.

"Oh. My. God!!!!" Lisa screamed. "I told you. It's a sign. Open the card. Go on, open it!" Lisa said, barely containing her excitement.

"OK. OK. I am. I am. God, I think you're more excited than I am," Kristie said, smiling as she pulled the card out of the envelope.

"I think I might be," Lisa sang through her words. "I can't help it."

Kristie read the card.

Kristie,
I'm so sorry.
I miss you.
You are my world.
Without you, I am nothing.
Please let me make it right.
All my love,
Enrique
xxxxx

"Well?" Lisa said impatiently. "What does it say?"

Kristie showed her the card as she tried to read it to Lisa but was overwhelmed by emotion. Kristie's eyes filled with tears as she watched Lisa read the card from Enrique.

Lisa jumped to her friend, hugged her, and started to cry too. "I told you... this is meant to be. You have just found out you're pregnant, and within minutes you've just received a massive bouquet of roses from Enrique asking you to try again! It's fate," she said as she placed the card on the kitchen island in front of the vase bursting with flowers.

"It *is* strange that this has happened right after I found out about the baby," Kristie said inquisitively. "You may be right...." She said it but didn't feel secure enough to believe it, really. She needed to see Enrique and speak to him face to face. "I think I need to text Enrique." She paused. "What should I say?"

"Say thank you for the flowers and ask if he wants to go to dinner or something? Just keep it casual."

"That's a good idea," Kristie said as she reached into her black Birkin, which was sitting on one of the stools at the kitchen island. She found her iPhone, selected Enrique's number in her contacts list, and nervously began writing a text. Her hands started to shake a little; the shock of everything that's just happened was starting to show.

She was struggling to think about what she should text. Her whole world had changed in what felt like a nanosecond, and she feels all over the place. She was going to tell her estranged boyfriend that they were going to be parents and had no idea how he was going to react. He may want her back, but this changed everything. Although she knew he would support her, she was so scared of what may lay ahead. But Kristie was strong; so strong she surprised herself sometimes, and she would have to handle anything that came her way, just like she always did.

She began to text Enrique.

Thank you for the flowers, they're beautiful.
We need to talk.
Tomorrow night. 8pm. Komodo?
K
xxxx

She showed Lisa the text, as she wanted a second opinion before she hit the send button.

"Perfect," Lisa said. "Send it."

Kristie hit send. That's it. She'd done it. Now she had to wait for a reply.

The two friends sat on the balcony of her apartment, watching people enjoy the ocean and afternoon sunshine on the beach below, and a cruise ship was gliding gracefully along Government Cut to the right of them. Sipping their coffee, they talk about what steps Kristie should take next. "You need to schedule a doctor's appointment... just to check everything's OK and see what you need to do next. I can come with you if you like?" Lisa offered.

Kristie reached over and held her friend's hand. "You're such a great friend. Thank you. Thank you for being here for me and helping me through this. It means a lot to me. Yes, I would love you to come with me." She smiles gratefully. "I'll call my doctor now." Kristie picked up her phone. Finding her doctor's number, she called to make an appointment. They offered her one for the next morning, and she booked it. At least she could get it done before she met Enrique so she would have more information to give him. She would have to let her staff know that she wouldn't be in first thing in the morning. Although work was the last thing on her mind, she had a mountain of paperwork to do, and she left work early today too. This was not in Kristie's nature, but she needed to deal with this.

A couple of hours passed, and Kristie was beginning to wonder why Enrique hadn't texted her back yet. Although he was such a hard worker and sometimes got lost in the task at hand, he was usually quick to respond to her. "He's not replied," Kristie said to Lisa.

"He will... don't worry... he's probably busy at work. You know what he's like when he's working. He gets caught up in it all and loses track of time," She reassured her friend, although it was unusual for Enrique to take this long to reply. "He could be in a meeting or anything."

"Yeah, you're probably right... it is just strange, though." Then Kristie's phone vibrates on the table. It was Enrique.

Sounds perfect.
I can't wait.
See you then.
E.
xxxxx

"He's just text." Kristie showed Lisa the message.

"See. I told you. It's all gonna be fine... trust me."

Kristie still wasn't so sure herself. She would have to see it before she believed it. The flowers were a beautiful gesture, but she knew this situation would take a lot more than flowers to fix. She loved Enrique dearly, but could he really change, even with knowing they were going to have a baby? Enrique was a good man, but he had some deep-rooted issues that needed to be addressed. Kristie wondered if he could ever face up to them and deal with them. She tried so hard to help him, but he had to be ready to help himself.

Kristie feared that Enrique was right when he told her that his demons were bigger than he was. The only way he seemed to cope with them when they got too much to bear was to bury them with work or alcohol. Could Kristie really go back to him and deal with that again, especially with a baby to think about? She really didn't know. In an ideal world, she would love to tell Enrique she was pregnant, and he would say to her he would seek the help he needed, and they would live happily ever after; but real life wasn't always like that. Real-life wasn't like it was in the movies.

Trying not to let her insecurities get the better of her, she took a deep breath and looked out to the horizon, trying desperately to calm her racing mind.

Chapter 16

Enrique wakes from the most peaceful sleep he has had in a long time, if not ever. He's cuddled up to Kristie from behind with his hand resting on her stomach. Kissing her shoulder, he snuggles up even closer to her, relishing in his feelings of contentment and peace. Kristie has always had a way of making him feel this way, and he's missed this so much.

The couple lay together for a while longer, and Enrique drifts in and out of sleep with his girl. He can't stop smiling. He can't believe she's here with him, and they are going to have a baby; he's ecstatic.

It's very true to say that having a child hasn't really been on the top of his list of priorities; how could he look after a child when at times he couldn't even look after himself? But now it's happening; he couldn't be happier. He's going to make damn sure he will not only be the best father in the world, but he will be the best partner in the world to Kristie; he will be there every step of the way.

As he holds Kristie close, he gently rubs his hand over her stomach. He wonders what it will feel like to feel their baby move. His heart brims with love and joy as he imagines how beautiful the moment will be; he simply cannot wait.

Kristie stirs and opens her eyes slowly. She reaches her hand down to his and holds it with hers. She smiles sweetly, absorbing the beautiful moment of togetherness with her man and their unborn baby. Enrique kisses her shoulder and whispers. "I love you... I love you both so, so much."

She turns slightly to face him and whispers back. "And we love you so, so much."

They kiss, and Kristie shifts around to face him, wrapping her arms around him as she does.

"I can't believe we're going to have a baby. I'm so excited." He smiles; his eyes are sparkling with joy and happiness.

"I know... me too," Kristie says, smiling excitedly, mirroring his emotions in her eyes.

He kisses her, and they smile against each other's lips, and then out of the blue, Kristie has a look that makes Enrique worry.

"What is it, baby?" His face is full of concern. He reaches his hand to her cheek and holds it tenderly.

"I uhh... I just...."

"What's wrong, mi amor?" Enrique's tone grows urgent. "It's OK. You can tell me anything... you know that."

"I know... of course I do... I just... I was so scared." She looks down, trying to find her words.

"Scared of what?" Enrique's heart is racing. He's so worried about where this is leading. Is she having second thoughts? He tries to remain calm. "What were you scared of, baby?"

"I was scared of how you would react... like, I don't know... of course, I knew you would support me... it was nothing like that, but I just worried about what it would do to you... ya know, you were going through so much... you still are...."

"Baby, I know I was behaving terribly, but I would never leave you to cope on your own... never."

"I know, I know. I just think I was worried as everything was so strange between us... like, we'd broken up... I knew you were still struggling. I knew us breaking up was having a toll on you, too... it's been so difficult. When I found out about the baby, I was so confused. It was such a shock... I mean, I even waited a week to take the test... I couldn't face it. It would have been different if we were still together, but we weren't, and so much had happened."

"I know, baby, I know." He sweeps her hair out of her face and looks deeply into her dark brown eyes. "I'm so sorry... I'm so sorry for all of this... for the way I treated you... for us breaking up... for not being there for you the way I should have... and for not being with you when you took the test... you should never have had to go through that alone. I should have been there."

"I know you're sorry, babe, and I know you couldn't help the way you were behaving... that's what made it so hard to leave you. I knew it wasn't your fault... but... I...." Kristie starts to get upset.

"Hey... baby." He kisses her lips softly. "None of this is your fault. You were right to leave... in fact, you should have left sooner... I was so terrible to you... but things are going to change."

"I know... and I know you mean that." She pauses for a second. "At the time... it was just super important to me that we didn't get back together for the sake of the baby... I didn't want that... I mean, I've always wanted us to get back together, but as you know, I needed to see changes... like you going to therapy or something... I needed to see you trying to fix what was going on with you... I couldn't keep going around in circles like we were. Now we have a baby on the way; it's even more important to me."

"Baby, I have always wanted us to get back together, too... I just didn't feel right saying it... it wasn't fair on you... I knew it was better for you to be without me because I couldn't give you what you deserved. You deserve the world, and I couldn't give it to you... but now it's like something has clicked, and as scared as I am... I'm going to do it... I'm going to get the help I need... it's time." He kisses her soft full lips. "And as far as us getting back together for the baby's sake is concerned? I had already seen the light before I even met you the other night... I realized how ridiculous I was acting by running from my issues... I knew what I needed to do... that's why I sent you the flowers... it was my way of making the first step to fixing what I had broken so spectacularly."

Kristie smiles as her tears fall. She can't believe what she's hearing. She had a feeling that that was the case, but she couldn't help but feel insecure about their situation.

Enrique wipes her tears away and kisses her. "I will never let you down again... never." He whispers with certainty.

Kristie smiles and nods, gazing into his glistening deep blue eyes.

"I've always wanted us to get back together... before the baby... but now we have our little baby... it just makes things even more special." He whispers with deep meaning.

"Oh, Enrique…" Kristie holds him close and sobs into his chest.

"Baby, don't cry." He strokes her dark silky hair as he holds her close. "Don't cry… I love you… it's all gonna be OK… I'm so, so sorry."

Kristie nods. She's unable to speak, as her emotions are taking her over. She's been so upset, worried, and confused over the past few months, and finding out about the baby only compounded things. But now, she actually feels hope for their future, and she couldn't be happier.

They hold each other for a while longer, and Enrique keeps reassuring Kristie as they lay together in each other's arms.

"You know, it was so strange." Kristie begins.

"What's that, baby?"

"I received the flowers you sent me straight after I did the test and found out I was pregnant."

"Really?" Enrique pulls back to look at her with wonder.

"Yeah… like, I don't know… the timing…." She pauses, trying to get her words straight. "Lisa came over… she made me do the test…." She smiles, Enrique smiles back at her. "Lis' told me that it was the universe telling me that we should get back together."

"I think Lisa is right." He kisses her lips. "Life has a funny way of making things work out. The universe works in mysterious ways."

"It sure does." Suddenly, her stomach starts to growl a little.

"You're hungry. I'll fix you some dinner." He turns to check the time. He's shocked to notice how late it is. "Baby, it's 8:30."

"Really?" Kristie replies with surprise. She can't believe that they have slept for so long, but they have both been so exhausted. She tells herself it's not really a surprise.

"Yes, babe. I need to get you some food." He shifts, starting to get up. "Wanna go out for dinner... or do you fancy staying in?"

"What I need right now is a shower." She smiles.

"OK, baby. Shall we shower, then have dinner?" He suggests as they both get ready to get up. Enrique stands and helps Kristie up.

"Perfect." She replies.

He walks over to the bathroom door, reaches to the back of it, and takes her long black silk robe from the hook. She had left it behind when she moved out. He holds it open for her and, she slides it on, then ties the belt.

"Thanks, babe." She replies, taking Enrique's hand as he leads her to the bathroom.

Once in the bathroom, Enrique walks over to the glass-enclosed shower and turns it on with the chrome tap on the wall. He walks back over to Kristie, leans down, and kisses her on the lips. Enrique is a foot taller than Kristie's petite, 5'4" height; she always jokes that this is the reason why she has to wear skyscraper heels, otherwise, she can't reach him.

Standing on her tiptoes, she holds his face in her hands and deepens their kiss. Still kissing her, Enrique wraps his arms around Kristie, lifts her up, and then he sits her on the marble vanity between the two basins. Kristie's silk robe slips open, revealing her full, pert breasts. Enrique slides his hands down her throat and slowly down to her breasts, caressing them and teasing her nipples at the same time.

He starts to move his kisses down her neck and to her breasts until his mouth finds the nipple of her right breast, and he begins to lick and suck it gently. Kristie moans with pleasure, tipping her head back as she does. She leans back on her hands, arching her body in a way that drives Enrique crazy; he feels like he is about to explode.

Standing naked before this seductive goddess, he glides his hand from her throat down over her chest and in between her full breasts to her stomach; he is on the brink as he watches her chest rise and fall with every breath she takes. Kristie is so seductive and sexy, and even more so now she is carrying their baby.

He unties the belt on the already open silk robe, and it slides off her shoulders. Enrique lifts her from the vanity and carries her to the already warm shower. With her legs wrapped around his waist, he can feel how ready she is as his erection presses against her.

As they enter the shower, their bodies are drenched by the warm water as it pours over them both. Enrique holds his hand out to cushion Kristie from the tiled wall as he holds her up against it, and their kiss grows more and more passionate. And with one swift move, he's inside of her.

"Ahhh!" Kristie cries before biting down on his shoulder; her grip tightens on him. "Fuck! Hmmm! Fuck!"

"You OK, baby?" He asks quickly.

"Yes! Yes! Fuck! Fuck me... fuck me." She needs this; after everything she's been through, she needs this more than anything.

And with that, he starts to thrust, sliding in and out of her with vigor. His breathing is ragged. With her arms around his neck, and her legs still wrapped around his waist, she can feel every inch of him, and he feels so good. His firm body is pressing against her and pushing her against the wall; she can't get enough of him. She never can.

Enrique begins to move faster and harder. Their bodies are damp from both the shower and perspiration. They're both building, closer and closer, higher and higher.

"Come with me, baby. Come with me." Enrique says with a demand.

And with those words, it pushes Kristie over the edge. Her orgasm takes over her entire body, and Enrique follows, letting out a long, loud groan as he does.

Praying his legs won't betray him, he helps Kristie slide down the wall to her feet. "Are you OK, baby?" He asks, trying to catch his breath, with one arm holding Kristie, the other leaning on the wall.

"Yes. Oh my God, Enrique. Yes." She replies, resting her head on his dark tanned, muscular chest as he holds her with his strong arms.

Relief washes over him; he was worried he had gone too far. They make love in so many different ways, and this is nothing out of the ordinary, but

Enrique is more aware of how rough he's being with Kristie now she is pregnant. He would never forgive himself if something happened to her or their baby.

After a short while, he brings her under the warm water coming from the rain shower above and begins to wash her. He lathers up his hands and massages the foam over her glorious curves.

Once he has washed her, he begins to wash her hair and rinse it. He then gets some conditioner and runs it through her hair. He quickly gets a comb from the vanity, gently combs the conditioner through her long brunette tresses, and then rinses it off.

"I've missed you doing this... you have such gentle hands... it feels so nice," she says as she begins to wash him. This is something they used to do often.

"I love doing it, too, baby," he replies before kissing her. "So, any ideas on what you'd like for dinner? It's getting late... do you want to order takeout, or shall I cook something?"

"Shall we get Chinese?" She suggests as they both step out of the shower and dry off.

"Perfect."

They finish drying off, and Kristie puts on her black robe, and Enrique slides on a pair of black pajama pants before they head downstairs and through the living area. Enrique notices their clothes on the floor near the door and picks them up, smiling at the memory. He neatly places them on the back of one of the sofas, ready to take them upstairs to the closet later.

"Would you like your usual?" Enrique asks with a smile once they're in the kitchen.

"Yes, of course," she smiles back at him, pulling out a stool and sitting at the breakfast bar.

Enrique dials the number for their favorite Chinese takeout and places the order. He discreetly checks to see if there is any news on his father; but there's nothing. He's still very angry with him, and right now, he wants to focus on Kristie; she and their baby are his main priority.

Once he ends the call, he says, "It will be here in thirty to forty minutes. Do you want a little something to eat while we wait? I know you were hungry before we had a shower,"

"No. I'll be OK to wait. Thanks, babe."

"OK... only if you're sure."

"I'm sure." She smiles.

"Would you like a drink?"

"Yes, please... water."

He reaches into the stainless-steel refrigerator, gets out two bottles of Fiji, breaks open both bottles, and hands one to Kristie. He sets up the black quartz breakfast bar so it's ready for when the food arrives.

Once the food is delivered, Enrique serves it up, and they eat their meal while talking mostly about their relationship, the direction they want it to go in, and the baby. This is a great distraction for Enrique, a positive one from the nightmare that's going on with his father.

He still hasn't told Kristie anything about the situation with José. How can he even begin to explain it to her? Right now, it's better not to burden her with any of it, plus he doesn't want her to worry. He would rather carry the weight of it himself to save her from the heartache he knows it will cause her if she knew. They're safe in his penthouse with the building's security as well as Ziv in the apartment below, or so he hopes, plus he's enjoying being in the moment with Kristie. He feels relaxed in their bubble and is enjoying her company. Around Kristie, he feels at ease and can be himself. Conversation flows easily, and they can just be together; things are always so simple, well, most of the time. Kristie seems to be relaxed too. She's asked to stay the night. Of course, he agreed. If he had his way, she would move back in right away, but he knows he has to take things slowly and not push his luck.

He can't help but feel like he wants to stay in this dream world where it's just the two of them and their little baby and never have to face the real world again, but he knows that's impossible, so right now, he's going to enjoy the moment.

* * *

The following morning, Kristie and Enrique wake refreshed. Their only interruption was more passionate lovemaking at who knows what time, but neither of them is complaining.

Once they're ready for the day ahead, they both head to the kitchen for breakfast. Gabriela, Enrique's housekeeper, is in the kitchen preparing food. She looks up to see Kristie and smiles; she's so pleased to see her again.

"There will be two of us for breakfast this morning, Gabriela," Enrique says to his housekeeper, smiling widely and sounding more than pleased with the situation.

"Of course," Gabriela says, full of cheer. She walks around the breakfast bar and hugs Kristie. "It's so nice to see you again. I've missed you."

"I've missed you, too," Kristie replies sweetly.

"What would you like for breakfast? Would you like me to fix you some fruit and whole-wheat toast?" Gabriela asks, recalling Kristie's usual breakfast.

"Yes, please, Gabriela. That would be perfect." Kristie smiles, pulling out one of the barstools and taking a seat at the breakfast bar. "So, how are you? How are the children?"

"We are all great, thanks," Gabriela replies. "How are you, mami?"

The two ladies catch up while Enrique checks some work emails quickly on his cell. Still no news on his father; he has already decided to check in with Ziv once he gets to work.

Gabriela has the Cuban coffee ready and pours them both some into espresso cups before preparing their breakfast. Enrique is having scrambled eggs and avocado on whole wheat.

Once breakfast is ready, Gabriela places the plates down on the breakfast bar and leaves the couple to eat their food. Enrique puts his phone down and starts to eat his breakfast before turning to Kristie and saying nervously. "So, today's the day," the anxiety is evident on his face. "I'm calling to schedule the therapist."

Kristie can see how scared he is, so she tries her best to reassure him. Looking deeply into his eyes, full of love for this beautiful man, she says. "It will be OK, babe. Think of it as a good thing. It will give you the tools to help you deal with everything you've been suppressing for so long... you know, your feelings about your mom and her passing." She takes his hand and holds it. "I'm here for you too. If you'd like, I can come with you. It's up to you, babe... I'm happy either way... I just want to help."

"Thank you, baby... thank you so, so much." Pressing his lips together, he raises a tiny smile. "I'm eternally grateful for everything you have done for me... but... I uhh... I'm probably better going alone to start with." He looks down, trying to put his words into order. He worries that she'll feel like he's shutting her out again, and this is definitely not the case; he's just concerned it will add to the pressure. "I... I uhh... I don't know how to explain what I mean."

"It's OK, babe... I totally get it. This is a huge deal to you... and you feel like you need to do this on your own... like, it's going to be a lot to actually talk about your grief after all this time, and to have somebody else there, even me, would only put you under more pressure?"

"How do you always know how to put my feelings into words, baby?" He says, full of wonder.

Kristie reaches her hands up to his face and holds it tenderly before kissing him. "Because I know you… and I love you." She kisses him once more. "You need to do this by yourself, and I completely understand that… but if your feelings change… I'm here for you… just like always."

Enrique shakes his head in disbelief. "How did I ever get so lucky to have you?"

"I could say the same about you, Mr. Cruz." She smiles. They're falling back into the way they used to be, and it feels so, so good.

They kiss tenderly. Enrique glides his hands down over her curves and places one on her stomach. Looking at her full of adoration, he says. "The last twenty-four hours have been so amazing… I haven't felt so relaxed and happy in a long time… and that's all because of you." He kisses her lips before looking down at her tummy. "And you, little one." He says to their unborn child. Looking back up into her eyes, he says. "I can only hope I've made you feel as happy as I am."

"It's been wonderful… I've had the best time, and I feel the same way too… I mean, I know we have work to do, but I'm more confident that we'll get through this now… I do feel things are different between us… they feel more… I don't know… more balanced," she explains.

"I do too. I feel the very same. I already feel a lot more open than I did before,"

"I've noticed... and I love it... it feels so good, babe."
They kiss once more. "It makes me feel so happy to
see you like this." Insecurity swoops in for a
second, and her eyes suddenly tinge with sadness.
"Please don't shut me out again, babe. I couldn't
bear it," she pleads with a whisper.

"I promise I won't, my darling." His eyes are telling
her he means what he's saying. "I'm serious about
this. Once I get to work, I'll make the call, OK," he
says sincerely before kissing her again.

"I know you are, babe. I know."

They finish their breakfast, and Enrique asks the
valet to bring his car around before they head
down.

Once seated in the SUV, Enrique selects a song on
his iPhone, drives out of the valet and onto Brickell
Avenue. "Que Precio Tiene El Cielo" by Marc
Anthony plays over the car's sound system. Kristie
and Enrique love Marc Anthony and have seen him
many times at the American Airlines Arena, and
this is one of their favorite songs. Enrique reaches
for Kristie's hand, holds it tightly, and she
squeezes his hand back. Kristie smiles as Enrique
sings along with the song. He sings a lot, and she
loves it; he has a good voice, too.

"Thank you for an amazing day and evening, babe.
I had such a wonderful time," he says, looking at
Kristie with a huge smile.

"Thank you too, and you're right; it was the best time." Kristie smiles. Although she feels nervous yet really excited about the future, she's starting to feel a little more at peace with things now.

As they head over the MacArthur Causeway, vibrant and colorful South Beach comes into view, and it's spectacular. They feel so lucky to live in Miami; it's paradise. Glorious sunshine, tropical climate, beautiful waterways, and the most breathtaking blue, green, crystal clear ocean, which laps onto the white sandy beach that goes on for miles. The architecture is extraordinary. Pastel-colored Art Deco delights fringe palm tree-lined pink sidewalks, with the deep blue sky as their backdrop; it really is incredible.

Miami is a melting pot of multiple different cultures, mostly Hispanic, but people from all over the world live in Miami; this is part of the magic. You can hear every language from all over the globe being spoken around the city, but Spanish is the most predominant. Living in Miami is something that Kristie and Enrique never take for granted, and they're so thankful that they live in such a fantastic city.

As they make a right onto Alton Road, Enrique drives leisurely down past various condos and onto South Pointe Drive. He feels sad to be leaving Kristie, but he feels a little more confident to ask her when he can see her next.

Nerves start to bubble up inside of him as thoughts flood his mind. The therapist! Oh, God! The dreaded therapist! He feels nauseous. Then suddenly, something even more horrifying hits him like a ton of bricks from out of nowhere. He's going to have to leave Kristie alone after everything that's happened with his father... the marine stadium... Stiltsville... everything! Fuck! He can't do this. Their bubble is about to burst, and reality is creeping in. He's going to have to stay with her... to keep her safe. But how is he going to explain that to her? She will get suspicious as she will know that something's wrong. He can't tell her... he can't put her through this, especially now she's pregnant.

Although Ziv said he'd arranged security for everybody, the thought of leaving Kristie alone worries him sick, and right now, something doesn't feel right. It might be paranoia, but he isn't going to leave anything to chance where Kristie's concerned.

Quickly he decides that he will go up to her apartment with her and walk her to work. That way, he will know she'll be safe once in the spa; surely nothing will happen to her there as she'll be around a lot of people? Then he will offer to meet her tonight, so he can continue to keep a close eye on her. As soon as he leaves Kristie, he will pull over somewhere and call Ziv to make sure he hasn't forgotten to cover the spa. He scolds himself mentally as he wonders why he hasn't thought of this already? He should have double-checked this with Ziv when he texted him about the security.

His fear is only being exacerbated by the fact that he hasn't seen any security tailing them this morning and can't see anybody around Kristie's building either. Ziv said they would be discreet, but you can usually still spot something when you know what you are looking for, just like he did yesterday. As he pulls into her condominium's parking lot, he stops the SUV by the elevator doors.

"I'll come up with you, babe," Enrique says like it's the most normal thing in the world.

"Why?" Kristie looks confused. "I'm only getting changed. Then I'll be going straight down to work. I'm gonna be late and so are you. It's 8:45, and you need to get back over the bridge during rush hour to downtown, plus I have a client at 9... I don't have time for anything else." She smiles with a glint in her eye. He smiles back at her with a look she knows only too well. "Christ, Enrique, you're insatiable." She giggles.

This is good for Enrique, as she isn't getting suspicious about anything. Well, not yet anyway. She thinks he wants to go up to her apartment to make love, which is actually a fantastic idea. He'd be more than happy to oblige, of course; why wouldn't he? Plus, he could make sure she's safe. Perfect! Besides, it doesn't matter if he's late for work. For the most part, he can come and go as he pleases.

"Around you, Miss Carrington... yes, I am," he says, with eyes sparkling with desire. "Your client can wait," he teases.

"No, they can't. It's not professional," Kristie says, all business.

Frustrated, she has a client so early, which makes things more difficult for him; he settles on her texting him once she's at work.

"Really, Enrique? What is going on with you? You're acting strangely?" She's starting to get suspicious.

That didn't last long. He's about to get busted already. She's so damned smart. Nothing can get past her, well, most of the time. Enrique's surprised he's been able to hold himself together for her sake, as long as he has.

"I just want to make sure you're OK... you know, with the baby and all," he replies, trying to downplay everything. He knows she's suspicious now, and he needs to back off, or she's going to start asking questions that he really can't answer right now.

"I'll be OK, babe," she smiles, loving him even more for how concerned he is being. She can see he's worried about leaving her alone now she's pregnant. He's always been so caring, and she understands this is very new for him, too. She leans over and brushes his cheek with the back of her fingers. "Look, I feel fine... better than ever, in fact. I'll text you when I get to work, OK." She kisses his lips softly. Holding his face gently, she says, "And thank you again for the most amazing day ever. I've missed us being together... just us... no distractions. It really has been so perfect." She kisses him, and he wraps his arms around her, pulling her closer to him. He could make love to her again. Right now. In the car. He couldn't care less that they're in the middle of a parking lot. He wants his girl so badly, and she knows it. She pulls away slowly and looks into his summery blue eyes. "See you tonight?" she says breathlessly, with eyes smoldering with passion.

"Tonight, can't come quick enough. God, I've missed you," he responds, trying to catch his breath. She's so beautiful, and he really doesn't want to go. If he had his way, they would spend every waking moment together. "Shall I pick you up at about 6? After you finish?" he asks, not believing his luck that she wants to see him again so soon. "You could come back to mine again if you like... or we could go out to dinner?".

"Sure." She kisses him once more. "We can figure it out later." They kiss again. "I can't wait." She says, giving him one last kiss before she exits the SUV.

Pressing the button on the door, Enrique rolls his window down and watches her as she walks around the car toward the doors that lead to the elevator. He drinks in every inch of her perfectly graceful figure as she moves in front of him; he can't get enough of her. Her pretty face is framed beautifully with her glossy brunette tresses as they cascade down to just above her waist. As she walks in her four and a half inch heels, her hips sway deliciously beneath her elegant pink fitted dress; she really is a sight to behold, so feminine, so beautiful. "I love you, babe," he says with hunger in his eyes, leaning out of the window to kiss her again.

"I love you too." She smiles. "Have a good day!" She kisses him once more. "Now I really have to go, or I'm gonna be late for my client."

He wishes her a good day, too, then, before he knows it, she's in the elevator on the way to her apartment. Anxiety sets in instantly. He needs to call Ziv once out of the parking lot and ask about security. He needs to know that Kristie will be completely protected, not just in her apartment but at work too.

Reluctantly, he starts to drive toward the exit of the condominium and turns onto South Pointe Drive. He looks around to see if there's anything out of place or if anyone is hanging around looking suspicious, but there's nothing. It all seems as peaceful as it always is South of Fifth.

South Pointe is such a tranquil part of South Beach, and Kristie and Enrique used to go for long walks up the beach-walk or along the shoreline and around South Pointe Park. It's so beautiful, and there're some great restaurants within walking distance of her condo; it really has a sweet neighborhood vibe about it. South of Fifth is located right at the southern tip of the Miami Beach peninsula, away from most of the clubs on South Beach and away from the noise. But at the same time, they both love South Beach; it has such a fantastic energy about it, and they've had so many great nights out there together, along with friends and family.

Still keeping an eye out for any suspicious activity around Kristie's neighborhood, all of a sudden, he gets pulled out of his high-alert trance, by his cell ringing. Pressing the button on the steering wheel, he answers the call on the hands-free; it's Kristie. "Hey, baby! Miss me...." Enrique's cheerful greeting is halted in its tracks abruptly.

"Someone's broken into my apartment!!!! There's writing on my mirror saying...." She pauses. "Oh, God, Enrique!!!! Please." Kristie can barely breathe or get her words out as she hysterically cries down the phone.

"What??!! Babe. Slow down. It's OK. I'm on my way back." Enrique can hardly understand what she's saying, but he knows whatever has happened is not good at all. He turns the car around so quickly it causes the tires to screech on the road, and he accelerates back to Kristie's building. "What's happened, babe?" All he can hear is Kristie sobbing uncontrollably down the phone; she can't speak. "It's OK, baby... I'll be right there... breathe, baby... breathe... try to take deep breaths... it's OK... it's OK," he says, trying to help her calm down, but he doesn't succeed.

"On... the... mirror... it... it... says... it says... you and your baby next. Why would anyone do this?! WHY?" She screams.

Chapter 17

Enrique slams on the brakes outside Kristie's building, jumps out of his SUV, runs through the lobby, and presses the elevator call button. Once in the elevator, he types in the security code and selects the fortieth floor. The elevator is taking an eternity. This is way too familiar to him from only a few days ago when he found out about his father's abduction.

As he travels up to Kristie's apartment, so many thoughts are rushing through his mind. What's happened to Kristie? What about the baby? Is anyone still in the apartment? What have they done to her? She will be OK, he tells himself. She has to be. He feels nauseous as bile rises in his throat. Is this the other cartel from the marine stadium? Is it tit for tat? They take my father, Gutiérrez takes Manolo's family, now they take my girlfriend, the mother of my child? No way! This isn't happening. No way! Why the fuck didn't I just insist on going up with her? What the hell am I going to say to her, and what the fuck do they mean by "You and your baby next"? Next??? What the fuck??

Finally, the elevator arrives at Kristie's floor. He runs the short distance to her apartment and rings the bell. She opens the door for him. Standing in the doorway, she looks devastated and frightened. Her gorgeous brown eyes are red and puffy from crying, and her beautiful face is stained with tears.

Enrique is heartbroken. He throws his arms around his girl and holds her as she sobs into his chest, soaking his shirt with her tears.

"It's OK, baby... it's OK... I'm here. Don't worry... I'm here," he says, holding her and stroking her hair as she cries uncontrollably. "It's OK, baby... I'm here... it's OK."

Full of devastation for his girl, he holds her until she calms, and then they attempt to slowly walk through her apartment, which is now an absolute mess. Furniture is upside down, ornaments are smashed, and paintings are ripped off the wall and slashed. With his arm around Kristie's waist, he keeps her close as he looks around to see if he can find anything that would give him a clue as to who did this, although he has a pretty good idea. Fucking assholes, he thinks to himself. And how the fuck did they know about the baby? "Show me the message on the mirror, baby. Which mirror?" he asks, trying to keep calm. There is no way that he can give in to the rage he is feeling inside; rage mostly at himself for allowing this to happen. He should have taken better care of her. He should have known.

"It's the one in my closet. The large one on the wall," she says, holding back more tears.

"OK, baby. Let's have a look." Still holding her close, he walks with her to the closet.

Kristie's closet has also been ransacked. Clothes are everywhere, bags and shoes are all over the floor. Drawers are all pulled open, and some have even been ripped out of their units and emptied onto the floor. Everything has been pushed off the long white dressing table, which is always so perfectly organized, just like the closet and, in fact, the entire apartment. Enrique's eyes fix on the mirror on the wall. The message is written across the mirror with red lipstick.

"YOU AND YOUR BABY NEXT"

Enrique looks at the mirror in horror as the color drains from his face. Kristie starts to cry again uncontrollably. He wraps his arms around her and holds her once more, kissing the top of her head as she cries, looking up at the message on the mirror simultaneously. He is enraged. I'm going to find those fuckers and kill them myself. How fucking dare they!

Knowing this has to be something to do with the marine stadium meeting, he knows he needs to get Kristie out of there now. "Come on, baby. Let's get out of here. You're coming back to my apartment... you're not staying here or going to work. I'll make the calls and let the spa know. Don't worry... I'll take care of all of this. I'll get people over to sort out this mess and fix anything that's broken," he says way more calmly than he actually feels.

"We need to call the police," she says.

Oh shit! The police. He knows with the current circumstances that's the last thing they should do. But how's he to explain that to Kristie? Any sane person would call the police if their apartment were broken into and vandalized. But this isn't a normal situation. He needs to talk to Ziv and Gutiérrez to find out what the fuck's going on. Ziv said he had everything covered! Like fuck! He should never have trusted them. But first and foremost, he needs to get Kristie out of there and to his apartment.

"Don't worry about that... I'll deal with it. Let's pack you some things, and you can stay at my place. Let me help you," he says, finding a suitcase that's been thrown on the floor. Opening it up, he starts to get some clothes and shoes together for her. "What toiletries do you need, baby? What about make-up?" he asks, trying to keep her mind occupied and distract her from the idea of calling the police.

"Aren't we supposed to leave everything as it is... for the authorities to come and take photos or whatever they do?" she says to him, looking and sounding completely dazed.

"It's OK, mi amor... it'll be OK for you to take some things now. Anything we forget, I can get you from the store," he reassures her. He knows this is the wrong thing to do, but he has no intention of calling the police. He simply can't. It would blow everything with his father to shit. "What do you need from the bathroom, baby? I'll get it and pack it for you."

She follows him into the bathroom and selects a few essentials like toothpaste, a toothbrush, deodorant, and some skincare; she has her make-up in her purse already. Enrique notices a pregnancy test resting on top of the marble surface as they walk back past the vanity. He manages a small smile as he sees the word "pregnant" on the stick. Then suddenly, it dawns on him that this must've been how they found out about the baby. He's just about to mention the test but decides against it for now; he doesn't want to upset Kristie anymore.

Back in the closet, Enrique places the rest of the items in a wash bag, puts it in the suitcase, and zips it up.

"Ready?" he asks.

Kristie nods, looking around in horror; she's devastated.

"Come on, baby... let's get you out of here," Enrique says, reaching out to take her hand.

They walk out into the living area and past the breakfast bar. The roses Enrique had sent her only a few days ago have been pushed off the marble surface and smashed on the tiles. The crystal vase is shattered into tiny pieces all over the floor. As Enrique notices this he chooses not to say anything. Material things can be replaced; Kristie and the baby could not.

"Be careful, baby. Follow me," he says as he guides her around the glass.

They exit the apartment, and Enrique walks Kristie to the elevator. He puts his arms around her and kisses the top of her head. She's quiet. She's stopped crying and seems a little calmer, but he knows she's distraught.

Enrique can't believe it. Only forty-five minutes ago, everything seemed so good. They were both so happy, singing in the car, flirting and kissing each other in the parking lot, and now it's like everything has been turned upside down.

He remembers his feeling of unease before he left Kristie at her apartment. His instincts were telling him something was wrong. Why didn't he just go up with her? He may not have been able to change what had happened to her apartment, but at least he would have been there for her. Shaking off his thoughts, Enrique pulls himself together. He has to be strong for Kristie. He needs to take care of her. He'll contact Ziv once they get back to his apartment, and there will be hell to pay.

Leaving the elevator, Enrique holds Kristie's hand while pulling her suitcase with the other. Once they get to the SUV, he opens the passenger door for her and helps her climb in; she's unsteady on her feet as she's shaking like a leaf. Closing the door, he heads to the trunk, opens it, puts the suitcase inside, and closes it, then climbs into the driver's side.

"Are you OK, baby?" he asks as he takes her hand; it's freezing.

Kristie nods her answer as she's unable to speak.

"It's OK... it's all gonna be OK. I'm gonna take you to my place and make you some hot tea," he says, looking into her eyes, trying to reassure her. Her beautiful brown eyes are still red and puffy, and she looks so pale. This is the last thing she needs, Enrique thinks to himself. He feels absolutely terrible. He's pretty sure this is to do with his father, and he is disgusted that his shit is now involving the love of his life, the mother of his child. Amongst his thoughts of fury, he tries to keep level-headed and put Kristie at ease. "I'll draw you a nice hot bath with some of the oils you like," he says with a smile, looking over at her and squeezing her hand at the same time.

"Thank you," she says quietly. Her eyes are filling with tears again.

On the way back to the penthouse, he calls the spa to let them know that Kristie won't be in as she's sick. He doesn't know what else to say, and there's absolutely no way he's going to tell them the truth.

Kristie stays quiet on the drive back, a stark contrast to how they were on the way over the bridge earlier this morning. Enrique doesn't let go of her hand as he drives her to the safety of his apartment. He intermittently lifts her hand up to his lips and kisses it softly, continually reassuring her everything will be OK.

He looks calm and in control on the outside, but on the inside, it's a very different story. Inside he is raging. How on earth could everything get so out of hand so quickly? Ziv said everything was covered. Why the hell did I trust him with this? I should have vetted the security Ziv provided. How can I expect anything less, with the type of people that are involved in this hellish situation? I'm dealing with cartel members and gangsters, not rainbows and fucking unicorns. These guys aren't gonna play nice and throw fairy dust around singing fucking Kumbaya! Enrique tortures himself with his own scorching thoughts of regret.

He would never usually trust others to deal with these sorts of things. Enrique likes to be in control of decisions so important. Why didn't he just use his own security? They are some of the best in the country. Why use Ziv's? Oh yeah, that's right, because he can't let anybody know what's going on with his father. If he uses his own security, they'll see what's really going on, and he can never let that happen. He can't involve any of his people in this shit storm. For fuck's sake! Why has his father put him in this position? What a fucking mess. This could ruin everything for him and Kristie. This is not a world he wants to be a part of, and he sure as hell knows Kristie wouldn't want any part of it either. Just as he felt things were looking up with Kristie, he feels like his world has been destroyed all over again. When will this ever stop?

Enrique is beginning to hate his father for what he has done to him. So much is on the line because of José's sick and selfish actions, not to mention his lies and deceit. He has caused so much damage, whether he intended to or not. Hate isn't a feeling he's used to when it comes to his father; it feels so alien to him. They were so close and had a bond Enrique always thought was unbreakable; how wrong can he be?

He had such great respect for José. He looked up to him and went to him for guidance. He loved his father so much and trusted him with his life. But that love, trust, and respect are starting to erode to hatred, disgust, and disappointment.

The barrage of shit that keeps being thrown at him since his father's disappearance never seems to end. How the fuck is he supposed to explain any of this to Kristie? He wants to protect her from it all by not telling her, but now, it would seem, he doesn't have a choice. Then his greatest fear hits him like a lightning bolt: What if she leaves me for good this time?

Chapter 18

After an agonizing thirty-minute drive, thanks to rush hour traffic, Enrique pulls the SUV into the valet area, and Jorge is there to greet them. They exchange pleasantries, and Enrique rushes Kristie toward the elevator, glad that Jorge didn't ask any questions like "You're back so soon?" and so on.

Enrique holds Kristie, who's now in a state of shock, and still very quiet. Once the elevator arrives on his floor, they enter the penthouse. Right now, Enrique wants nothing more than to get on the burner phone and contact Ziv, but he knows he can't do this in front of Kristie. He will have to wait for the right moment, and this is killing him; he needs to get onto it right away. What else are these monsters capable of? This has to be dealt with pronto.

He quickly works out a plan. He's going to get Kristie a cup of hot tea and draw her a bath; then, hopefully, she will be relaxed enough to get some rest. He will then call Ziv. As he can't leave her alone in the apartment, Ziv will have to come up to the penthouse discreetly. He feels like he is out of his mind for even considering this, but as per usual with this disgusting situation; he has no choice.

"Enrique… is everything OK? Can I get you anything?"

Shit! Gabriela! He forgot that she would still be there, although he only left her there a short while ago. So much has happened this morning; it slipped his mind.

"Hey, G... everything's fine. Krissy isn't feeling too well, so I'm going to fix her some hot tea and look after her," Enrique says, stumbling over his words. What the fuck is he supposed to say?

"I'm so sorry to hear that, Krissy," Gabriela says sweetly. "I'll make you some right away. Is there anything else I can get you?"

"It's OK, G... I'll fix the tea." Then Enrique has an idea. "In fact, why don't you take the rest of the day off, Gabriela?" He says, forcing a smile. "It's OK... I've got this."

"Oh... uh... well, only if you're sure?" She looks at the couple, who both look desperately upset, and she's really concerned about them. "Is everything OK?"

"Everything's fine... honestly. You go and enjoy your day," Enrique says with another fake smile.

She looks back and forth between Kristie and Enrique, she's worried about them, but she doesn't want to pry. "OK... well, let me know if you need anything." Gabriela isn't one to take time off, but she knows there's no point in protesting. Enrique never takes no for an answer with his kind gestures; she got to know that a long time ago.

As Gabriela leaves, Enrique takes Kristie into the kitchen, and helps her up onto one of the white leather bar stools at the breakfast bar. He then fills the kettle, and switches it on, before preparing some Cuban coffee for himself. Placing a white china teacup and saucer on the sparkling black quartz counter, he asks if she would like chamomile tea?

"It will help relax you, babe," he says to her with hope in his eyes.

"Thanks, babe... but I remember the doctor saying I have to limit herbal teas. Oh, I also remember him saying something about aromatherapy oils too. At the spa, we can't use certain oils and things on people who are pregnant... for this reason," she manages. Still dazed, she wonders if she's making any sense. "It can be harmful to the baby. I think I'll just have an English Breakfast, babe,"

"Very strong, with a dash of two-percent milk and some sugar?" he smiles. He knows her too well.

"Yes, please." She manages a smile back. She loves how he remembers all these things about her. He's so caring toward her. This is why it was so hard for her when he would shut down and drink too much. She always knew he was a good guy, a good guy with issues; issues that she knew could be sorted out with some help.

Kristie is happy to give Enrique all the time he needs to fix himself. After all, he's already started to open up to her and agreed to get help; this is progress. Enrique's always struggled to talk to her about his issues, especially about his mom's passing. As he makes their drinks, Kristie's lips lift into a tiny smile, as she can't believe how far he has come already. She casts her mind back to how difficult he finds opening up about his pain and grief.

When they first met, Enrique had told her that his mom passed when he was six, and he found it far too painful to talk about. He tried so hard to confide in her over the years, but he just couldn't do it; the words just wouldn't come out.

This became such an issue throughout their relationship as he felt something of a failure because he couldn't open up to her. He felt he should be able to do this, as she was the only person he had ever felt like he could do this with, but he still couldn't. This only compounded the problem, and he became more and more frustrated with himself. Over time, whenever she tried to broach the subject, he would start to get agitated and do anything he could to divert the conversation.

Enrique had a pattern, and Kristie began to learn it very quickly; his drinking would usually get more excessive around certain dates. These dates were his mom's birthday and the anniversary of her passing. Of course, Christmas and his birthday are also a challenge for Enrique, but nothing to the magnitude of these two specific dates.

Things would start off slowly, and he would work all the hours God sends and spend hours upon hours in the gym. He would start to become distant, and when he was at home, he would either spend more time in the office or the gym. It was like he was avoiding Kristie because if he wasn't around her, he couldn't be reminded of what he thought was his failure, his weakness, which was not being able to be completely open with her about who he was, in terms of his pain and grief.

Of course, Kristie never felt this way about him, she just wanted to help, but unfortunately, she was helpless. He didn't know how to open up about his pain as he had buried it for so long. He suffered terribly from insomnia too, and Kristie would wake up in the middle of the night and find him working in the office.

The next stage of his pattern was going out on the weekends, getting wasted, and then sleeping it off until noon. At this point, his workout regime would slip a little, and he would then get angry about that. It was like he hated himself at times; he would be so angry at himself for not being able to control his emotions.

For the most part of their relationship, Enrique was the gentle, kind, caring, and fun-loving man he is, but when the pain got too much to bear, he would slip into this darkness, and there was nothing Kristie or anyone could do to stop it. Over time, things got worse. It was like the pain he had pushed down for so long was forcing its way out of him, and he had no idea how to deal with it.

Kristie is super close to his auntie, Arianna, Enrique's mom's sister, and she told her that Enrique hasn't cried since his mom's funeral. It was like he had locked it in a box and threw away the key. When he was growing up, whenever anybody asked him about his mom, he would tell everyone he was OK, and she's happy living in heaven; no matter how hard anybody tried to get him to talk, he wouldn't.

During the months leading to their break up, Enrique got worse and worse. Gina, Enrique's mom's anniversary is in January, and her birthday was in March. With these dates being so close to Christmas, it only made things worse, and Enrique became intolerable. He was working around the clock during the week, and then on weekends, he was going out and getting so drunk he could barely stand.

Kristie hardly saw him, and when she did, he was distant and isolated himself. When he was at home, he would either be in his office working or sleeping off the alcohol from the night before. Every time Kristie tried to get Enrique to talk about it, he would change the subject or walk away. He couldn't bear to talk about what was going on inside of him. If Kristie pursued him to talk, he would cause an argument. Kristie knew this was his way of making sure he didn't have to talk about what was bothering him. This went on for nearly three months, and there were no signs of it getting any better. Kristie couldn't live like that anymore. She had no other choice than to leave. She found this so hard to do, as she knew it was all down to the pain he had inside.

Kristie would try to explain to him that all the pain he'd been suppressing for so long was trying to force its way out of his body and was finally giving him no choice but to face everything, but he wouldn't listen, and he just carried on ignoring it. Her only hope was that he would realize what was happening before it was too late.

She can see that he's started to realize it now and is open to dealing with it. She's so happy he's finally recognized this, even if it did take a while. He's beginning to change, and she loves him even more for it.

"Here you go, babe." Enrique places a cup of hot tea in front of her. "I'll never understand the milk."

He chuckles a little, trying to make light of the situation.

"Thanks, babe," she replies. Her hands have finally stopped shaking.

Kristie started to drink English Breakfast tea when they were on vacation in London nearly three years ago. Although Kristie's distant family originates from Britain she had never been there, it never really interested her, until she met Enrique and they began talking a lot about her family. When her family moved to America all those years ago, they loved and adopted the American life and have never returned to the U.K.

When the couple were in London, they stayed at Claridge's hotel in Mayfair and had afternoon tea there one day. Kristie has always been a coffee drinker, never tea aside from herbal varieties. They served the tea with a side of milk, and she decided to try it; she's been hooked ever since. Enrique's never seen anyone put milk in tea before, but if that's what Kristie wants, then that's what she will have.

"Maybe you should try it? It's delicious," she says to him, reaching the cup over to him, knowing that he never would. She knows he hates tea and only drinks coffee or water mostly.

"Ummmm...no!" He screws his face up at the tea as he sits beside her. "I'll stick to my coffee, thanks.

I'm Cuban… Cubans don't drink tea." He jokes. Enrique's trying really hard to make Kristie feel at ease now that she's in the safety of his apartment, although he's in complete torment. He needs to call Ziv. Time is getting on.

They finish their drinks, and Enrique stands and tucks a loose strand of hair behind Kristie's ear and kisses her lips softly. "A little better?" he asks, hopeful that he's helped relax her after such a scary ordeal.

"Yes… thank you, babe. You really are so good to me. Thank you for looking after me," she says, kissing him back.

Enrique smiles. "I love looking after you, baby." He kisses her forehead. "Shall we go upstairs? I'll draw you a bath, and perhaps you can have a laydown? Get some rest?" he asks, hoping she'll go with it.

He needs to check the burner phone, and he also needs to make that call. He hates not being honest with her, but there's no other way at this stage; this is a conclusion he keeps coming to recently, and he's beyond furious about it. He needs to know what the fuck is going on. How the hell could Ziv miss this? On top of it all, he's still furious with himself; furious he allowed this to happen and furious he even trusted that vigilante moron. He also has to find out the lay of the land. Enrique has absolutely no idea what's happened since he last had any contact with Ziv and Gutiérrez. Plus, he needs to know if there's any news on his father, although he's sure they would have let him know if they had heard anything, or so he hopes.

"Yes. That will be nice," she replies gratefully.

Carrying Kristie's suitcase with one hand, Enrique takes her hand with the other. They climb the stairs and walk through the bedroom, leaving the suitcase on the chaise longue. As they arrive in the bathroom, Enrique walks over to the white standalone bathtub and turns on the faucet. He then walks over to the stainless-steel and glass cabinet on the wall and opens it. "Is your favorite coconut bubble bath OK to use, mi amor?" he asks softly, taking it out of the cabinet and showing her the bottle.

"Yes. That would be lovely," she replies. Kristie loves anything coconut or mango. She's impressed he kept it after she left. In fact, he's kept everything she left behind, including her black silk robe.

"Couldn't bring myself to package it all up and return it to you," Enrique says, reading Kristie's thoughts. "It made me feel less lonely after you'd gone. Like you were still here, in some way. Sounds silly, I know."

"Oh, Enrique," Kristie bursts into tears, putting her hands over her face as she does; it's all too much for her. Enrique runs over to her and wraps her in his arms, and she sobs uncontrollably into his chest.

"It's OK, baby... it's OK. I'm so sorry... I'm so, so sorry... I didn't mean to upset you... I'm so, so sorry, baby... you're safe now." His voice is soothing to her as he holds her close. "Everything will be OK... trust me, baby... everything will be OK."

"I'm so scared, Enrique... I'm so scared." Kristie manages through her sobs; her voice is trembling. "I just... I just... don't understand... why... why anybody would want to do that?" She looks up at him. Her beautiful tear-drenched face is etched with worry, and her glorious dark brown eyes are full of fear and devastation; it's heartbreaking for Enrique to see her this way. It's too much to bear.

Looking back at her with eyes full of love and concern, he reaches his hand to her hair and sweeps it out of her face, gliding his fingers gently down her cheek and wiping her tears. "Baby... don't worry about that now." He whispers. "It's OK... we'll get to the bottom of this... please... try to relax and get some rest... you need...."

"And that message...." Suddenly she loses her words, she can't bring herself to say it, and she feels so confused as to why anybody would want to say that to her. And more to the point, how did they know about the baby? Only her parents, Lisa, and Enrique know.

"Baby... please, don't think about that now." He cups her face gently with his hands and kisses her lips. "I'm sure it's just some stupid idiots playing games," he tries to reassure. The guilt he's already feeling about what's happened is taking over his entire being, and he feels sick to the stomach that he could have anything to do with this. Although he doesn't know for sure who did this, he has a pretty good idea his assumption is right, and right now, he's blaming himself for it all. He should have just called the cops in the first place and left it up to them to deal with instead of fueling the already blazing fire of hell that his father ignited only days ago. He tries to keep level as he has to be there for Kristie. "Try not to think about it, mi amor... we'll get to the bottom of this, don't you worry... I'll deal with it." With his voice still in a calm and soothing tone, he says. "You need to try to be calm... for you... and the baby." Still holding her face in his hands, he looks deeply into her eyes. "It's not good for the baby." He kisses her lips softly.

Kristie smiles and nods.

He kisses her soft lips once more. "Come on, baby... the bath's ready... it'll help you relax. Would you like me to get in with you?" Enrique asks, trying to divert where the conversation is going. He's worried she'll bring up the police again.

Kristie nods in agreement. Enrique gets undressed, then helps Kristie out of her clothes, and they climb into the warm, soothing bath. As they sink into the warm bubbly water, it feels so comforting, and the smell is delightful.

Sitting next to his girl, Enrique puts his arm over her shoulders and kisses her on the cheek. It feels surreal to them as they sit quietly, gazing out of the floor-to-ceiling windows, and watch life go on as normal below them outside when things are far from normal for them both right now. Kristie reaches over to the small cabinet next to the bath and gets a hair elastic. She ties her long dark hair up in a bun, so it's out of the water.

Enrique puts his arm back around her shoulders, kisses her cheek, and then her lips. He looks at her with teary blue eyes full of love. "I love you, baby." He whispers.

"I love you, too, babe." She kisses him again then slowly moves so she's sitting astride him. As their kiss grows deeper, Enrique slides his hands from her hips, up the center of her back, then to her shoulders. He pulls her closer to him, and he can feel her firm breasts and erect nipples pressing into his toned chest. Sliding his hands back down her body, following the shape of her curves, he holds her hips as she starts to move back and forth on top of him, rubbing herself on his erection, before sliding him into her.

Not breaking their kiss for a second, Kristie grips hold of the edge of the bath, steadying herself as she rocks back and forth in perfect time with Enrique. As they begin to move faster, his grip on her hips is getting tighter and tighter as he accepts the overwhelming surge of ecstasy that is flooding through him.

Water begins to splash over the side of the bath with their every move, and Kristie tips her head back, letting out a cry of passion. Enrique's mouth finds Kristie's breasts, and he begins to suck and bite her nipples one at a time, moaning with appreciation as he does. She feels so good, and she's so sexy; he worships her.

Their bodies tense as they move as one; they're getting closer and closer, and their moans are getting louder.

"Ahhh... fuck... fuck!!" Kristie screams as she comes explosively.

"FUCK!!!" Enrique hisses through gritted teeth as he explodes inside of her.

Kristie's head falls on Enrique's shoulder as he holds her trying to catch his breath.

"You OK, baby?" Enrique asks softly.

"Yeah... yes." She's breathless. "Are you?"

"Yes, baby." He kisses her cheek. "I love you."

"I love you, too."

He holds her as she sits astride him. As much as he wasn't expecting that to happen, he's glad it did. Getting lost in her is always a good remedy for him, and by the looks of things, it was just what she needed, too.

Eventually, she shifts herself off him, sits next to him again, and starts to wash. Then she begins to wash her man, admiring his beautiful body as she does. He's so handsome, and his muscles are so perfectly defined; his body really is a work of art. She will never get over how lucky she is to be with somebody as gorgeous as Enrique. When they first met, at times, she really felt intimidated by how perfectly handsome he is, and at times, she still does.

Once she's finished washing her gorgeous man, she kisses his lips and holds him close. With her head resting on his chest, she closes her eyes and starts to yawn; she's exhausted.

Enrique asks her if she would like to get out and have a laydown. She agrees but asks Enrique to lay with her. Of course, he wants to cuddle up in bed with her more than anything, but the problem is, he really needs to find a way to contact Ziv before anything happens to anyone else.

Climbing out of the huge bathtub, they both dry themselves off and walk into the bedroom. Enrique slips on a pair of black pajama pants, opens Kristie's suitcase, and pulls out a white floor-length Agent Provocateur silk and lace nightdress. He helps her to slide it down over her perfectly tanned figure and stands back to admire her. Kristie looks back at him, with a little shyness.

Although she looks the way she does, Kristie can still get a little insecure. Enrique has never given her any reason to feel this way, but unfortunately, men who she dated in the past did. Thankfully, she overcame these issues, but at times, they still come back to haunt her.

"You look so beautiful." He whispers with a sweet smile. He knows how Kristie is feeling, as he can read her, so he does what he always does at times like this; he reminds her how beautiful she really is. "You know how I love white silk against your tanned skin, my darling." He kisses her lips, closing his eyes at the same time before whispering. "You look delectable."

"I could say the same about you." Kristie smiles, glancing down at his perfectly toned body.

He smiles and holds Kristie tightly for a few moments. "Let's go to bed." He whispers. "You need some rest."

He walks Kristie to the bed with his arm around her and pulls back the luxurious white sheets, ready for her to get in. Once Kristie lays down, he covers her and leans down to kiss her on the cheek, before walking around to the other side of the bed. He presses some buttons on the iPad on the nightstand, and then the blinds begin to close out the late morning light; once completely closed, the room is dark and peaceful.

He climbs in next to Kristie and takes her into his arms, holding her from behind. He sweeps her hair away from her neck and kisses it, sliding his hand down over the silk of her nightdress, and holds her tummy, caressing it gently.

Within minutes, Kristie begins to drift off slowly and peacefully. Enrique stays holding her; he doesn't want to go anywhere. He wants to stay with her like this forever, just him and her with their tiny baby. Loving this moment of peace and tranquility, he wants nothing more than to savor every second, but he knows he has business to attend to. His painful reality is giving him no choice but to have to pull away from this harmonious embrace with the love of his life and get some answers. But for now, he will allow himself some time to enjoy lying next to his girl, breathing in her scent, watching her slow and steady breathing as she sleeps peacefully in his arms.

About a half-hour later, he reluctantly pulls away from his sleeping beauty and climbs out of bed, careful not to wake her. Checking back to make sure she is still asleep, he smiles. He loves her so much and can't believe she's carrying their baby. He's going to be a father, and he is brimming with elation. Glad that his beautiful girl is sleeping peacefully and getting some well-deserved rest, he takes a deeps breath and tries to prepare himself for what he is about to face.

Suddenly feeling like he has the weight of the world on his shoulders, he strolls into the closet to get a t-shirt, slips it on, and quietly heads down the stairs to his office to call Ziv. Anxiety grips his chest as he considers what lies ahead; yet again, he has no choice. Does he ever?

He needs to find out what the fuck is going on! But does he really want to know?

Chapter 19

On the way to the office, Enrique stops by the kitchen and grabs a bottle of Fiji from the refrigerator. He's hardly had anything to drink today and probably should think about having some lunch, but he doesn't care about that right now; there are more important things at hand, like getting his entire family protected against these assholes and getting some answers.

He can't understand why his father hasn't been found yet. If Ziv and Gutiérrez are as great as they make out, why the fuck is José still missing and why the fuck has his girlfriend's apartment been broken into? They should have eyes everywhere; this is what they promised, and to say Enrique is pissed off is an understatement.

He steps into his office and closes the door behind him. Just as he's about to sit down, he realizes he's left the fucking burner upstairs in the inside pocket of his blazer!

"For fuck's sake!" He exclaims a little louder than he wants. He's glad the penthouse is fully soundproofed, and Kristie won't be able to hear him, although he still worries.

Full of agitation, he exits the office and creeps upstairs quietly. He will now have to go back into his bedroom and try not to wake Kristie. He can't believe his luck. He's just finally managed to get her relaxed enough to sleep and get out of the bedroom without waking her, and now he has to go back in there and risk ruining it all.

Once upstairs, he opens the bedroom door slowly, keeping his eyes on Kristie as she sleeps peacefully on the super-king-sized bed, draped in luxury white linens. To his relief, she doesn't move. He glances around the bedroom, looking for his clothes; he can't find them anywhere. Then he remembers he left both of their clothes on the bathroom floor. Shit!

Looking at the main bathroom door, he notices it's closed, so he opts for the closet entrance instead. The closet has its own entrance to the bathroom and will be quieter, as opening the closed bathroom door could make noise and wake Kristie.

He tiptoes through the closet and into the bathroom, finds his Armani blazer in a heap on the floor, and searches for the burner phone. It is so unlike him to leave his clothes like this, but right now, he has more important things to worry about, like keeping Kristie and his family safe.

Once he's found the burner and his iPhone, he tiptoes back through to the bedroom. As he enters the bedroom, he stills and checks Kristie; she's still sound asleep. Just as he reminds himself to breathe, his iPhone chimes, alerting him he has a message. Fuck! His phone is always on vibrate! For all the times this could happen. Why now? Fuck!!

He checks on Kristie again. She stirs. Fuck! Fuck! Fuck! He stands frozen to the floor, staring in Kristie's direction. Thankfully, she settles again, looking beautifully calm and dreamy, as she lays on her side dressed in white silk underneath the sheets.

Thank fuck for that, he thinks to himself. Before he can cause any more reason to wake his sleeping beauty, he tiptoes out of the bedroom, closes the door slowly and very quietly, and heads back downstairs again.

Once back in the office, he closes the door and makes his way to his glass desk. God, what he would do for a fucking drink right now! How could so much go wrong and keep going wrong for him? He takes a deep breath and opens the flip phone, finds Ziv's number, one of the two that's stored in it, the other being Gutiérrez, and dials. He better fucking answer, Enrique seethes in his mind.

"Yes," says the voice on the end of the phone. It's Ziv.

"It's me. Enrique. You need to come up to my place now! Don't let anyone see you," He demands.

"I know what this is about. I tried to call you."

"What?" Enrique says. He's puzzled.

"I called. You didn't pick up. I will be there in two minutes."

"Don't ring the doorbell. Kristie's here... she's sleeping. Call me when you're outside," Enrique instructs.

"You think I don't know that?" Ziv says.

Enrique can't help but feel like Ziv is mocking him and acting as if there's nothing he doesn't already know. This irritates Enrique beyond measure. "Just get the fuck upstairs! This needs to be dealt with once and for all! This is bullshit!! You said you were onto everything! Clearly not!" he says, infuriated. "Just get up here now!" Enrique demands, hanging up the phone and throwing it on the glass desk. He can't tolerate any more of this shit. His internal voice is screaming. "FOR FUCK'S SAKE!!!"

Ziv calls him in what seems like two seconds. Enrique walks over to the front door of the penthouse and opens it to find the burly Russian standing there. Before he even gets the chance to enter the penthouse, Enrique steps out and pushes the bigger man in the chest, causing him to move backward. This obviously catches Ziv off guard as he takes a couple of steps back.

Enrique snaps. Pointing his finger at Ziv, he keeps his voice low, but his venom and rage are palpable. "What the Fuck!" His face is dark and almost menacing. "This is all on you and Gutiérrez! 'We've got it all handled' my fucking ass! That's my girlfriend... if something happens to her... I'll fucking kill you myself... the fucking pair of you!"

"We didn't have the condo under surveillance at that point. We were setting up with the rest of your family. Her condo was last because we knew she was with you!" Ziv responds in an all too calm fashion.

"I don't want your fucking excuses. You and Gutiérrez said you had this handled. It looks a long fucking way from handled to me. I should have never trusted you with the security detail... I only did because I didn't have a choice. I thought the reason you took Manolo's family was so this shit wouldn't happen!" Enrique's rage is beginning to explode inside of him; he's struggling to contain it any longer. The thought of anything happening to Kristie and their baby doesn't bear thinking about. The mere thought of this pushes him over the edge; he's had it with this shit. "D'ya know what? I need you out! Out of my building! I can't have you here. It could jeopardize everything. If anybody sees you here... how the fuck am I supposed to explain it? It's too close to home. Having you here is like putting a target on my back! What the fuck was I thinking?"

"Look, calm down and let's talk about what's going to happen next." Ziv attempts to appease Enrique, but it doesn't go over well.

"Calm the fuck down? Fuck you! Fuck all of you! This is my family! Imagine if it was your family! How the fuck would you feel? I'm serious... pack up your shit now and get the fuck out!" Enrique snaps back.

"OK. OK. I understand. I'm sorry for what happened to Kristie. This is on me, and it won't happen again. Let's go inside so we can discuss what we need to do next. Once we are done, I will clear out of the apartment, if that's what you want? But I think you're making a mistake." Ziv gestures for them to head into the penthouse.

Enrique reluctantly proceeds to head inside. The fact of the matter is, he doesn't want him anywhere near his home, let alone inside of it, but this isn't something he wants to discuss on his doorstep. He turns back to Ziv and says, "We're going to my office! I don't want Kristie to be woken up or to find out about any of this."

Ziv nods. "OK."

The two men move quickly and quietly to the office. Opening the door, Enrique enters and holds it open for Ziv to follow him inside. Enrique closes the door behind him, makes his way around his desk, and sits in his chair.

"OK. What do you have to say then? Make it quick... I don't need to be explaining this to

Kristie," Enrique says dismissively, keeping his voice low despite the fact that he's fuming inside. He's had his fill of this shit, and he just wants to get this over and done with as quickly as possible. If he never sees any of this lot again, it will be too soon, and right now, that includes his father.

"Look, we have everything set up. All of your family now have the most discreet guards on them twenty-four seven. Just like you asked, they won't even know that they are there. This can't and won't happen again. You have my word!" Ziv promises.

"You said that this wouldn't happen in the first place, and here we are. Kristie is fearful for her life... and I'll be honest with you... so am I. How can you be so sure it's not going to happen again?"

"I've spoken to Manolo... he's onto it... it could be retaliation for us taking his family... but Manolo is unaware of anybody in his organization being involved... but if it is anything to do with him... he's under no illusion that if something like this happens again... it will be his family that will pay the price."

"No! I will not have someone's family harmed! That is not the way it's going to happen. Do you hear me? Threats are all that this will be. If anyone else is harmed in any way, I'm going to the police about all of you." Enrique's stern tone emphasizes his seriousness to Ziv.

"Look, I have no intentions of bringing harm to anyone unless it's totally necessary. But if the need arises for us to make our point, trust me when I say that I will."

"I'm going to say it one more time," Enrique says in a threatening tone. "Nobody, and I mean NOBODY, is going to be hurt or killed. Do you understand me?" He raises his eyebrows and stares at Ziv.

"Fine if that's the way you want it," Ziv says dismissively. He has absolutely no intention of listening to Enrique. He will do what needs to be done. "Manolo is going to be in touch soon with the information about how we can get your father back."

"He fucking better," Enrique says sternly.

"He will," Ziv replies with certainty. "For now, try to go about business as usual. I know this isn't easy, and it was never our intention for things to turn out this way. But everything is under control now." He stands to leave.

"You better make fucking sure it is."

"You have my word... I will arrange for people to get Kristie's condo cleaned up."

"You've got to be fucking kidding me. No way are you stepping foot in her apartment. I will deal with that." Enrique is in total disbelief at Ziv's suggestion.

"OK. I was only trying to help. Have you managed to keep her from contacting the police?"

"Yes," Enrique replies with a disgusted look on his face. "I've lied to her and said that I would get it all sorted with the police. But believe me, when I say this, I am not going to keep lying to her to cover up your shit."

Ziv nods his response, turns and heads to the door. Enrique stands to follow him. "Don't worry. I'll see myself out. I will be out of the apartment within the hour. I will be in touch soon." He pulls the door open and turns back to Enrique before he heads out of the office. "Don't worry... we will get your father back safely, and everybody is under close surveillance... nothing will happen to anybody... trust me." Ziv attempts to reassure Enrique.

"I hope you're right." Enrique follows him to be sure that he leaves. "No more fuck ups." He warns as he closes the door behind him.

Reminding himself to breathe, he rests his forehead on the back of the door and asks himself silently, "What the fuck am I doing?"

Chapter 20

After checking on Kristie, who is still sound asleep, Enrique decides to go through his emails and catch up on some work. It's his way of taking his mind off things. But first: cafécito.

Once his coffee is made, he pours it into an espresso cup and gets another bottle of Fiji from the refrigerator before heading back to his desk.

As soon as he gets into his office, he places his coffee and water down on the glass desk. Finding the remote, he switches on the wall-mounted television, presses mute, and selects the news channel. There's still no news on the murders at the marine stadium. He's pleased about this but unnerved at the same time. He should have asked Ziv about where the bodies have gone. But then again, does he really want to know? Probably not. The less he knows, the better.

Sitting at his desk, he turns to his iMac and shakes the mouse gently to bring the screen to life. He signs in and loads up his work emails. Although there's still been no word about his father, Enrique's phone has been going crazy with email alerts, but they haven't been a priority due to what is happening. This is something he's usually very much on top of, but not over these past few days.

His email screen loads; nine hundred and fifty-two emails!! What the fuck?? Holy shit! I may be here some time, he thinks to himself. But this isn't unusual. He averages around two hundred per day, and with being out of his office for nearly three business days, plus there's been the weekend too, it's to be expected.

Sipping his coffee, he starts to plow through them, glancing up at the television from time to time. He has the subtitles on so he can see what they're talking about and flips between the regular news and the business news. He watches the business news a lot, as he likes to keep up to date; it's in his interest to.

He stops for a break from the screen and checks his voicemails. There are only a few. Petra has been great at keeping everyone at bay. Thank God, he thinks. He calls her to say he won't be in at all today and possibly the rest of the week. He asks her only to contact him if it's urgent and to cancel all of his upcoming meetings. This is a shock to Petra, but he explains he has a family emergency. Thankfully, he's made it so the business can run itself without him there. He feels it's a sign of good management; although he still likes to be in control of everything, he knows they can manage without him.

Having said that, there are certain things only he can do, but they will have to wait. He knows developers will be going crazy, but he's in no frame of mind to be sitting in business meetings right now. He will have to take the hit and pay whatever the cost for delays, etcetera; he honestly doesn't care right now.

He calls the rehab clinic to check on Leon. He's pleased to know that his friend is doing good and responding well to the treatment. Unfortunately, Enrique is not allowed to visit him throughout the duration of his treatment, but this is completely normal when people are in rehab.

Finally, he sends Gabriela a text telling her she has another paid day off tomorrow. He ends the text with "no arguments" and a smiling emoji. Glancing at the television, which still has no news on the marine stadium, he notices the time is 1pm. He must get some lunch prepared soon; he's actually getting hungry, plus, he wants to prepare something for Kristie when she wakes. Then he remembers he should have called a therapist today.

With dread swirling in his stomach, he loads up the internet. He needs to do some research first to find the best one. As he enters the information into the search engine, his feeling of hunger begins to disappear. Uggghhh this is so daunting. Where the fuck do I start, he thinks to himself.

After searching through various websites, he begins to find some therapists with good reviews that may be suitable to help him. Taking his Mont Blanc Blue Hour LeGrand fountain pen, he begins to write their information down. He doesn't know much about it all; it's an absolute minefield. He's not sure what he was expecting when he told Kristie he would call a therapist today, but he sure didn't expect it to be this complicated.

Saving the details of the ones that look the best, he decides to wait for Kristie to wake and ask her if she wouldn't mind going through them with him when she's ready. Of course, he understands that she may not feel up to it after today, but at least she will know that he is serious about going to see one.

He navigates back to his emails, replying to the ones that require it and deleting the junk. This is why he likes to keep on top of them. Some only need a short answer, but it's taking an eternity to get through them. Completely focused on the screen as he types a response, suddenly he feels someone watching him. Looking away from the screen toward the door, his eyes adjust, and to his delight, he sees Kristie standing in the doorway. She's looking beautiful as ever, wearing her white silk nightdress and black silk robe draped over the top.

"Hey, baby!" Enrique says softly; he's so happy to see her. He gets up from his desk and walks over to her. Holding her face gently, he kisses her sweet, full lips, then he asks. "Did you sleep well?"

"I slept good, thanks, babe. I woke up and found you weren't there... so I came looking for you," she replies, then looks down sadly. "I woke up feeling great... then I remembered what happened at my apartment. Oh, Enrique, I'm so scared... I can't believe this has happened. It doesn't make any sense," she starts to cry.

"It's OK, baby, everything is in hand," he says, holding her as she cries. "I know it was an awful thing to happen, but I really believe it was just some morons trying their luck. I've arranged for people to go with the police to show them the apartment, so they can do what they need to do... then they will fix it all up for you... it will look like nothing ever happened when you go back there." He kisses the top of her head. "You can stay here as long as you like. OK?" He hates the fact that he's lying to Kristie, but he doesn't know what else to do right now, plus he needs her to be calm for her and the baby's sake. But it feels so wrong to him, and it's getting harder and harder to keep things from her. He doesn't know how much longer he can keep this up; it's torture.

"Thank you, babe. I'm so grateful that you're doing all of this for me," she says, her voice is shaking.

"That's what I'm here for." He holds her pretty face in his hands once more and looks deeply into her eyes. "I'm so glad you're letting me do this for you. It means the world to me... I'm so lucky to even have you here... even if it's under these horrible circumstances. I'll look after you, baby... don't worry about anything. Once everything's been dealt with, I will have the security improved in both our apartments," he says. "It's all gonna be OK, mi amor... it will all be OK."

"Thank you, babe. I can't tell you how much this means to me, too." She says, sounding a little brighter now.

"Don't thank me, baby... I love you."

"I love you, too."

He holds her a while longer, and he can feel her body relax against him. Looking down at her, he says. "Shall I make you some lunch, baby?"

"Yes, I'm starving."

"OK, baby... what would you like?"

"Ummm... well, I really fancy some feta and watermelon salad?" Kristie suggests.

"Sounds absolutely perfect." He smiles. "I can't think of anything else I'd rather do right now. I've just gone through over nine hundred emails," he says, laughing. "I need a break, and I can't think of anyone I'd rather spend my break with." He smiles before putting his arm around her and walking with her toward the kitchen. "Wanna get some sun... we can eat up on the pool deck?"

"Perfect... shall we get changed into our bathing suits? We can go for a swim too?" Kristie suggests, feeling like a bit of sun will help make her feel better after what happened this morning.

"Sure thing, baby. Do you want to get changed first, then I can make lunch for us?"

"Sure. I can help you make lunch," Kristie responds. They always enjoy cooking together.

"Of course," he says as they walk upstairs.

Kristie opens the suitcase, wondering if Enrique had thought to pack a bathing suit when they left her apartment in a hurry earlier this morning. To her surprise, she's pleased to find her multi-colored Agua Bendita bikini. As she puts on her bikini, Enrique slips on his pale blue swimming shorts. She glances over at him, checking out his sculptured physique; the color compliments his flawless dark skin tone beautifully. He's so unbelievably hot, and she's missed admiring his handsome looks.

Once dressed, they both head back downstairs and prepare lunch.

In a bowl, Kristie places a mixture of lettuce leaves and chopped cherry tomatoes. Then chops up an avocado for the side. She likes it on its own with some lemon, not mixed in with the salad. She eats most things but can be a little fussy with certain foods.

Enrique puts Sade on over the sound system, which reaches the entire penthouse, including the pool deck, all operated from his iPhone. Then he starts to help Kristie make lunch. He carves up a watermelon, slices some feta, then cuts some wholegrain bread. First, Kristie remembers she needs to make sure the feta is pasteurized. She's still getting the hang of what she can and can't eat now that she's pregnant. Thankfully it is, as she really has a craving for her favorite salad.

Kristie mixes the lettuce, tomatoes, feta, and watermelon in the salad bowl, then pours a mixture of balsamic vinegar and olive oil over the top. She gets the salad servers out of the drawer and silverware, and Enrique puts the bread in a bread basket and gets out some plates and glasses. Enrique makes two journeys carrying the food and drinks up to the pool deck as he won't allow Kristie to carry anything.

Once on the sun-drenched pool deck, Kristie lays the food and dishes out on the outdoor dining table in the shade of a large white hexagonal parasol. It's another beautiful Miami day; glorious sunshine and the humidity is high in the eighties. They sit down to enjoy one of their favorite meals.

"Lunch is amazing, thank you, my darling," he says.

"It was a joint effort, Mr. Cruz." Kristie smiles.

"And we work so well together, baby." He reaches his glass across to her, and they toast their glasses full of sparkling water.

"We do."

Taking a sip of his drink before placing down the glass, he says. "So, you'd like to go to the Maldives?" He remembers her telling him this yesterday at brunch and wants to keep Kristie's mood upbeat after how upset she was earlier.

"Yes, babe... I would love to go there one day. It looks so beautiful... I was looking at the Sanchester resorts there... they look incredible."

"Sounds incredible... I'll take you there, baby." He smiles sweetly. They could use a vacation right now. When all this is over, he's going to take her on a much-needed break away from all this, of course, that's if she would like to. He can't be too sure just yet; it's still early days. "Ya know... I got an email today about their property in Bora Bora. That also looks phenomenal. I want to see the world with you...." His voice goes quiet. "That's if you still want to...."

"I would love to, babe... of course I would... we just have some things to work through first, that's all," she says softly as she finishes her salad.

"I know...." He presses his lips into a hard line. Fear creeps across his face as he feels that overwhelming feeling of dread in the pit of his stomach again. "I... uh... when you were sleeping... I... found some therapists online." He pauses, not sure if he should ask her this now. He looks at Kristie, who is looking back at him with a mixture of hope and sadness as she listens to what he has to say. "I... uh... I'm not sure if... if I should ask you this... but...uhhh...."

"What is it, baby?" Kristie shifts in her chair so she's facing him and holds his hands on his lap. "It's OK... you can ask me anything."

"I... uhh... just with everything that's happened today... I don't feel right asking you... but when you're ready... would you mind having a look at which therapist would be best for me... when I was looking earlier... it was like a minefield, and I have absolutely no idea about any of it... so...."

"Of course, I will, babe."

Enrique breathes out a huge sigh of relief. "Thank you." He lifts one of her hands to his lips and kisses it. Looking into her eyes, he tries to get his words out. "I... uhh... just with everything... I didn't feel right asking... but... I... uhh... umm... I don't know... like... what if...."

Kristie can see he's getting frustrated with himself as he can't say what he means. "You're worried that you'll choose the wrong one and have to find another... and go over it all again?"

She gets me. She totally gets me, he thinks to himself. Tears fill his eyes. "You always know...."

Kristie reaches her hand to his cheek and looks into his eyes with sincerity. "Because I love you." She smiles. "Just like you get me... because you love me... we have a connection... so powerful... we always have... you always know how I'm feeling and what I'm going through... I don't have to say anything... you just know." Her eyes sparkle with tears as she smiles at him. Running her thumb across his cheek, she looks deeply into his teary blue eyes and says. "I'm so proud of you."

"Proud of me?" Enrique looks confused.

"Yes, babe... I'm super proud of you. You've made the first step... you did it... and you did it by yourself."

"I would never have been able to do it without you." He shakes his head with wonder as he looks at the beautiful lady sitting before him.

"You did it without me, babe. Even with what happened this morning... you still stuck to your word and started to research things... and it means so much to me that you have... I mean, this time last week, I would never have thought you'd be researching therapists."

"Well, yes… that is true… but I would never have been able to do this without your support… your guidance."

Kristie stands and sits astride him, draping her arms around his broad, muscular shoulders. "You did this." She whispers into his ear. "And I'm proud of you… so, so proud." She kisses just beneath his ear. "And I love you."

"And I love you." He kisses her cheek and holds her tightly, breathing in her scent.

Surprisingly, Enrique feels calm and at peace as he holds Kristie close to him; this is the effect she always has on him, and he can't get enough of it. With the looming fear of going to therapy and actually talking about his grief for the first time in his life, Leon in rehab again, and the hurricane that is José's situation, Enrique needs her peace more than ever. She has the ability to calm any storm, no matter how treacherous, and right now, he is more than willing to allow her.

After a short while, the couple decides to go for a swim. With the rooftop being as private as it is, they often swim and sunbathe naked up there. Today is no exception. They love to swim naked. It feels so liberating, plus it means that they don't get tan lines. Tan lines are a pain for Kristie, especially when she wears strapless dresses; they look unsightly.

Before they jump in the pool, Enrique slips off his shorts and places them on the double sun lounger. Then he sits on the edge of the bed while Kristie takes off her bikini. As she places it down with his swimming shorts, Enrique takes her hand and guides her to stand in front of him. He looks at her body and glides his hand from the side of her breast and down toward her stomach. He notices her breasts have become slightly fuller, and her stomach has the tiniest of bumps. He looks at her in awe as he runs his hand along her tummy, caressing the tiny bump. He gazes at her stomach in disbelief; his baby is inside there. He leans forward and places a kiss on the bump, and looks up at the love of his life with complete adoration.

"Your body is changing, baby... and you look so beautiful." He kisses her stomach again. "It's very sexy to me, ya know... so, so sexy." He gently caresses her tiny bump once more.

Kristie looks down and smiles at him, running her hand over the bump with him. Enrique leans in, kisses her hand, then kisses down her stomach and continues lower. Slowly he trails his kisses over her smooth skin just above her clitoris before traveling down further. He gently puts his hands between her thighs, guiding her to part her legs. She steps one leg sideward slightly as he continues to kiss her soft skin finding his way to her clitoris, then he starts to lick and suck her sweet spot.

Kristie's hands glide through Enrique's jet-black hair, gripping and pulling as the pleasure starts to run through her body. She begins to moan as she tries to absorb the extreme pleasure as it rips through her. Consumed by the intensity of her feelings, her body starts to bow as her legs betray her. She leans her hands on Enrique's strong shoulders, trying and keep her balance. He steadies her with his hands as he holds her behind, and his grip tightens with his fingers digging into her flesh.

He continues to lick and tease her, relishing every second of her glorious taste and the feel of her on his tongue. He absolutely loves doing this to her, it's the ultimate turn-on, and she looks so unbelievably sexy. Gliding his tongue from her clitoris, he slides it inside of her, and she cries out as her orgasm nears. Fuck she is so goddamn hot, he thinks to himself, as she floods his mouth with her arousal. He loves watching her body move as he pleasures her this way; in fact, he loves the way her body moves with anything she does.

Kristie screams out his name as she comes wildly, trying to keep her balance, but Enrique holds her up with his darkly tanned, muscular arms as they flex and glisten in the blazing sunlight.

"It's OK, baby… I've got you… I've got you." He whispers.

Once her orgasm subsides, he stands, picks her up, and lays her on the sun lounger. Hovering over her, he starts to kiss her deeply. Kristie reaches up to him, desperate to deepen the kiss further. She loves tasting herself in his mouth. She moans loudly as she devours him, drinking every drop. He slides his erection up and down over her clitoris, and she moves in time to meet his rhythm.

Enrique is getting even harder as her arousal soaks him; this drives him so crazy. Kristie opens her legs wider and wraps them around his, so they're intertwined. Enrique needs to be inside of her; he can't wait any longer. He slowly slides into her, tipping his head back as pure ecstasy explodes within him.

He buries his face into her neck, breathing out through his gritted teeth, as he tries to accept the painful pleasure coursing through his veins. He lightly grazes his teeth over her neck and bites it gently; Kristie bites into his shoulder as her legs grip him tighter and her nails scrape down his back.

The sheen of perspiration on their skin is shimmering in the sun as they move together as one. He kisses her again, then travels his kisses down her throat, intermittently licking and biting her skin. Kissing, licking, biting, and tasting his way down to her breasts, and as he reaches each nipple, he licks, sucks, and bites. She moans loudly, enjoying every second of Enrique tormenting her nipples. Her back arches off of the bed, pushing her breasts up to him as he teases her.

"Fuck!" Enrique groans with appreciation. She looks so incredible, so feminine. He's close, and he knows she is too.

"Fuck... babe... oh god... fuck!" Kristie screams. "Please... oh God!!!" She comes over and over again. "I can't... it's too much... fuck... oh... please...." She comes again.

"That's it, baby... that's it... fuck... Christ, you're soaking... you're all over me... so fucking beautiful... so sexy and beautiful."

Kristie comes again and takes Enrique with her to the point where he can barely take it.

Laying entwined with their eyes closed, they bathe in the afterglow of their lovemaking. Wrapped in each other's arms, they kiss softly and intermittently as their bodies calm in the warmth of the afternoon sun.

"I love you so much," Enrique says, looking deeply into Kristie's eyes. He kisses her once more. "You're so goddamn sexy," he feigns a growl as he squeezes her tightly in his arms.

Kristie giggles. "I love you too... and so are you, babe," she replies with a dreamy smile.

He pulls her into a spooning position and holds her, kissing her shoulder and he rubs his hand on her tummy, feeling her little bump; their little bump.

He sweeps his hand up to her left breast, and starts to glide his fingers around it, then starts to pull and tug at her nipple. He kisses her shoulder and then across the top of her back as the sun beats down on them from up above. It feels so good, enjoying each other, just like they always used to.

Enrique can feel Kristie has scratched his back as it's stinging in the sun, and he loves it; he always has. It only adds to how aroused he's getting as he lays with his girl, feeling her beautiful body next to his.

He's so hard; his erection is pressing into the cleft of her behind, and she begins to push herself into it. Enrique moves down the lounger a little, and Kristie tilts her body so he can enter her, and he slips into her with ease. Still caressing her breasts and pulling and squeezing her nipples, he starts to move in and out of her, feeling every inch of her as she wraps around him.

Kristie rolls onto her front, and Enrique follows. She lifts herself off the bed with her elbows and knees, with Enrique still inside of her, and he begins to move; Kristie wants more.

"Fuck me hard and fast!" she demands.

Her wish is his command. He starts to thrust in and out of her, holding her by the hips, as he fucks her as hard as she's begging him to. Their breathing is ragged.

"Let me see your face," he demands. "I want to see your face." Enrique loves to watch Kristie when they make love.

Kristie leans down closer to the bed and turns her head to the side so that Enrique can see her face, and he watches her as she takes everything he gives her; this is so fucking hot!

"Fuck! You're so fucking sexy!" he breathes, as he continues pushing into her hard and fast. Fuck, she feels so fucking good. Their moans and cries of passion are getting louder and louder.

Then, leaning over the top of her, he whispers in her ear. "I want you on top." Kristie pulls away and moves on the lounger so Enrique can lay on his back. His back stings as he lays down on the bed, which only adds to the blazing carnal desire that's burning inside of him; fuck, he's about to explode!

Kristie climbs on top of him and slides down on his rock-hard erection. But this time, she's facing away from him. She leans forward, allowing him to watch himself slide in and out of her; the ultimate turn-on. She knows he loves this, and she does too; she loves him watching her, she finds it very sexy.

Enrique grabs her hips and holds her firmly in place as she moves up and down on him.

"Fuck babe... you look so fucking incredible... hmmm... you know how much I love watching you... so fucking sexy... fuck!!"

"I love you watching me, babe... hmmm...." She moves oh so slowly, only making the pleasure more agonizing.

"Ahhh... babe... fffuuuccckkkk!" Enrique throws his head back... this is too much to take... she's driving him to the point of no return, but he wants it to last forever.

She moves up and down on him, keeping her rhythm slow and sensual, giving him no choice but to accept what she's giving him, and then she shifts herself, so she's facing him, and their bodies begin to move in unison.

They're both so close, and Kristie can feel him expanding and getting harder inside of her as she leans over him, resting on her elbows. He can feel her beautiful hard nipples brushing up and down his chest as she bites his shoulder, and suddenly, she's screaming through her orgasm, then Enrique follows. His fingers are digging into her behind as they moan through the intense surge of ecstasy as they climax and their bodies shudder as one.

They lay on the sun lounger, kissing each other, unable to move, as they try to gain some sort of equilibrium.

"Wow, baby... that was so amazing... what the hell are you doing to me," he says breathlessly, with a sexy smile. "Christ, I love you so much,"

"I could say the same about you, Mr. Cruz." She giggles.

"Ahhh... that giggle." His smile grows wider. "Gets me every time... ever since I met you...." He kisses her lips. "Hmmm... my beautiful girl."

"My handsome man." She kisses him, then smiles at him, biting her lower lip. "That was incredible."

"It sure was, Miss Carrington... it sure was." He looks down with eyes tinged with sadness. "Ya know... I never thought you would come up here again... let alone do this with me... I feel so blessed. Thank you," Enrique says, reaching his lips to hers and kissing her.

"I feel blessed to have you too." She kisses him once more. "Ya know, I feel the same... I mean, I always hoped I would come back here... be with you... sharing moments like this...."

"You did?" Enrique's eyes are sparkling with hope as he smiles with delightful surprise.

"Yes, babe... I did."

"You don't know what that means to me, baby."

"I know, babe... and it means the world to me to be here with you, too... you know that." She smiles.

The truth is, both Kristie and Enrique made no secret that they missed each other and wanted to reconcile, but it always seemed so impossible when they were apart. Although Enrique knows this, he's never felt it's something he should be sure of ever happening; he's never felt that he's had the right to, after the way he treated Kristie. But now they're here, together, it feels so incredible, and it's like the most natural thing in the world.

"I'm so excited for things to come... for our future," Kristie says. "I really can see a change in you... and it makes me feel so good inside. And to think that even with all this other stuff going on, you've still managed to investigate therapists."

"I told you that I was serious, baby... I want to make this work... and I want to be the best father and boyfriend I can be." He tucks a loose strand of hair behind her ear as they lay entwined, facing each other. "You make me want to be better... to be a better person. I couldn't go on like I was anymore... you were right all along." He pauses for a second before continuing. "It's just always been so hard for me to talk about my problems... you know... Lord knows I've tried... but in the end I thought it was easier not to, as it always made me feel so sick when I tried. But actually, it's harder not talking about them because it meant I lost you. And if I carry on drinking like I have been... when things get too much... I won't be here much longer either... and I want us to live a long, healthy, happy life together." He smiles, although he's extremely serious about what he's saying. "And, if you'll have me... I want to get married one day and have more children," Enrique says, with hope in his voice.

Kristie smiles back at him. "You're a good person, Enrique... you do so much, not just for me, but for lots of other people. You're so kind and caring... and you'll be an amazing father; I know you will. It means the world to me that you're willing to go to therapy for us and get better for yourself. It's not about me being right about anything; it's about wanting the best for you... for us." She kisses him and smiles against his lips. "And yes, once we've got through this, I would love for us to get married and have more babies."

"Oh my God, really?" Enrique's face lights up with extreme joy; he's smiling so widely, you can see it from space.

"Yes, baby." Kristie giggles and kisses him again.

Enrique pulls her into a tight embrace. He buries his face in her neck and tries desperately to hold back the floods of tears as they well up in his eyes. He feels on top of the world right now, and he couldn't be happier. He will get past this; they will get past this, and he's going to push through the agony to heal himself once and for all.

Submitting to their tears, they hold each other closely as they cry their tears of joy together.

"Oh, baby, I love you," Enrique whispers.

"And I love you, too."

"I'm going to make you proud, baby… so, so proud."

"I know you will… you already do." Kristie looks up into his summery blue eyes through her tears.

"Thank you, baby, and so do you… you always have."

"Thank you, babe." She smiles. "Just give us some time… we'll get there… we'll get through this… I just don't want us to go a hundred miles an hour, then crash… I want us to build a solid foundation… something we can build a strong relationship on," she explains.

"I know, baby… I understand… and I will be better… for you… for us… for this little one." He reaches his hand to her stomach as she lays beside him. "And you're going to be the best mom in the world... and it makes me so happy to hear those words coming from you... I would love to have the privilege of calling you my wife, as well as the mother of my children." He smiles sweetly. "It would mean so much to me... especially after everything... everything I've done," Enrique says, kissing her one more time. He brushes his fingers over her cheek and kisses her again.

They lay side by side, face to face and gaze into each other's eyes, with pure love.

"I love you, Miss Carrington."

"I love you, too, Mr. Cruz."

They kiss tenderly, enjoying their magical moment together, as they bathe in the afternoon sun.

Chapter 21

Once they have cleared away all the lunch dishes, Kristie and Enrique have a shower and then get dressed; they both decide on leisurewear. They're going to spend some time together around the penthouse and try to relax, but first things first, Enrique has to find a therapist and schedule an appointment. Ugh, he feels nauseous and super anxious at the mere thought; how the hell is he going to feel when he actually has to go? He looks at Kristie with eyes full of fear and takes a deep breath.

"Shall we go look online and get this therapist appointment scheduled then?" He says, his voice is almost trembling. He wants to do this, and he *will* do this, but he's petrified all the same.

"It will be OK, babe. I'm gonna be here for you every step of the way," Kristie replies, trying to reassure him. She knows more than anybody how big of a deal this is. She walks over to him and takes him in her arms.

"I know, baby... and thank you for everything you've done for me so far... thank you for helping me find the right therapist, too," Enrique says, holding her tightly and kissing her cheek. He knows he has to make this call, but right now, he wants nothing more than to go to bed and make love for the rest of the day. Losing himself in this most gorgeous girl is the best therapy there is.

"You don't have to thank me. I love you... I want to help." She shifts back to look at him with a smile. She looks so sexy and beautiful dressed in her black yoga pants and light blue camisole top.

"And I love you for that... I love you so, so much, baby," Enrique replies. Knowing he has to distract himself, or they will never leave the bedroom, he suggests, "How about we go down to my office and load up the computer then?"

They head downstairs, stopping for some bottles of water in the kitchen on the way. In the office, Kristie gets a chair and sits beside Enrique at his desk. She slides on her black-framed cat eye Prada glasses and looks toward the screen. Enrique glances over to her, holding his gaze for a few moments. He loves her wearing her glasses; he finds it so damn sexy. She catches him looking at her with blue eyes glittering with wanton desire, and they smile at each other. They both want each other so badly right now, but they know how important it is to deal with the task at hand, so they shift their focus back to the computer. Enrique loads up the large iMac screen, and as efficient as ever, not only has he written down the possible therapists, he has also saved their websites on the computer.

"There are three that I've narrowed it down to; however, I'm open to your suggestions, of course," Enrique explains. He's now feeling extremely anxious; borderline panic. "I'm not sure what I'm looking for... I'm not sure if I need one in a specialized field or what? I don't really know which category I would fit into?" As he says this, his hands start to shake.

Kristie notices this right away, and takes his hands in hers, and looks deeply into his eyes. "Baby, it's gonna be OK... I love you, and I'm here for you." She leans over and kisses him tenderly. "Please... I know how hard this is for you... but please don't be scared... it will all be OK... try to think of this as the first stage of healing... your first step toward being free of feeling the way you feel when things get out of hand... that feeling of spiraling... the one you used to say about." Enrique nods slowly as he listens to her. "This is your first step toward helping yourself with that darkness... the agony you feel in here." She holds her hand on his heart, looking at him with eyes brimming with love and understanding. Kristie knows him oh so well, and she knows what he goes through, even though he struggles to open up to her.

Holding her hand with his over his heart, Enrique smiles and nods, with eyes full of tears. She's right, she always is, but he can't seem to put a stop to this fear and dread as it forces its way through him. Gripping her hands tightly, he says. "I don't know what I would do without you, babe. You get me... you understand me... even though I've shut you out the way I did... you know... you know me and what I'm going through." Regret swoops in.

"Why did I treat you the way I did? How could I let you go?"

"That's in the past now, babe," Kristie says softly. She gestures her hand to the computer on the desk. "This is our future... you going to therapy is our future." She looks down at her stomach and glides her hand over it. "Our baby is our future, too."

He holds her hand with his on her tummy. "And I will do anything for you and our baby... anything." He leans over and kisses her lips. "I will do anything for us... to be happy... to live life to the full... and to never do what I did ever again... to never feel that way again... the darkness... my pain... I will do anything to never feel that way... you deserve better... our baby deserves better, and I deserve better."

"You don't know how much that means to me to hear you say that, baby." Kristie smiles as tears fall from her eyes.

"Hey, baby," Enrique whispers, reaching across to her and lifting her onto his lap. "Please don't cry." He holds her close. "I only wish I had done this sooner... a lot sooner... to save you from all the heartache and pain... I'm so sorry... so, so sorry... I love you." He strokes her hair as he holds her, kissing the side of her head as he does.

"I know, babe, I know... it's just... I've waited so long to hear you say this... I... I know how difficult it is for you... I know how hard you're finding this now... but you're still doing it... and it means the world to me."

"Like I said, I will do anything for us... I love you... I love you so, so much... you are my life... my world... my everything."

"And you're mine too... you're everything to me... you always have been."

They hold each other a while longer before turning to the screen and checking out the therapists.

Kristie leans toward the screen, resting on her elbows. As he shows her his findings, she can see what Enrique means; it is a minefield. They all deal with most things, but some specialize in P.T.S.D and others with drug and alcohol abuse or grief.

Kristie strongly believes that if you peel back all the layers, grief is at the root of Enrique's issues, anger, and frustration. He has never been able to handle the pain of losing his mom at such a young age. As he was only six, he had no way of understanding what he was feeling, so he suppressed it and did everything he could to forget about it. For the most part, he does a great job of hiding his pain, but at times, it becomes bigger than him and explodes out of him in different ways.

When he would get quiet and distant, Kristie always knew that it was his way of avoiding losing his temper; if he wasn't around people, he was less agitated; felt less pressured. When he would snap and get angry, on the surface, it looks like he's just a very angry and frustrated person, but behind that anger is actually somebody who is living in intolerable agony.

Not that she's a professional, but Kristie doesn't believe Enrique has a drinking problem per se; she doesn't think he's an alcoholic. Although he sure can drink to excess when things get too much for him. It's true to say that he uses it as a crutch, but not all the time. It happens in phases. Most of the time, he can have a few glasses of wine and chill, but when things get too much, it's like alcohol numbs the pain he's in.

"Look at this guy. He helps with everything... and specializes in grief... he looks really friendly, too." Kristie points to Dr. Xavier López on the screen. "Let's have a look at his reviews." Enrique loads them up, and they start to read. As she reads on, Kristie likes the sound of him. People are saying that he was their first port of call, that they had never been to therapy, and he was so kind and helped with their fears of going. A lot of people sound just like Enrique, and he has helped give them the tools to deal with their issues. "I think he sounds the best." She looks at Enrique and asks. "What do you think?"

"I agree." He smiles through his nerves. He lets out a long calming breath. "OK. I'll give him a call?" He picks up his cell. Taking a deep breath, he dials the number on the screen. He has to do this. He has to take the first step to fixing himself. He knows he needs to do this, but it's still torture for him. He feels so nauseous, but it's for the greater good. Here goes, he tells himself as he hears the dial tone.

Still sitting on his lap, with one arm around his shoulder, Kristie holds his hand for reassurance. She's so proud of her man. He's taking the first step toward something she thought he would never do. She's always hoped he would do this, but this is the first sign of him actually taking action. She's so happy to do this together with him, to be there with him during his first step on his journey to recovery, and she will be there every step of the way, for as long as it takes.

Once the appointment is arranged, Kristie shifts herself, wraps her arms around his shoulders and kisses him. He holds her more tightly than usual. "That wasn't so bad, was it?"

"No… I think a lot of it is the anticipation." He lets out a sigh of relief, smiling at her sweetly. "Thank you for helping me find someone… I couldn't have done this without you," Enrique says, grateful the ordeal is over, well, for now at least. He needs to get through the appointment next. But until then, he's going to put that right out of his mind. He's with Kristie, and he's going to focus on spending time with her and their little baby.

"I know what you mean... things are never as bad as you think they'll be... I'm happy I'm here, babe... and I'm so proud of you for doing this."

"Thank you, baby." He kisses her lips before looking at her with concern. "How are you feeling? I know you like to distract yourself with things when you have a problem... I just want to check you're OK after this morning... I worry about you," He knows Kristie tends to throw herself into something to take her mind off of difficult situations. If she has a problem that she can't fix, she would busy herself with something else. They aren't dissimilar in that respect, but unlike Enrique, Kristie can talk about things that are bothering her. After the break in this morning, he wants to make sure she is really OK, as she has a way of putting on a front. Kristie is unbelievably strong, and sometimes that makes it hard for Enrique to look after her. Of course, he knows she can look after herself, but Enrique is the type of man who likes to take care of her; he wants to be her protector. It's just who he is.

"I'm OK. It's just that message that got me, that's all. I don't understand it. I know break ins happen every day, but that message made it more personal to me. Plus, I don't understand how they got into my apartment with the security we have at the condo… ugh… I just want them caught," Kristie says with a look of sadness as she strokes her tummy. "How would they know about the baby? I don't understand," she says, looking down at her stomach, then at Enrique.

"Ummm… well, when we were in your bathroom, I noticed there was a pregnancy test on the vanity… I didn't want to mention it, as I didn't want to upset you anymore… I was worried about you." He explains.

"Oh right, I see." Kristie feels a little calmer now. She didn't think about that. "I kept it… for us… as a keepsake…." She smiles sweetly.

"Oh baby, that is so beautiful." He smiles back just as sweetly. "I must admit, in the midst of it all, it was a ray of light… like, as I wasn't part of it… it felt so special to me to actually see it… sounds silly, I know."

"No, it doesn't… I know what you mean." She holds his face in her hands and kisses his lips. "I must admit, I do feel a little more at ease now I know that… it's really been bugging me."

"I'm sorry, baby… I just didn't want to bring it up at the time as you were so understandably upset, and I didn't want to make things worse… plus since then, we've been distracted with other things… I would have mentioned it sooner, but I didn't want to keep bringing up what happened… it's important to me that you try to relax."

"I know… I understand. I just hope the police find them."

"I'll get to the bottom of this; I'll make damn sure of it, baby, don't you worry," Enrique says, trying not to raise his voice, revealing the anger he's feeling inside about the situation. Seeing Kristie so upset is torture for him, and he hates that he's keeping things from her, and he doesn't know how much longer he can keep it up. This isn't who he is; he's no liar. But he has to do this for the time being. The alternative is much worse, as far as he's concerned.

"I know, babe, I know." She looks at him full of love. "Why don't we just try to enjoy our time together in our little cocoon… just you, me, and this little one," she says, brushing her hand over her tummy again. Reminding herself, she needs to stay calm for the baby's sake, if anything, and talking about it isn't going to change what has happened. She will leave the authorities to deal with it and stay at Enrique's until it's over.

"Baby, if I had my way, we would never leave this place and stay in our little cocoon forever." The thought is very appealing to Enrique. He's had enough of dealing with the outside world. When he's in his penthouse with Kristie, he feels at peace. Like he can shut out all the horror of his father's situation, or even just the stresses of daily life. It's very easy to forget about what's really happening in his life, ninety floors up in the sky.

All of a sudden, he feels really hungry. Patting Kristie's behind playfully, he says. "Shall we cook some dinner? I don't know about you, but I'm so hungry. I can't believe how quickly time's gone today." He tilts his head to the side and gives her a sexy grin. "But then again, time always flies when I'm with you, mi amor."

Kristie giggles. "Time flies when I'm with you, too, Mr. Cruz." She kisses his lips. "What shall we make?" She asks as Enrique gets up out of his chair, lifting her at the same time. She slides down his body and lands on her feet. "I fancy something Cuban," she giggles once more.

"You always fancy something Cuban," Enrique says, chuckling with her.

"Yeah, I do," she smiles and grabs his firm backside with both of her hands before kissing him once more.

They both head to the kitchen arm in arm, and Enrique puts on some salsa over the sound system.

"Vaca frita de pollo?" Enrique suggests.

"Oh yeah! That sounds great."

"Your favorite," he says with a smile.

He gets some chicken out of the refrigerator, along with an onion. Then gets garlic, oil, oregano, salt, and limes out of the pantry. He chops the onion and minces garlic, places it in a saucepan with the chicken, adds some salt, and pours some water on top of the ingredients. He places the pan on the stove and waits for it to come to a boil.

Kristie gets the rice ready, chops up a salad, and puts it in the refrigerator ready for when dinner is served. She then starts preparing some Cuban coffee. She knows Enrique is more than likely ready for his next fix, and she could do with one, too, although she has started to limit caffeine since she found out she's pregnant.

Enrique starts to make the espumita ready for when the rest of the coffee is brewed. Héctor Lavoe is singing "Mi Gente" over the sound system, and Enrique is singing along to the words and dancing as he cooks. This is nothing new. Enrique loves to dance. A lot. He never really sits still. He says he was born dancing.

He grabs Kristie's hands and starts to dance with her. He swirls her around and brings her into him before twirling her around again. Then they stop and kiss tenderly, closing their eyes and savoring the moment. Then the coffee signals that it's brewed, forcing them to break their embrace.

"Damned coffee," Enrique complains playfully.

They smile against each other's lips and kiss once more before preparing the cafécito.

As they sit at the breakfast bar sipping their coffee, Kristie's cell vibrates on the shimmering black quartz counter. Glancing over at the screen of her gold iPhone, she notices it's a text from her friend, Lisa. She will be worried about her, so she decides to text her back.

Hey!
How are you?
I take it brunch went well?
Haven't heard from you.
Fancy coffee this week?
We must catch up.
Let me know.
Lisa xxx

Kristie texts back.

Hey!
I'm so sorry I haven't got back to you.
Everything's Good.
Hope you're OK, too?
Brunch was amazing.
Stayed at Enrique's.
Shall we say Friday?
Krissy xxx

I knew it!
I'm so happy.
I can't wait to hear all the deets.
See you Friday.
Text me when you finish.
Lisa xxx

Sure.
See you then
Krissy xxx

"That was Lisa," Kristie says to Enrique as he checks the chicken on the stove.

"Oh yeah. How is she?"

"She's good. She wants to meet up… so, I said Friday… to give things a chance to settle down a little… ya know… with everything that's happened… I don't want to worry her. Plus, I need to contact the spa… they'll be worrying about me, too."

"Of course, babe." He smiles. "I'm sure by Friday, things will be a little less up in the air," Enrique says with hope. Surely his father will be found by then, plus this break in should be dealt with by then too? As tempting as it is, he would love to stay in his penthouse forever; it's not like they don't have everything they need there, but it's not realistic. Plus, they both like to go out and enjoy Miami. They love the beach and going to all the amazing bars and restaurants Miami has to offer.

Above all, they both have businesses, plus all of their charities to run; they both need to be at work. He thinks about his company for a brief second. He knows there's so much he needs to do right now, but he just doesn't have it in him. For the first time in his life, work isn't a top priority. He knows he has developers and heads of other companies he needs to have meetings with. He also knows he has multiple construction sites to oversee and asses to kick. Mostly, his staff is on point, but not always, and sometimes he has to push them to get the job done; they have deadlines to meet. The trouble is, working in the kind of heat you have in Miami isn't for everybody; it sure isn't for the faint-hearted. The pay may be exceptional, but it's extremely hard work doing manual labor in over a hundred degrees, day in day out. With this in mind, Enrique has the utmost respect for all his people on the ground, even the ones he has to push from time to time. As much as a blissful fantasy as it is, Enrique knows locking themselves away in the penthouse is impossible to maintain.

"She's so excited that I stayed last night... she's always wanted us to get back together," Kristie says as she walks over to the stove where Enrique is standing.

"I've always wanted us to get back together... and I was a fool for leaving things as long as I did," he says, kissing her forehead as he holds her.

"Well, we're here now," she says. "And I'm glad we are."

"Me too," Enrique replies, taking the chicken off the stove and straining the water over the sink. He puts the chicken and onions on a plate to cool.

Once the chicken has cooled, he breaks it up with a mallet, pours the juice of limes over it, adds some garlic, oregano, and a bay leaf, covers it, and puts it in the refrigerator.

"Would you like a drink, mami?"

"Sure." She smiles. "I'll have water, papi."

He reaches into the refrigerator, gets out a Fiji and a Dos Equis beer. He gets a glass and pours Kristie's drink. Handing her the water and he takes the top off his beer.

"While the chicken is marinating, would you like to go up to the pool or the balcony? Get some air?" he suggests.

"Shall we sit on the balcony? See what's going on over the bay?" Kristie responds, taking a sip of water.

"Sure."

They walk out to the balcony and curl up together on the circular double lounger and look out over the bay. The sun is starting to set, and the sky looks so beautiful, painted pink, orange, and yellow; nature's art. Enrique holds Kristie, thinking how special this moment really is. These are the moments he missed the most when they were apart. He loves that with Kristie, he can sit quietly and just be with her. Like they say, "the best things in life are free." He can afford anything in the world, but money could never buy moments like this; this is what life's all about.

Once the sun has set, they go back to the kitchen and finish off preparing their meal while Celia Cruz is singing "La Vida Es Un Carnival" over the sound system. Kristie boils some rice, sets the table, puts the dressing on the salad, and Enrique browns off the shredded chicken and onions on the skillet. They've decided to eat out on the balcony, and Kristie lights the candles, which are in lanterns around the balcony and standing on crystal holders on the table.

Deciding on something more relaxing to listen to for their meal, Enrique selects the "Amar Sin Mentiras" album by Marc Anthony. It's such a beautiful album full of ballads, and it's one of their favorites.

As they sit next to each other at the candlelit table, Enrique leans over and puts his arm around her shoulder, pulling his girl closer to him and kisses her. "So beautiful."

"You're so handsome," Kristie says, holding Enrique's cheek with her hand and kissing him again. "I love this song. Well, I love the whole album. Holds a lot of happy memories for me," she smiles.

"Tu Amor Me Hace Bien." begins to play.

"So many happy memories." He says with agreeance. "And this is our song, too."

"How could I forget." She kisses him softly. Holding hands and resting them on Enrique's lap, they both start to eat their meal.

"Oh my God, this is so good, babe. It's delicious," Kristie says, as she takes the forkful of food Enrique has just passed her.

"Cuban's make the best food and coffee," Enrique teases, putting his arm around her shoulders and bringing her in for a kiss. Kristie looks so beautiful in the candlelight. "Te amo, mi amor," he whispers, with eyes glistening with love for her.

"Te amo," she whispers back. She reaches her hand to his face, finds his lips with hers, and gives him a long, slow kiss; a kiss, which feels like they're being transported to heaven. They reluctantly breakaway, with their eyes still closed momentarily. Enrique kisses her lips again and then rests his forehead on hers; this has always felt so intimate. Slowly opening their eyes together, they look at each other with pure love and desire.

"I'm the luckiest man alive," Enrique whispers. "I'm so, so lucky."

"I'm so lucky too," Kristie smiles as she whispers back.

They eventually continue to eat their dinner, enjoying the music, the view, and each other's company. Then a thought crosses Kristie's mind.

"So," she says, with a naughty look in her eyes.

"Sooo...." Enrique says, wondering where this is going.

"Do you still have the box?"

"What? *The* box?" Enrique replies, thinking he knows what she means. They have a box that contains various sex toys, handcuffs, blindfolds, and a few other things. They like to dabble in a little S&M from time to time. Nothing too extreme, but Kristie enjoys Enrique taking complete control of her pleasure in the bedroom on occasion. He would drive her crazy, and it would drive him just as crazy doing it to her.

He has a thing for watching her beautiful body move, responding to his touch, and when she's handcuffed and blindfolded, this only makes things even more intense. Because she can't see what he's going to do next and being restrained means that she has to absorb whatever feeling she has; it's unbelievably erotic.

"Yes, Mr. Cruz," she says, with a naughty smile. "*The* box."

He raises his eyebrows, looking at her with that sexy grin of his. "Of course, I do... I said I kept everything after you left... and I still have everything," Enrique says, kissing her again. "Why do you ask?" he teases expectantly. He's starting to feel aroused just thinking of the idea. Erotic memories run through his mind of Kristie being cuffed and blindfolded as he teases and torments her to the point of insanity; he shifts in his seat as his thoughts are almost too much to bear.

"I just wanted to know, that's all," she says, smiling at him, trying to look all innocent. She knows what she's doing.

"Oh, OK," he replies with a playful tone, gazing at her with his glorious blue eyes glistening in the candlelight; he looks so undeniably handsome. "Well, Miss Carrington, now you know."

"I sure do, Mr. Cruz." She teases, biting her lower lip, gazing back at him with eyes smoldering with anticipation; her eyes always give her away.

Locked in their gaze, Enrique reads Kristie correctly. He knows exactly what's she's doing, but he desperately tries to refrain from surrendering to his burning desire to carry her upstairs, cuff her to the bed and drive her wild. He worries that perhaps taking things to that particular level, may be a little premature at this stage; he's still concerned about pushing Kristie too far at the moment, plus she's pregnant, and he's not sure he feels right about doing those kinds of things to her while she's carrying their baby.

After their meal, they clear the table and put all the dishes in the dishwasher. Enrique changes the music to Al Green. Then he gets another beer, Kristie another water, and they sit back down on the balcony, cuddling up on the circular double lounger again.

Kristie's head is resting on Enrique's firm chest as they look out at the twinkling lights of South Beach over the bay. Key Biscayne is on their right, and Enrique can vaguely make out the marine stadium, which is located on Virginia Key.

He doesn't allow himself to think about what happened there for one second. He's spending time with the love of his life, and she's all he's going to think about. With his girl in his arms, Enrique takes a sip of his beer and kisses the top of her head as he quietly sings the occasional line of the love songs as they play.

"I love you," he whispers.

"I love you too," she replies. Kristie's feeling so good, despite everything that's happened today. This moment is so incredibly romantic; she feels at one with Enrique, like they've turned a corner. To her relief, he's arranged a therapy appointment, but even without that, things are very different between them. Like Lisa said, they broke up for a reason. They needed this break for things to change, and they're already changing for the better. Enrique seems more focused on fixing his issues, something he always avoided before now, and she feels so incredibly positive for their future.

As Kristie tightens her hold on her man, Enrique sets his beer down on the nearby table. He rolls onto his side and kisses her lovingly, running his hands down her body as he does.

"You look so sexy," Enrique says with admiration. He loves her dressed this way; she looks so beautiful. She has no make-up on, and her dark hair has been left to dry naturally. He loves her dressed up too, but there's something he finds very sexy about her in yoga pants and a camisole.

As he glides his hands over her gorgeous curves, he sweeps his fingers around the swell of each breast. Her top is tight enough to reveal that she isn't wearing a bra; he finds this so alluring. When they were getting dressed earlier, he couldn't help but notice the only thing she's wearing under her clothes is a tiny black thong, and he has to be honest; it's been driving him crazy all day. She is intoxicating.

He deepens his kiss and holds her face with his hands. Then his left-hand glides down her throat and over her chest to her right breast. Gently squeezing her breast, he brushes his thumb over her erect nipple as it pushes through the fabric of her top.

"Ahhh...." She moans, pushing her breasts up to him. Her breasts are always so sensitive, but it would appear they're even more so now she's pregnant; this only turns Enrique on even more. He pulls her top down, freeing one breast, then kisses and sucks its nipple, then does the same with the other. Her upper body lifts off the lounger as pleasure floods through her.

As Kristie presses herself into him, she can feel his erection pressing into her. She reaches down and grabs it through his pants.

"Fuck!" He hisses through gritted teeth. "I wanna take you upstairs," he says urgently. After the day they've had, this is just what they need. He pulls her top up for her, picks her up off the circular lounger, and carries her up to the bedroom.

Once in the bedroom, Enrique lays her on the over-sized bed, dressed in luxurious white linens, and hovers over her. Resting on his elbows, he starts to kiss her again. "I've wanted you all afternoon." He breathes. "I've needed you... to be with you... to feel you." He kisses her again and then travels his soft kisses down over her silky tanned body, stopping at her erect nipples and biting them gently through her top. Kristie cries out. She's so close; she needs him too.

As his lips travel down over her curves, he stops at her bump and kisses it tenderly. He looks up at her and smiles. Kristie runs her hands through his jet-black hair and smiles back at him.

"I love you." He whispers.

"I love you, too." She whispers back.

He continues to kiss further down her body until he reaches the waistband of her leggings; pulling them, he slides them down her legs. Leaning down to her clitoris, he kisses it through the lace of her thong, and his lips dampen with her arousal.

"Hmmm...." He groans as he licks his lips.

Gazing down on her sensual figure, he pulls off his T-shirt, then his sweat pants, and throws them on the floor with Kristie's yoga pants. He is now naked. He climbs up back on the bed and lays on his side next to his girl. Reaching his lips to hers, he kisses her with fervor and pulls her top down so her breasts are pushed up, making them look even fuller. Enrique runs his fingers over them softly, following the curves of her breasts, then squeezes and pulls at her erect nipples.

He then glides his hand down to the junction of her thighs and over her thong; it's soaking wet. Lifting his hand up, he puts his fingers, which are covered in Kristie's arousal, into his mouth. She tastes so good. Then he kisses her hard, and Kristie moans as she tastes herself as they kiss.

He leans to her ear and whispers. "Play with yourself... I want to watch you make yourself come."

Kristie reaches her hand down her body and slides it into her thong, finding her clitoris, and starts to rub it with her middle finger. Her body starts to respond, and she begins to moan. Enrique watches on, enjoying every second; this is such a turn-on for him. He kisses and teases her breasts, then kisses down her abdomen and then to her thighs.

Stopping just above her knees, he moves so he's lying on his front, in between her legs. He watches closely as Kristie plays with herself with one hand, and the other is playing with one of her breasts. Fuck! This is so erotic, but being this intimate with her means so much more than that. When they first got together, Kristie wasn't so at ease, with her body, for reasons before she met Enrique, and the fact that she's comfortable enough to do this with him means the world to him. It may be erotic as hell, but it's very special and meaningful too.

Enrique pulls her thong to one side so he can see exactly what she's doing. He kisses the inside of her thigh as he watches. Fuck she is so beautiful. "Finger yourself, baby."

Loving every minute of this erotic intimacy, Kristie reaches her other hand down and slides two fingers inside herself. Her moans are getting louder as she does. Enrique could come just watching her do this, and he knows she's close; he can tell by the way she moves her body.

He can see she is getting wetter and wetter; it's pure ecstasy to watch. She's on the brink, and so is he. Then before he knows it, she screams out as she reaches her climax. Enrique just about manages to control himself as he watches her beautiful figure rise and convulse with pleasure.

As her body calms, Enrique kisses her thigh, then up to her soaking vagina, before kissing and licking her. Kristie's hypersensitive body starts to quiver as he tastes her, driving her to another orgasm. He lets out a moan as he lifts his head up and says, "You taste so good."

He sits back on his heels before hovering over her, grabbing both her hands together and pulling them over her head, holding them in place. She looks at him expectantly. She would love nothing more than for him to tie her up and fuck her into oblivion.

"So… were you suggesting what I think you were when we were having dinner earlier? When you said about the box?" His tone is breathy, yet demanding.

"Yes, I was," Kristie replies breathlessly. This is very true, but she wants him inside her right now. She can't wait any longer. Her body is literally begging for him.

"Really? You want me to blindfold and cuff you? Drive you wild?" He asks suggestively, still holding her hands in place. The fact that he's holding her this way only adds to her need.

"I just want you inside me. Now!" She demands. "Please!" Kristie is so turned on right now. "Fuck me… I want you to fuck me… so hard… I need you… I need you now." And with those words, Enrique slams his rock-hard erection inside of her; his hands still holding her arms above her head.

Kristie gasps then lets out a loud moan. She's so close again already. Every time she tries to move her arms, Enrique holds them down harder; this only makes things more difficult for her to pace herself. She has to absorb every single ounce of pleasure her body is feeling from every thrust Enrique is giving her.

She can feel another orgasm building, and she can't stop it; it's taking over her entire body. She screams out Enrique's name as she climaxes; he can feel every muscle inside of her tighten as she comes and comes and comes.

He slows his pace. He wants to feel everything. He releases her hands, and she wraps her arms around his back. Looking into Kristie's eyes with love and adoration, he says, "I love you more than anything in the world, my beautiful girl."

"I love you with all my heart, baby. You mean so much to me," Kristie replies. She's so in love with this gorgeous man. She can never find the words to express how she feels for him and he for her. Their bodies move together slowly and tenderly. Kristie's hands move down Enrique's muscular back and grip hold of his firm buttocks.

Enrique kisses down Kristie's neck to her throat, breathing in her scent. It's intoxicating; she is intoxicating. He then kisses down to her breasts, stops for a moment, and pulls her top off, freeing her breasts completely. He kisses her breasts tenderly and caresses them, then starts to kiss her again. This feels so special and so sensual. Enrique feels so connected to Kristie when they make love. She feels so good, and he loves feeling her skin on his.

He was enjoying being lustful with her, but now he's making love to her... a love so pure, a love so profound; a love he can only feel for Kristie. They're lost in each other's eyes, and it feels so intimate. Enrique holds Kristie's face, and her arms are draped over his shoulders and her fingers running through his hair.

As he feels her body tighten beneath him, he can't hold back any longer. Kristie's moans start to get louder, as does Enrique's, then they both come loudly together, with pleasure igniting through both of their bodies as they connect as one.

Once they float back down to earth, he pulls Kristie into his arms, and they lay beside each other. He gently tilts her face to him and kisses her lips. "I love you." He whispers.

"I love you, too, baby." She whispers back as they hold each other.

They lay together for a while, holding each other, and then Enrique draws them a bath. He changes the music, and Marvin Gaye is now playing love songs over the sound system as they sit back and relax in the tub.

Enrique quietly sings the lyrics of the chorus to "Precious Love" and looks in Kristie's direction. He leans over, kisses her lips, and says, "The words to this song are so perfect for this moment, baby. It so perfectly explains how I feel about you and our baby."

"And it so perfectly explains the way I feel about you and our baby, too," Kristie replies, feeling so full of love and happiness.

Enrique smiles against her beautifully full lips. "How are you feeling, my darling?"

"I feel good," Kristie replies, kissing him before he sits back down opposite her.

He can see her placing her hand on the little bump underneath the water. He finds it so adorable. "When is the next appointment with the Doctor? I want to come with you," he says, looking excited.

"I've scheduled another for next week... so you can come with me... I thought you would like to see the scan... so I wanted to wait." She smiles.

"Dios mio, cariño! I can't wait... we're going to see our baby for the first time! Oh my God!" He gets up and sits beside her. Kissing her cheek, he says. "Thank you for waiting so I can come with you." He's so excited; his stomach is doing somersaults. Placing his hand on her tummy, he looks at her with adoration. "I'm so lucky. Thank you," he says, so grateful that Kristie has done this for him. "I thank God every day for blessing me with you and our little baby." Kissing her again, he starts to feel his eyes well up. Right now, he's on such an emotional rollercoaster.

"I wanted you to be there too. Even if we were still apart, I wanted to give you the chance to be there for the first scan. I told the doctor I wanted to wait to speak to you first... I just wanted him to check things and give me advice. Like I said, I didn't believe it was true at first. I just kind of wanted him to confirm it for me," Kristie explains. "I was going to tell you on the pool deck earlier, but I got distracted... it's been a bit of a day."

"I know, baby. Well, I want to be there every step of the way. I don't want to miss any of it," Enrique says, getting more excited.

"I know, babe. I love seeing how excited you are. It makes me so happy."

"That's because I am happy, baby... in fact, I'm more than happy... I'm ecstatic."

"Me too... ya know, I love being pregnant. It feels so good. I've not had any sickness or anything. I've been so lucky." She smiles. "It's such an amazing feeling carrying our baby... it feels like I'm never alone... I always have our baby with me. It's such a special feeling," Kristie says, getting emotional.

"That sounds so beautiful," Enrique says, hugging her at the same time. "You will never be alone," he whispers into her ear. "I will be here forever."

Kristie starts to cry with happiness. "I'm so happy right now," she says through her tears.

"Me too." He continues to hold her. "I never want this to end… the feeling of us being together and our baby growing inside of you, it's so special and pure… it makes me want us to have many more babies together."

"Perhaps we will." Kristie smiles sweetly.

"Ahhh… Miss Carrington… my beautiful girl… I would love that more than anything; you know I would." If he had his way, he would get the jet, run off to Vegas with her, and get married right now. But he knows he has to pace himself. Although Kristie seems to be opening up to him more and more, he doesn't want to push his luck. Plus, he knows he has a long way to go in terms of dealing with what's going on with him. Kissing her once more, he asks. "When will we be able to feel the baby move? I can't wait."

"I think it will be around five months. I've been researching things online a little. I think I saw something saying it will be around five months… I need to get more clued up. Things have been a little crazy since I found out," Kristie says, starting to yawn.

"I'm so excited to feel it. It will be another special moment with you," Enrique says with a smile. Kissing her again, he says, "You're tired. How about we get ready for bed?"

"I'm exhausted... I think we'd better." Enrique stands and helps her up, and then they start to get ready for bed. He picks up Kristie's white silk and lace floor-length nightdress from the chair in the bedroom, walks over to her, and he asks her to put her arms up before sliding it down over her curvaceous body. He kisses her lips and says, "Perfect."

Kristie smiles and kisses him again. Enrique slips on his black pajama pants, and they climb into bed. He checks his cell for any updates on his father; but still nothing. Placing his cell down on the nightstand, he turns off the already dimmed bedside light and turns off the music. Guiding Kristie into the spooning position, he holds her from behind and kisses her shoulder. She holds his hand up to her lips and kisses it. Still holding hands, they place them together on Kristie's stomach.

"Good night, baby. Sweet dreams. I love you."

"Good night, babe. Sweet dreams. I love you too," Kristie replies.

Then they drift off to a peaceful, dreamy sleep together.

Chapter 22

Enrique is lying awake. He's just woken from a nightmare. He was at the marine stadium, and instead of the cartel members lying in pools of blood, dead on the floor, it was Kristie and his mother too. Covered in their blood, he was kneeling on the ground next to them, screaming in horror. "NOOO!! NOOO!! NOOO!!" over and over again. Then they just disappeared. He woke shaking from head to toe, with his heart pounding in his chest, sweating and crying.

He glances over at Kristie; she looks so beautiful. She stirs slightly, then rolls onto her side, facing him, and puts her arm over his chest. He's glad he didn't wake her, as she needs to sleep. He checks the clock on his nightstand. It's 2:30am. He's been awake for the past hour, with his mind racing with thoughts about how the world he knew so well or thought he knew so well, has been shattered to pieces. Yet, at the same time, Kristie is back in his life, and they're going to have a baby. How fucked up can things get? It destroys him that he can't enjoy this moment with her fully, as he has all this other shit going on in the back of his mind. He can't take it anymore. He has to do something.

He slowly climbs out of bed, holding Kristie's hand up before gently placing it on the bed. Then he tiptoes out of the bedroom, closing the door quietly behind him. Once downstairs, he needs a drink. He gets a bottle of Perrier from the refrigerator, snaps it open, and drinks it from the bottle.

Then out of the corner of his eye, he sees his favorite bottle of Havana Club rum. This will help calm my nerves, he thinks to himself. Getting a tumbler out of the cupboard and a sphere of ice out the freezer, he places the ice in the glass and pours himself a generous helping of rum. He takes a long slow sip, swallows, and then breathes out, feeling the warmth of the liquor as it travels down.

Carrying the glass, he walks to his humidor, chooses a Cohiba, and picks up his lighter from the coffee table on the way to the living room balcony. Opening the sliding glass door, he pulls up a chair and places his glass on the nearby table. He lights his cigar and inhales the rich, smooth smoke. The warm early morning air feels good on his skin as he sits wearing just his black pajama pants.

Alone with his thoughts, he sips his rum and puffs on his cigar as he stares out over the bay and into the darkness; a darkness he feels he's all too familiar with right now.

He can't stop thinking about all the horrific things he's been subjected to over the past few days. This is not for him; he has to do something, but he doesn't know which way to turn. He hates that he's hiding this from Kristie, yet if he tells her, she'll probably leave, and he can't face losing her again. He knows he should go to the police about his father's situation, but he's scared to; he has no idea what might happen if he does. They could kill his father plus, he's worried sick about the rest of his family and not to mention Kristie's family too.

Against his better judgment, he allowed Ziv to organize the security, as he didn't want to involve the legitimate company he uses, in such vigilante dealings. How can he even begin to explain any of this to them? But most of all, he's petrified about what they might do to Kristie. They've already vandalized her apartment and threatened her; what else are they capable of? Was that just a warning?

His hands start to shake, and his heart races even faster than it already was, and his chest grows tighter. Suddenly, he can feel these horrific pains in his chest, so much so, he raises his hand and presses on the pain. His heart feels like it is pounding out of his chest, and he's struggling to breathe.

This has never happened to him before. Yes, he's been stressed in the past. Hell, he runs a multi-billion-dollar construction company; stress is something that goes with the territory, but this is different. He's never felt anything like this before in his life. This is frightening to him; he feels like he's going to die.

What the fuck is happening to me, he asks himself. Placing his cigar on the ashtray, he tries to calm the anxiety that's exploding inside of him, but nothing is helping. He's still struggling to breathe, and the pain in his chest is getting worse. Is it a heart attack? It feels like a fucking heart attack! No. It can't be. Can it? Fuck!

He tries desperately to focus on the horizon. He can just about see ahead as his eyes adjust to the darkness. He forces himself to breathe through it, slowly taking back control of his body. Thankfully, his breathing is beginning to slow. Fuck, that was scary. What the fuck just happened? He sits back in his chair, telling himself that this can't go on a moment longer; he has to do something. But what, he doesn't know.

He takes a sip of his rum, picks up his cigar, and inhales the smooth smoke into his mouth. He breathes out the smoke with a long calming breath. He will have to tell Kristie; he has no choice. He can't keep this from her any longer. It's killing him, destroying him inside. This is his chance of a fresh start, and starting it off with secrets and lies is not going to work. It isn't fair on her. She doesn't know anything, and it isn't right to keep her in the dark, plus it's even starting to involve her now, whether she knows about it or not.

He can't carry on this way; it's eating him up inside. It sickens him that he's kept this from her for the past few days since it happened. He feels disgusted with himself for lying to her when they're sharing such special moments like they had by the pool yesterday when they talked about their future and the possibility of marriage. Kristie has been so good to him, and he's lucky that she's even there. He feels so ashamed; this isn't the person he is. He may have issues, but he's never been a liar.

The nightmare and panic attack have made him realize that his body is reacting to the extreme pressure of acting like everything is OK, when it's far from OK; it's torturing him. He can't bury things anymore, and living in denial is no longer working; in fact, it never has, he was only ever kidding himself, and he knows that now. It's almost like his body is forcing him to deal with everything he's been suppressing, not just over the past few days but for most of his life.

Enrique feels like it's trying to spill out of him, giving him no choice but to face his demons... his pain... his grief. Everything has been building and building, and finally, it's bubbling over. Like a pan of water on a stove; things have been bubbling for a while on full heat, now it's boiling over, and he has no way of stopping it. He feels like he's being forced to deal with it all, like a force of nature.

For a second, he considers if his mom is trying to give him a sign; after all, she was in his horrific nightmare too. His eyes find the black and white photo of Gina on the glass side table in the living area close to the sliding glass door. "What do I do, mom?" He whispers to the picture framed in platinum. "What do I do?"

Enrique knows his mom would be devastated if she knew what was happening. His parents were so in love and devoted to each other. For her to find out about José's supposed secret life would destroy her as much as it's destroying Enrique. Closing his eyes, he shakes his head as a searing pain rips through his heart, leaving scorching agony in its wake. How could his father do this to his mom... to the family... to him? Opening his eyes slowly, his eyes focus on the photo again. "I'm so glad you're not here to live through this, mom." He whispers.

As he studies his beautiful mother in the photograph, he knows what he has to do. He has to tell Kristie everything, from start to finish. She has a right to know. He isn't prepared to lie to her any longer, even if that means losing her, although just the thought of losing Kristie feels like a knife being stabbed through his heart, it's a sacrifice he will have to make. She deserves better than a relationship based on lies.

Then another horrifying thought shoots into his mind. What about the baby? He's now petrified that all of the shock and stress will harm the baby too. Kristie adores José. She will be devastated. Telling her will not only risk losing the love of his life, but they could lose their baby, too. His heart smashes into a trillion pieces as he contemplates the possibility. Tears flood his eyes and pour rapidly down his cheeks. He can't bear this anymore. Whichever way he turns, there's nothing but heartache and devastation. What the hell is he going to do?

He feels so nauseous to the point where bile starts to rise in his throat as tears continue to pour down his face and roll onto his bare chest. Holding the glass and cigar in one hand, he wipes the tears from his face with the other, but they keep coming; they're relentless. He leans forward with his elbow resting on his knee and his head in his hand, still holding the glass and cigar in the other; tears are still flooding out of his eyes. He can't stand the thought of losing Kristie, especially now. They've already come so far in such a short space of time; what on earth is he going to do?

Then suddenly, he hears a voice.

"Are you OK, baby?"

He lifts his head from his hand and turns his tear-drenched face toward the direction of the voice, and his eyes try to focus through the tears. Standing just inside the living area, wearing just her white silk and lace nightdress, with her voluminous brunette hair cascading over her shoulders, is Kristie. His guardian angel; an angel that's come just at the right moment to guide him out of his darkness and into the light.

Chapter 23

"Enrique?" Kristie says urgently as she rushes over to him. She pulls up a chair and sits in front of him. Seeing him cry when she told him about the baby is one thing, but seeing him cry this way is devastating. These are not tears of joy, these are tears of agony and pain, and Kristie has never seen Enrique this way before. He's such a strong man, yet so broken, and it's heartbreaking to see.

"Baby, what is it? What's happened?" She looks at him with deep concern as she tries to get him to talk to her. Aside from the crying, Kristie has been here so many times before, and she knows that getting Enrique to talk about his pain is nigh-on impossible, but after everything they've recently discussed, she hopes this time will be different. Holding one hand in hers, she reaches the other to his face and gently wipes his tears away, giving him time to find his words.

"I... I... oh... ba...by...." He's sobbing uncontrollably and heaving through his tears, which is making it difficult for him to speak. He so desperately wants to talk to her, but his throat is closing up with panic and pain. He starts to shake even more. He puts down the glass and places his cigar in the ashtray beside him. He looks back at his girl, his angel who has come to rescue him once more, but this time, he is ready to allow her. The only problem is, he's petrified that the first time he has ever done this will be the time he loses her for good, but he has to do this. He has to talk to her.

Kristie pushes the chair back, kneels in front of him, and pulls him into her arms. She holds him and lets him cry it out. Tears start to fill her eyes as she holds her man. She doesn't understand what's happened. Everything seemed great when they went to bed. He was so happy. Something has to be seriously wrong. After a short while, he calms a little. She gradually pulls away and looks into his gorgeous blue eyes, which are full of pain and trauma.

"Please, baby... talk to me... tell me what's wrong," she asks again, hoping he will confide in her. "I'm here for you... I love you... it's OK... I'm here for you." She whispers.

"Oh... baby...." He manages, running his fingers through her hair and gliding them down over her cheek. He can see his pain reflecting back in her eyes, they have always felt each other's pain, but he knows that the pain she's feeling right now is about to get even worse. For a moment, he thinks about keeping it all to himself so he can save her from it, but he knows that's impossible. He has to do this, and he has to do this now.

"Something's happened... well, in fact... a lot's happened... and I'm so scared to tell you." As he watches the color drain from Kristie's face, more tears flood down his cheeks; he can't bear it. He wipes his tears and takes a deep breath, attempting to tell her what he has to say. He shakes his head with disbelief. "I'm so scared… so scared you'll leave… that I'll never see you again… oh God… and our baby…." He looks down and rests his head in his hands. I can't do this, he thinks to himself. I can't fucking do this.

Kristie lifts his face to hers and looks at him with eyes full of anxiety. She has no idea where this is going, and she sure as hell doesn't like the sound of it, but Enrique needs to talk about whatever is bothering him. "Enrique… please… I'm not going anywhere… baby… I love you… I'm here for you… there's nothing we can't fix together."

"I love you, too… so, so much… more than anything in the world… but… what's happened is so awful… I'm petrified that it will destroy our future together… and you will be so devastated… something will happen to our baby…." He wipes more tears as he studies Kristie's beautiful face, taking in every detail, every feature, as he fears that once he tells her what's happened, she will never look at him the same way again. He shakes his head again and holds his clenched fist to his mouth. "Ughhh…." Removing his hand, he says. "I have no other option… I'm between a rock and a hard place… if I don't tell you and you find out… I'll lose you… and if I do tell you… you'll most probably leave, and I will never see you and the baby again. I can't bear it… I'm just so scared… I don't know which way to turn."

"Enrique... babe... I love you...." She looks down at her tummy and caresses it softly. "We love you... we're not going anywhere...."

"Please don't make promises you may not be able to keep, baby," Enrique says, sounding way calmer than he actually is. As agonizingly torturous as it will be, he wonders if the best thing for Kristie and the baby would be to set them free. It's not fair to tangle them up in this horror.

"Enrique, just tell me for Christ's sake... you're worrying me now." Kristie says nervously, wondering what on earth he's been keeping from her. Her heart is sinking. She's been so open to him, so soon after getting back together, and she's starting to worry that she's made a big mistake. What the hell can it be? Questions flood her mind; questions she knows the answers to already, but she can't help but entertain them anyway. Has he found somebody else? Is he having second thoughts about us... or the baby? What could it be?

"I'm so sorry... I'm so, so sorry... I'm just finding this so hard... please baby... try to prepare yourself for this... you're not going to like what I have to say, but I can't keep this from you any longer... you have a right to know everything," Enrique pleads.

Still kneeling in front of him, Kristie holds his hands and rests them on his lap. "Baby... talk to me... I'm here... here for you... whatever it is...."

"Darling, I know." He sweeps a loose strand of hair behind her ear. "And that's why I love you so much." He kisses her lips softly.

Kristie knows in her heart that this isn't anything to do with them directly. She can tell that it's something outside of their relationship, but unfortunately, this doesn't give her any comfort, as Enrique is clearly tortured by whatever he feels he needs to tell her. "I love you, too, babe." She whispers against his lips. "We love you."

Enrique manages a tiny smile as they rest their foreheads on each others. He closes his eyes and takes a deep breath before opening them again and kissing her lips once more.

Kristie sits back on her heels and looks at him expectantly.

He takes a gulp of rum and breathes out heavily. "OK. Here goes," he says, looking at Kristie, wondering if she'll ever look at him the same way again. Hell, he doesn't even look at himself the same way anymore. "José's been kidnapped."

"Sorry, what?" Kristie's eyes widen in shock. She puts her hand to her mouth as she tries to take in the news.

"He's been kidnapped... a few days ago... I didn't want to worry you... I thought we could get him back sooner... but it's not been that simple... it turns out that this is just the tip of the iceberg."

"Oh my God, Enrique... no... I can't... I... I... oh God... he must be so frightened... and you... is he...." Tears fill Kristie's eyes as she can barely get her words out.

"Hmmm, well... it seems this is something he brought on himself... I mean, I don't know for definite... but it's sure as hell looks that way with the more time that goes by."

"What do you mean? Why on earth would he bring this on himself?" Kristie's confused. She's not only confused at why Enrique would say such a thing; she's confused at Enrique's reaction. He loves his father, and he seems upset about his disappearance, but not in the way she would expect.

"Ummm... well... remember years ago... he used to live a particular lifestyle...."

"Yes, I remember you telling me about it." Kristie starts to feel nauseous as she wonders where this is going.

"Well... I uhh... oh God, Krissy... this is what I'm struggling to tell you about... ugh...." he shakes his head, trying to find the words, but he knows the only way to say them is to just say it. "I uhhh...

well... I've... ugh... I've just found out... uh that he never left...."

"Never left?"

"Yes... he never left... and uh... it gets worse... much worse...." He pauses for a second before saying. "He's... he's um... he's head of a cartel... and has been for my whole life apparently." The words just pour out of Enrique's mouth. Oh, fuck! What have I done?

The look of complete shock, confusion, sadness, and disgust on Kristie's face is too much to bear. Oh, Fuck!! I should have never told her!! Oh, Shit, he thinks to himself. She says nothing. He looks at her as she sits before him, with her mouth slightly agape, and she's staring at him with a look of dazed fear in her eyes. It's like she's frozen and can't move. What the fuck shall I do?

His brow furrows as he contemplates what to do. He has no idea. He feels responsible. He should never have told her. He should have set her free and lived with the agony alone; it would be a small price to pay to save her from this. What the hell was he thinking?

Knowing that it's out there now and there's nothing he can do to take it back, he grips her hands tightly and looks deeply into her espresso-colored eyes, which are full of tears of pain and confusion. "I'm so, so sorry... baby... I'm so, so sorry... the last thing I wanted to do was burden you with this... but I... I just don't know what to do... I... I... uh...." Kristie still says nothing. She's speechless, and this is worrying Enrique like crazy. "Please... baby... say something."

She's gone very pale, and tears start to fall from her eyes. Enrique wipes them away, but they keep coming. It's too much for her. Kristie loves José, and after the past few days, he worries she's feeling cheated; cheated because he knew this and kept it all from her. But he didn't know what else to do. Please, God. Please don't make her leave me, he silently prays in his head.

"Are you OK, baby? Should I get you some water?" Enrique says with extreme concern. What the fuck have I done? I'm so selfish for putting my shit onto her, he scolds himself. He kneels in front of her and takes Kristie in his arms. She's rigid as he holds her. Oh, fuck, this isn't good. "Please... baby," Enrique sits back and looks at her expectantly.

"I... I... can't believe it," she finally says. "José's one of the sweetest people I know... how can he have anything to do with a cartel? He doesn't even like drugs... it doesn't make any sense."

"I know... I know... I can't get my head around it either."

Enrique explains how he found out about José's kidnap, what Raúl had told him, and about the note telling him not to go to the cops.

"So, is there a ransom? They obviously want money, right?" she asks, a little more responsive than before.

"That's another thing." Enrique's still kneeling on the floor, holding Kristie's hands. He's starting to feel the overwhelming panic in his chest again. He tries to ignore it. Please, God, give me the strength to get through this, he prays silently again. "There's more."

"Go on," Kristie says in total disbelief. She's hoping that any minute now, she's going to wake from this nightmare. There's no way this can be true. Not José. He's so gentle and caring. He could never be involved in anything like this. It must be a mistake. Yes, he used to be a bit of a hustler back in the day, but that was before Enrique was even born. She's more worried about where he is and if he's safe than anything else.

"There's no ransom." He stops for a moment. Perhaps he needs to break down the information. It's not fair for him to pile it all onto her all at once, but at the same time, he's not great at this either. He's trying hard to express himself and be open, which feels alien to him, but he has to keep going. He has to break down the barriers, as keeping everything inside is doing no good, and it has to stop. Talk about being thrown in the deep end, he thinks to himself. In the world of Enrique Cruz, nothing is ever straightforward or easy when it comes to difficult emotions, and this situation is only confirming it.

Enrique goes on to explain about the message José had so obviously left with the charity documents for him to find and how he had to meet Gutiérrez at the Monastery.

"So, you think your father may have known something might happen to him?" Kristie's totally confused.

"It would appear so... I don't know... the whole thing is like a blur to me at times. It's like my entire life... as I knew it... wasn't real... it was all a lie." He looks down solemnly.

"I can understand that... this is unbelievable." Kristie is in complete shock at what's she's hearing. "I'm so sorry, baby... this must be awful for you... I can't imagine."

"I'm more worried about you." He whispers.

Kristie manages a small smile. "I'm OK... just a little...."

"Shocked? Disgusted?" Enrique's face is deadly serious. He's disgusted, disgusted to the core that his father could do such a thing to him... his mom... to Kristie, to their families.

"I'm shocked... not disgusted... I mean... it's crazy... like a movie or something." Kristie explains. "I mean, I can't believe this is your father you're talking about." She shakes her head in disbelief. "It's like this has to be a mistake or something, babe. I mean, are you sure about all this? Like, how do you know he's head of a cartel? It doesn't add up. I just can't believe it." Kristie knows she keeps saying she can't believe it, but she really can't. This is not the José Cruz she knows and loves so dearly.

"I'm sorry to say this... but I'm practically certain, babe. As far as I'm aware, everything I'm telling you is one hundred percent true... and I promise you... I wish I had better news to tell you."

Kristie shakes her head again.

"Are you OK... do you need a break?" he asks softly as he holds her beautiful face in his hands.

"I'm OK... carry on, baby," she replies, with a vague expression on her face.

She seems to be taking this better than he thought she would, but then he remembers how he reacted when he first found out; the shock made him go into denial mode. It was like his mind's only way of dealing with such horror was to pretend it had never happened. That's how he managed to get through the last few days; for the most part, he pretended it hadn't happened. Is this what's happening to Kristie? If it is, he can't blame her.

As he prepares himself to continue, another wave of torturous fear and anxiety consumes him. He's scared to death that the shock will do something to her, like make her sick or harm the baby. On top of that, he's so frightened he will lose her, that she will leave him again. But he knows if he doesn't do this now, it will be worse in the long run. He has to get this poison out of him, once and for all. It's like a force bigger than him. Kristie deserves the right to all the facts so she can make the right decision for herself. He doesn't want their relationship and maybe marriage to be based on lies. He wants a strong, solid, healthy relationship, not just for him, but Kristie deserves that too. As much as he's in complete torture right now, and it must be for her too, it's better to get this out of the way now. Then if she stays, which he prays to God she will, they can move on without any secrets; there won't be a lingering worry of her finding out at a later date. He knows if that happened, he will probably never, ever see her again. So, he pushes through this hell and continues to tell her the rest of the story.

He tells her about his meeting with Gutiérrez and how he received the text at the Monastery requesting he go to the marine stadium.

"So, I went to the stadium... this was... uhh... Saturday morning." He takes a deep breath before he continues. "I met these guys… and they told me they wanted drugs… my father's drugs. They knew who my father was… this confirmed to me that Gutiérrez was telling me the truth." He pauses, looking at Kristie full of concern. She's looking shell-shocked. Is she just quiet because she's letting me talk, or because she's thinking about running, he asks himself. As he studies her face, he can see she's struggling with all of this. She's overwhelmed. Who wouldn't be? He runs the back of his fingers down her cheek and asks. "Are you OK, baby? Shall I make you some tea?" He angles his face downward slightly and looks up into her tear-filled eyes. "You look pale, my darling. Shall I stop? I… I just want you to know everything. I want our relationship to be based on truth, not lies. That's if you still want to be with me after all this… which I pray you will." Enrique is almost begging.

"I don't feel good, Enrique. I think I need to go to the bathroom," Kristie says miserably. She's in a complete daze. Everything is spinning. She feels very nauseous and really unwell. She's so glad Enrique's opening up to her and being honest. Not that he was ever a liar, he just struggles to talk when there's something wrong. He never has been a dishonest person, and it isn't like him to do something like this.

It's clear to see that he's been pushed way beyond his limits with this situation. She knows that this is way beyond anything Enrique could ever imagine his father doing. Although she believes he should have called the police, she understands the position he's in; he's scared the kidnappers will kill his father. Even though it seems José isn't the person they all thought he was, she knows how much Enrique loves his father. She completely gets it, and she understands why he kept it from her. She knows he's coming from a good place: a place of love. She can see how much it's killing him inside, plus she knows how confusing and scary this whole ordeal has been for him. Kristie really feels for Enrique, but it doesn't stop her from being angry at the situation, not to mention devastated that José is not the person she thought he was. This devastation and the fact that Enrique has been going through this, and has been alone, is what's making her feel sick more than anything.

Enrique gets up from the balcony floor. "Let me take you to the bathroom, baby. Come on, my darling... I've got you." He says as he reaches down to help her up. Kristie's holding her hand over her mouth and is looking paler and paler.

Enrique helps her walk to the downstairs bathroom, and they just make it in time and for Kristie to be sick; she only just makes it to the toilet. Enrique holds her hair back for her, rubbing her back at the same time, and reassures her that everything will be OK.

Once she's finished being sick, Enrique helps her up and passes her a towel from the vanity near the toilet. Kristie wipes her mouth, shaking her head as throwing up always grosses her out. She wonders if it's something she will have to get used to now that she's pregnant.

Enrique finds a spare toothbrush, toothpaste, and some mouthwash in the cupboard of the vanity and passes them to her so she can freshen up. He's glad he doesn't have to leave Kristie to go upstairs and get hers. In his mind, he thanks Gabriela for always making sure he's prepared for almost every situation.

"I'll get you some water, baby... OK?" Enrique says, helping her keep steady on her feet.

They head into the kitchen, and he helps her sit at one of the stools at the breakfast bar before heading to the refrigerator to get them both a bottle of Fiji. Snapping the bottles open, he passes one to his girl, and she sips the water from the bottle. Enrique sits down next to Kristie and faces her. He looks at her with concern etched across his face and gently runs his hand down her cheek. Has he gone too far? Should he have told her? Again, he feels like he has no choice.

"How are you feeling now, my baby?" He whispers. "I'm so, so sorry... I feel like I've caused this... like I'm burdening you with all of this. I'm so sorry," Enrique says apologetically.

"This isn't your fault, babe."

"I think it is." He shifts back a little and says. "I should have just gone to the cops in the first place."

"I can understand why you didn't, though. I mean, my first reaction was, why didn't you tell the police, but now you've explained things, I get it. You've kinda been put in a very difficult situation… and it must be so hard for you."

"It's been rough… but I'm more worried about you."

"And I'm worried about you… I'm worried about José, too."

"Me too. It's like I'm so goddamn angry with him, but I get these bouts of extreme sadness and worry… it's so confusing. I'm so worried about what's happened to him, but I'm furious with him at the same time."

"It makes sense… after all, he's still your father."

"Hmmm…." Enrique nods his agreeance, although, at the moment, he feels that if he saw him right now, he'd kill him himself, as he's so angry with him for all of this. "I'll make you some hot tea, baby… hot sugary tea. It will be good for you… for the shock." He kisses her lips softly before getting up and beginning to prepare the tea.

"Thanks, babe," Kristie replies sweetly. She looks over at him as he makes her drink. She can't help but feel proud of him for being this open to her, especially given the circumstances. "You know, I don't like what I'm hearing... not at all... but I'm so glad you're talking." She manages a smile. "This is a first for us... it shows me you're trying."

"I feel like I'm failing miserably... I mean, telling you something like this... you've just told me you're pregnant, and here I am putting this on you...." He walks over to her and leans with his back to the breakfast bar. He looks down at her and glides his fingers down her cheek, following her jaw-line.

"You can't help this... or the timing... and I know you would never do anything wrong unless it were to protect somebody you love. I know that doesn't make it right, but I want you to know that I really do understand your predicament. This is such an extreme situation. I don't know what I would do if this happened to me, if I'm honest. I understand your anxiety."

"Baby... I love you... I can't believe how understanding you're being about all of this... but then again, you've always been the strong one out of the two of us."

"I don't know about that." She smiles.

"I do… I always have done." He leans down and kisses her soft, full lips.

"So, what happened at the marine stadium?" she asks, taking a small sip of water.

"Are you sure you want to know?"

"Yes. I need to know everything." Kristie doesn't want Enrique to stop until he's finished. Even though this story is so horrific, he needs to talk about it, and she needs to know everything. He's right. She needs to know the full story.

Enrique finishes making the tea, passes it to Kristie, and sits back down beside her, before continuing the torturous conversation.

"So, at the marine stadium, things get heated… and I hate to tell you this… but… I had to carry a gun… I didn't have a choice… I needed protection… just in case."

Kristie's eyes widen. "Oh no! You didn't kill someone? Please no!" she exclaims.

"No, babe, I didn't." He replies with reassurance. "But this is the worst part… I've been trying to block it out ever since it happened… but I have been getting flashbacks. Oh, God. I can't believe I'm telling you this." Leaning his elbow on the black quartz counter, he rubs his forehead with his fingers before rubbing his eyes. He lets out the deep breath that he's been holding in, before proceeding to relive the nightmare he was forced to live through. "That guy Ziv and some others shot seven men right in front of me... it was the worst thing I have ever seen in my entire life. It was so awful. These men... just lying dead on the floor... blood everywhere. I've never seen anything like it." Enrique shakes his head at the thought. He's numb, numb to it all, but he wonders if that's a good thing, as it's making it easier to get things out there.

"Oh my God, babe. That's terrible," Kristie says, looking at Enrique with concern. She pulls him into her arms and holds him tightly. "It must have been awful for you... I just can't imagine what you must be going through." Kristie is horrified by what she's hearing.

"I'll be OK... I'm just glad it's all over with... I'm sure I'll move past it," he says, trying to downplay the situation. Will he ever get those terrible images out of his mind? He hopes. But for now, he'll believe that with time he will.

Pulling back from their embrace, Kristie gasps out loud, putting her hand over her mouth.

"What is it, baby?" Enrique asks.

"My apartment? That's who broke into my apartment? It has to be? Oh no." She looks at Enrique accusatorially. "You knew this?"

"No, I didn't," Enrique replies with certainty. In the midst of all this, the break in had briefly slipped his mind. "I didn't know who did it at the time... I still don't... honestly, baby... aside from putting two and two together... I don't know for certain. I should have told you... but I didn't want to worry you." He looks down, feeling disappointed with himself, before looking back up at her. "Umm... but... there's one thing I need to confess though... I umm...."

Kristie looks at him expectantly; words fail her.

"I uhh... I didn't call the police... I couldn't... in case it blew everything with José. I'm so sorry I lied... but again, I didn't know what else to do. Whichever way I turned, I was wrong. It was torture for me to be dishonest with you. Please believe me... I did it for what I thought was the right reason." Enrique takes a minute and sips some water. He's desperately trying to read Kristie's expression. He hates that he's the cause of anything that would upset her or give her pain. He holds her hands and rests them on her lap.

"Enrique, this isn't good at all. We have to do something... it's pretty obvious it's got something to do with them... it's too coincidental." Her face creases as she tries to hold back her impending tears. "What if I was in there? What if...." She puts her head in her hands and surrenders to her tears. They soak her pretty face as they pour from her eyes. Enrique stands and takes her into his arms. His bare chest soaks with her tears as she cries.

"Don't even think about any of that, baby... I don't want you thinking like that." He looks down at her and holds her face in his hands. Looking deeply into her eyes, he says. "Nothing will happen to you... nothing... I have the best security in the country working for us now. I will get your apartment fixed up, but you can stay here as long as you want. You can stay here with me forever if you like. You know that's what I want."

"Thank you," she says through her tears. "So, you've told your security company? About your father?"

Oh fuck, things are about to get worse, he thinks to himself. Enrique knows he has to be honest; there's just no other way. But he hates that Kristie's so upset and doesn't want to worry her more, although he can't keep things from her any longer. Taking a deep breath, he tries to explain. "We have twenty-four-hour security for both of our families and us. The security is discreet, and our families don't even know they're there." Enrique tries to appease her as he holds her in his arms. "I uh... I couldn't use my security company... as I couldn't tell them about this." How the hell is he supposed to tell her this? He knows she isn't going to take it well, and he really can't blame her. But he has to do it. She needs to know everything.

"So, who are you using?"

"Ziv's arranged it."

"What?! You have got to be kidding me?" Kristie snaps out of her tears and is now looking at Enrique with disbelief that is turning to anger. "Are you crazy?" she scolds.

"I know how it sounds, but how was I supposed to tell a legitimate security company about any of this? I couldn't involve them. I couldn't risk it. You have to understand I was in an impossible situation. I know it's not ideal, but...."

"Not ideal?" Kristie can't believe what she's hearing. "Enrique, we can't have people like that looking after our families. It's ridiculous. It could put them in even more danger." She shakes her head in total disbelief at what he's done. "You're such a smart man... how can you be so stupid?"

"I know, baby, I know. It was against my better judgment, that's for sure. But I knew we needed security... and Ziv knows everything about this... so, I thought at the time, it was better to have him working for us rather than against us. I'm sorry... I know I was stupid, but I really didn't know what else to do."

"We need to arrange proper security, not these criminals. We need to deal with this first thing in the morning. I can't believe this is happening."

Kristie is fuming inside, but she keeps trying to remind herself that Enrique has been to hell and back with all of this, however, she's struggling to understand his logic with this one.

"Don't worry, babe. I will get straight on it. I'm so sorry to put this on you, but I want to be completely honest with you."

"I know. I just can't believe how much this has spiraled out of control." She pauses. "I can't worry my parents with this. It would scare them to death."

"Don't worry. Nothing will happen to anybody," Enrique replies. Hoping what he's saying is true.

"I hope you're right, Enrique. I couldn't bear it if anything happened to anyone in our family. Including you," she says with a worried look on her face.

"I know, baby." He holds her face with his hands and kisses her. "I'm so sorry." Tears start to fill his eyes. He can't believe she's still here. In his head, he thanks God she's still standing here in front of him.

"What else do you have to tell me then? Does it get any worse?" Kristie asks, hoping her suspicions are wrong. She takes a sip of tea in complete disbelief.

"I had to take this guy Manolo, who Ziv captured out to a Stiltsville dock. They did God knows what to him... trying to find out where José is... I wasn't there. I drove off in the boat... I couldn't stand to see anymore. They said they were trying to get information out of him about my father... I had to leave. Before I knew it, I was nearly in the Bahamas."

He tells her the rest of the story and how he came back to Stiltsville and how Ziv and Gutiérrez had taken Manolo's family as leverage.

"Oh my God! I can't believe all of this is happening. I'm in total shock. I don't know how to process all of this information." She sips some more of her tea before looking back up at him. "I must admit, I'm upset that you lied to me... you knew my life was in danger, Enrique, and you're only just telling me this now. I can't believe you kept all this from me." Kristie's starting to freak out. On the one hand, she's glad he's telling her, but on the other, she's angry, angry at the situation, but she's beginning to get angry with Enrique.

How could he do this to her? She was giving him another chance, and he's lied to her like this already. She knows it not as black and white as that, but she can't help how she feels. She has her own feelings to deal with in all this too. She doesn't want to judge him for his actions, and she's trying so hard not to, but she can't help it. How could he get involved in something so barbaric? This isn't his world. But then, he was pushed to extreme limits. She can see he felt he had no choice and that it's an impossible situation.

Kristie tries to look at things logically and push her anger and feelings aside. It's so difficult to do this, but she knows she has to. She doesn't want Enrique to stop talking. This is a breakthrough; she knows that much.

"I'm sorry, Enrique. It's just a lot for me to take in. I mean, this is José you're talking about. A man I love and look up to. I have the utmost respect for him, and I'm being told he's some cartel kingpin? It hurts me to think that he's lied to you... to us... all this time, and now he's putting you, his only son, in this kind of situation... in this kind of danger. My apartment's been broken into, and I've basically had a death threat for our baby and me. You're telling me you've witnessed seven murders and took some cartel member to be tortured or whatever... this is all too much for me to take in. What if you get sent to jail for being affiliated with all this? What then, Enrique?!" Kristie's voice starts to quiver. "What if something happens to you... I... I couldn't bare it...." Tears fall from her beautiful brown eyes once more. She's had enough. She can't take anymore.

Enrique pulls her into his arms; he feels terrible for putting her through this. "I'm so sorry, baby," Enrique whispers. "I'm so, so sorry."

"I know this must've been hell for you… I know you must feel like you're living a horrific nightmare… your father is your world, and it must be so devastating for you to find this out. I can't imagine what you must be going through," Kristie says as she holds him tightly. They have to do something. José still hasn't been found, and these people, whoever they are, don't seem to have made much progress as far as she's concerned.

In her mind, she's starting to think about what the next step should be. They need a plan, and she needs to get her head straight. This can't carry on any longer. This madness has to stop; it's already gone on way too long for her liking.

This is what Kristie is like in a crisis. She usually goes into complete shock at first, then she freaks out a little and then gets to work on dealing with the matter at hand. This situation is no different. She will find a way of getting them out of this nightmare and somehow get José home. With these thoughts, she starts to find strength.

Chapter 24

"It has been hell…" Enrique explains. "And I have to admit I was worried about getting into trouble with the police… but I honestly don't think anything will come of it. I've been watching the news since it happened, and nothing's been reported." He shakes his head with disbelief. "I don't understand… it's like it never happened." He looks at Kristie with eyes brimming with love and concern for this beautiful lady, a lady who is so strong and tenacious, a lady who he adores and worships with his entire being. He sweeps his fingers through her hair and says. "I'm so sorry for putting you through this, baby… I just didn't know what else to do. I had to tell you. You needed to know… you had a right to know… I couldn't keep it from you anymore. I was wrong to do so in the first place, but you have to understand what I've been dealing with. Also, I had worries about you and how you would feel. I know you love José, and I know you're against anything like this… I mean, you're against drugs… you hate guns… I…."

"And you can see why."

"I know, I know." His lips lift into a tiny smile before looking serious again. "I… I was struggling to find a way to tell you something so horrific, and selfishly, I was loving spending time with you. I felt so connected to you… it was like we were back to being us… and I didn't want to burst the bubble… I didn't want to ruin such beautiful moments, plus it was a glorious distraction from all the hell that was going on. You relax me. You make me feel calm, my calm away from the storm. I know it's wrong, but I couldn't help it... I got so caught up in it all." Enrique tries to explain. He then tells her about how he woke from his awful nightmare, came downstairs and had terrible pains in his chest, and was struggling to breathe.

"Oh no... that sounds like a panic attack. To think you were alone when it happened. I wish I were with you to help you... to be there for you. That must have been scary? I think your body is trying to tell you something, babe. You've been suppressing things for way too long. This is what happens if you don't deal with things that affect you mentally, they come out in you physically. Eventually, your body will force you to deal with things. I think this is why you're opening up to me like you are. It's like this has ripped you wide open... I don't know... I'm not a professional, but that's how I see it."

"I think you're right, baby." He smiles. "I keep telling you... you know me better than I know myself."

"I think that goes for both of us." She smiles back. "How do you feel now?"

"I feel very anxious. Like, my chest is tight... my mouth is dry... I feel shaky inside but numb at the same time. It's horrible... I can't really explain it."

He pauses for a second, trying to put his words into order. "I'm not good at this…. you know me…."

"I know, babe… but you're doing great… take your time."

He smiles and nods, looking at her with teary eyes. "It's just so hard… to explain… it's such new territory. I'm not quite sure how to deal with it all. But I know one thing for sure; you and our baby are my top priority. All I care about is your well-being and safety." He lifts his hand to her face, cups her cheek, and runs his thumb back and forth across her silky skin. "I'm so scared… scared you're gonna leave me after all this. But it's a risk I had to take. I couldn't base our relationship on lies and dishonesty. I didn't want you to find something out later on down the line. I wanted this to be a fresh start and make things work. I'm so excited about the baby and the possibility of our future together… I really don't want to mess it up ever again." He pauses again and swallows, gazing into her glorious dark brown eyes.

Kristie's eyes are sparkling with tears as she looks back at Enrique and shakes her head slowly. He takes this as a sign that she will stay, although he doesn't want to be too sure at this stage. He knows and understands the part he has played in this and has to give her time to process it all.

"What you said about me being ripped open makes perfect sense. I think that's what was happening to me on the balcony. It's like I've kept so many things inside of me for so long... now it's spilling out everywhere. It feels like poison is pouring out of me. It's painful as hell but liberating at the same time. It's hard for me to put into words." Enrique's struggling to say what he thinks and feels. But he's giving it everything he's got. He's in absolute emotional agony, but he keeps pushing on.

"You're doing really great, babe, honestly. This is the most we've ever talked about your emotions... the painful ones. I really feel like you've had a breakthrough. This may sound crazy, but everything happens for a reason. It's terrible what's happened to your father, but it's almost like this horrific event has happened to bring you to this point. I don't know if I'm making sense?" She stops for a moment, trying to get her mind straight. "I mean, I don't want you to think that I think your father's situation is a good thing... it most definitely isn't... but if that hadn't have happened, I'm not sure you would have been so talkative... so soon... about what's going on inside of you... you know what I mean? I'm not sure how to word what I'm trying to say." Kristie tries to get her point across. As tormented as she is about this whole situation, in a strange way, she's so happy to see Enrique finally talking. This is something she has wanted to see for the nearly four years they have been together.

"I understand what you mean... and I know you would never suggest my father's kidnapping is a good thing." He shakes his head slowly as his handsome face darkens. "But Krissy... I'm so angry with him... I'm actually beginning to hate him."

Kristie is shocked to hear this coming from Enrique, even given the circumstances.

"I really am... he's put so many people in danger. You, me, our families, the business, his staff, so much is at stake. It's been an emotional rollercoaster." He stops and raises a tiny smile. "And in the middle of it all, we met for dinner, and you told me you were pregnant... such beautiful news... such beautiful news in the middle of all this horror. It's what's kept me going through it all... it's given me hope," Enrique says with eyes full of tears. As he brushes his hand over her stomach, he can see the tiny bump through her silk nightdress. He smiles before kissing her on the lips. "The both of you are all I care about. I just want us three to be safe, healthy, and happy... I want you to be happy. You mean the world to me. I will fix myself... I know I will... in fact, I feel like this has changed me as a person... I feel so different now." Enrique is starting to feel a little calmer now that it's out in the open. He knows he can trust Kristie with anything, and even if she doesn't stay, he knows she won't breathe a word; this is one of the many things he loves about her.

Kristie closes her eyes as Enrique glides his hand over her stomach again. She reaches her hands up to his face and holds it, looking deeply into his gorgeous blue eyes. "I'm not going anywhere," she says sincerely.

Enrique bursts into tears. As Kristie holds his face, her hands drench in his tears. "Baby, I love you... and I'm here for you."

Enrique tries to smile through his tears and nods his response. He's so relieved, and his heart is full of love and joy; he can't believe what he's hearing. How did he get so lucky to have a lady like Kristie in his life?

"We are going to find your father... but we have to do this properly."

"You are so amazing." Enrique sobs.

Kristie smiles and kisses his lips. "And so are you... I love you... and I want to help."

"You do?"

"Yes."

Enrique pulls her into a tight embrace and cries hysterically; he can barely breathe through his tears.

"I love you so, so much... more than anything... more than words can ever describe... I always have, and I always will."

"And I feel the very same way about you, too, baby." She says softly as she holds him. "It's OK, babe. It's OK."

Enrique nods as he buries his face in her neck, breathing in her scent and feeling the tranquil peace that she always gives him.

Once Enrique has calmed a little, Kristie pulls back to look at him. She smiles sweetly and says. "I know someone... in the D.E.A... she's a client and a friend. I'll call her when we reach a more reasonable hour and ask her to come over." Kristie looks at him with seriousness. "No more vigilante stuff... we have to do this right. You can't carry on dealing with these kinds of people. You could end up getting yourself, and God knows who else killed. It's been nearly five days since your father's been kidnapped, and he's still not been found. All I can see is they've dragged you further into this mess. This is not the way to deal with this... but we will find a way, don't worry. I know you're angry with your father, but I also know you love him unconditionally... and behind all that anger... I know you want him back... and he can answer to you then," Kristie says with confidence.

"You want to help me?" Enrique responds. Although fearful about contacting the authorities, he knows it's the right thing to do. There's no other way. Kristie's right, this has gone on way too long, and it's only getting worse. Tears fill his eyes again. He's in awe of this woman. He can't believe she wants to help him after all of this. He tightens his hold around her and cries once more. He can't believe how lucky he is to have her in his life. She's his rock, and he's always known she's stronger than him, but this only makes him realize it even more. Kristie is always there for him, and just as he thought when he saw her standing at the door when he was on the balcony a few hours ago: she's his guardian angel.

"I will help you... of course, I will. I love you. I may be mad at you for the way you've handled certain things, but I'm angrier at the situation. I know you didn't ask for any of this, and I know you did what you thought was right at the time," Kristie says as she holds him.

"I love you so much too." He gazes into her glorious dark eyes, shaking his head in wonder as he glides his hands through her glossy brunette hair. "I can't believe how lucky I am to have you... I really can't. You're so strong and beautiful... you always know what to do. I'm so sorry I've shut you out for so long. I feel so foolish now... talking to you has made me feel so much better... and I'm so glad that I've finally managed to open up to you. I always thought that having a drink would help make me forget everything, but I was so wrong... all I needed to do was talk to you."

Although Enrique hasn't ever been able to discuss his grief specifically over the years, he had told Kristie that when his mom passed, it was so difficult for him to process; he found that not talking about it made him feel better. People would ask him questions about his feelings regarding her passing, and when he tried to talk about it, he would get so upset he could barely breathe. Over time, he quickly learned that if he didn't talk about it, he didn't get upset, and that's where burying his grief was born.

"I do wonder... as you got older and life got more complicated, it was even harder for you to express your feelings?" Kristie says with trepidation. "Then it compounded, and that's where the alcohol came in... I know your drinking gets worse around certain dates... dates relating to your mom."

"I think you're right." He agrees. "It all seems so easy now... if only it were when we were together... ugh... I hate that I behaved the way I did... and I hated being apart from you too. It was complete torture. All I wanted to do was make things right but didn't know how. I wanted to call you to tell you how much I loved you... or to ask you out to dinner... or just to be with you... cuddle up with you on the pool deck and listen to some music like we used to. There were so many times when we were on the phone, and I wanted to ask you for another chance... or even beg you... but I kept telling myself you were better off without me... you deserved better... and you do." He pauses. "I mean, I know there were a couple of times when I cracked and let my mask slip."

"I know… and I wanted to come back so desperately too, but you know I needed to see some kind of change, and I knew you weren't at that place… you weren't ready… but now I can see you are."

"I am, baby. I really am. I'm ready… so, so ready." He kisses her lips. "God, I'm so, so sorry to put you through what I did. I was so horrible, especially toward the end. It was getting harder and harder for me to deal with things. As you know, the insomnia was back… the way I had been dealing with the pain in the past wasn't working anymore." He lets out a long slow breath. "I would usually have a night out and few drinks… maybe work a little more, and I would be OK… I would forget the pain for a while… but it wasn't working anymore."

"I know, baby, I know," Kristie says softly.

"It was like mom's anniversary and birthday were harder on me more than ever this year… the pain was intolerable. I knew you were only trying to help me, but I didn't know how to express myself… I didn't know how to let you be there for me… and I would get so frustrated with myself for not being able to." He shakes his head slowly. "Then I would find myself pushing you away and arguing with you… it's like I knew you would leave me alone if I started an argument. It seemed like I just wanted to be left alone, but I didn't at the same time. I was desperate to open up to you, but the words just wouldn't come out. I was awful to you. I can't believe I treated you that way. I'm so sorry."

"I knew that's what you were doing, babe. That's why I stayed as long as I did… I knew what you were going through… and I was so hopeful that we would get there… that we would find a way." She presses her lips together, letting out a sigh. "Sometimes, I could see that you wanted to talk, but it was like you couldn't speak. Then you would get frustrated with yourself for not being able to say what you wanted to say."

"That's exactly what was happening. I would get so frustrated with myself, and for some reason, I would twist it, so it was your fault, somehow. It sounds crazy now that I'm saying it out loud. But I guess I was deflecting my issues onto you? I don't know. I suppose, if you can blame somebody else for what you're doing wrong… it makes you feel like you're not the one with the problem? I'm not sure if I'm making sense?" Enrique is struggling to explain what he means. He knows now that he was blaming Kristie for his shit. That way, he didn't have to deal with it, and he feels terrible that he did this to her: to somebody that loves him so much.

"You are making perfect sense, babe. I thought that's what was happening, but I just couldn't take it anymore. Although we still had some great times during those months." Kristie places her hand on her stomach and looks down at her bump with a smile. Enrique puts his hand on hers, smiling with her.

"Our little baby," he says to her.

"Yes, our little baby was made during one of those happy times." Kristie smiles back. "But all the bad times were making me so miserable. I had to leave. I know now that it was the right thing to do, as painful as it was at the time."

"You were right to leave me, babe. One hundred percent right. I don't think we would be here now if you hadn't left. I needed a shakeup. A shock to the system to drag me out of my own head. I'm so glad you're here now, though... and I hope you will stay with me." His eyes are full of hope. "Our conversation on the pool deck made me feel so good inside. The fact that we were even talking about marriage... I feel so honored... and thank you for being here and thank you for being you." He kisses her soft full lips.

"I'm not going anywhere, babe... and I loved talking about our future on the pool deck. It meant so much to me too... and I'm glad I'm here with you as well... although I would rather it not be under these circumstances, but we will get through this together."

"Thank you, babe. Thank you. Thank you. Thank you. You don't know how grateful I am to have you."

They hold each other close for a few moments, as the penthouse shimmers with pink and orange as the sun begins to rise, symbolizing a new day and new beginnings.

"I'm going to make some more tea for you and coffee for me, I think." He says.

"That's a good idea... well, actually, cafécito after a panic attack? Probably not."

"Baby, I've been drinking cafécito since before I was born." He chuckles. "I'm sure I'll be OK." He kisses her lips once more before he begins to make their drinks.

He notices it's 6:32am. Jeez, they've had a long night of talking. I'm exhausted, exhausted yet wired, he thinks to himself. Kristie must be tired, she's been up all night, and she is carrying our baby. "I should imagine you're tired, baby? Would you like a lay down after your tea? It's been a bit of a night. Also, you need to eat. It's nearly breakfast time," Enrique says, although he's not hungry in the slightest.

"No, I'm fine, babe. I feel strangely wide awake," Kristie replies. She knows it's the adrenaline. She has to get onto this and contact her client. She's on a mission. Now that she has a plan, she's starting to feel more in control of the situation.

"OK, baby... well, as long as you're sure?"

"I am."

Enrique makes their drinks and sits beside her at the breakfast bar.

"Ya know, another thing that's getting to me about José is I can't help but feel like he has something to do with mom's death... there's always been a big question mark over what happened... too many unanswered questions."

"Really? Do you really think José had something to do with your mom's passing? He worshiped your mom... he still does."

"Nothing surprises me anymore as far as he's concerned."

"I know it's hard, baby, but try not to jump to conclusions before you know all the facts."

"I know, I know." He takes a sip of his coffee. "Like, I always knew he did well back in the day, but I would have never put him in the category of being head of a cartel... I mean, I knew he made good money and had a good life, but he never mentioned anything to that magnitude. Mom gave him an ultimatum, and he quit that world and started the company... and as you know... as far as I knew, that's where it ended... they lived happily ever after until my mom's passing." He tilts his head to the side momentarily with a sad expression. "But it's now got me thinking about mom. If dad was still involved in that kind of world... would it have had something to do with mom's death?" Enrique's thoughts and fears are spilling out of him. They won't stop. It's like a faucet has been jammed on, and the water won't stop pouring out.

"I understand what you're saying... but we have to try to give him the benefit of the doubt for now until you can talk to him." Kristie tries to calm Enrique's racing thoughts. All the evidence may be pointing in the direction that José has been lying to everybody, but they still don't know for sure. These people could be anybody, and they need to find out hard facts, not hearsay.

"It's pretty obvious to me that it's the case, babe." He says, raising his eyebrows, residing himself to the fact.

"Babe, this is all speculation, and it's not helping anything at the moment... we need facts to go on. Try not to think about things like that just yet. Let's concentrate on getting José back for now." Although she worries he might be right, none of this is concrete evidence, and she can see Enrique's mentally drained and exhausted enough already. She doesn't want him wasting more energy on something that's speculation at this point.

"You're right. But there's something else... something I keep thinking about."

"What's that?"

"Well, do you remember me saying about how we had a family feud?"

"Yes, I remember you mentioning it a long time ago... you didn't really say much about it at the time."

"Well, it was when mom passed." He takes another sip of his coffee. "My grandfather... Pablo... he blamed dad for mom's death."

"Really?" Kristie is shocked to hear this as the family is all super close, and she's never seen any signs of tension between Pablo and José.

"Yeah... it went on for a while... they didn't talk for years. I really believe if I hadn't been born, he would never have spoken to him again... and things really are starting to add up for me now. And I know I've never told you how mom died... aside from the fact that there was a car accident... I've always found it too painful." Tears prick his eyes again, and before he can stop them, they fall down his cheeks. He's going to try to talk about this for the first time in his life.

"Take your time, baby," Kristie whispers as they sit facing each other, holding hands. "Take your time."

He takes a deep breath, trying to force his way through the agonizing grief as it slices through his heart. "Mom was on her way back from work… she was working late… and uh… she was driving down the I-95…." He swallows down the pain as it tries to grip his throat and steal his words. He's not giving in to it this time; he's going to push his way through this for the first time in his life. He wipes his tears and continues. "Her car… uhh… well, there was this truck… for some reason… it… it stopped… the driver slammed on the brakes… there were tire marks on the road… and mom's car… she… she…."

Kristie is totally heartbroken for her man. This is destroying him, but she can see he wants to do this for her… he wants to do this for them, and he's pushing through the intolerable agony for the very first time.

"She didn't have any hope… any hope of surviving… there was nothing she could do." His voice trembles through his tears. His grip on Kristie's hands tightens, and he tries so desperately to breathe through the torture. His chest is drenched with tears as they gush from his beautiful blue yet bloodshot eyes. He takes a deep breath and then proceeds. "She went… went underneath the truck… her car was jammed under it… when… when the Fire Department got there…

it was too late... she was already gone... she'd... she'd died from her injuries."

"Oh, baby, I'm so, so sorry... I'm so, so sorry." Kristie holds him as he cries. His whole body is trembling, and she can feel his heart racing against her as she holds him close. "I'm so, so sorry." She whispers again.

"Thank you, baby." He whispers. He pulls back for a second to look at her. "I can't stop thinking... what's making me think something is off about it all is the truck driver fled the scene... and he never got caught... there was no real investigation... it was just put down as a nasty accident... that's what I've never been able to understand... now I feel like pieces of the jigsaw are starting to fall into place. All these unanswered questions I've carried with me my whole life are now... it's all starting to make sense... it's all starting to make sense." He's finally said it. It's out there. He breathes out a huge sigh of relief. The tears won't stop. Kristie holds him so tightly, and his head's resting on her shoulder. He breathes in her scent. He feels calm at last. He feels at home.

They continue to hold each other, saying nothing. Kristie lets Enrique cry. She's so proud of him for finally doing this. She knows he's realized that he can't carry on the way he was; he can't bury his pain any longer. Finally, it has come to the surface, and he has no choice but to deal with it. And they will deal with it together.

Chapter 25

Enrique lifts his head from Kristie's shoulder and gazes into her loving brown eyes. "Thank you. Thank you for listening to me... for understanding me. I feel free now... free of all the pain... all the suffering I've been carrying and suppressing all my life."

"Baby, don't thank me... I'm here for you... always."

"I know, babe... and I'm always here for you." He tucks a loose strand of hair behind her ear, looking at her with eyes full of wonder. "And you didn't leave."

"I'm not going anywhere... it's you and me... and our little baby."

"Just you and me and our little baby." He repeats her words with a whisper before kissing her lips tenderly. "I love you."

"I love you, too."

Reaching her hands to his face, Kristie kisses him softly.

"You're so beautiful." He whispers against her lips before kissing her deeply, pouring everything he's got into their kiss. He needs to feel as close to her as he can; he needs her.

Enrique's hands follow her delicious curves, and as his fingertips reach below her hips, he glides her silk nightdress upward and lifts her to him; Kristie wraps her legs around his waist as he does.

He sits Kristie on the breakfast bar, not breaking their kiss for a second, and he runs his hands down her back, caressing her silky skin, revealed by the low cut back of her nightdress. Sweeping her long dark hair into his hands, he pulls her head back slightly and deepens their kiss as their breathing accelerates.

Kristie's fingernails dig into Enrique's already tender back from yesterday on the pool deck; this only turns him on even more. He can't get enough of her, he never can, and he never will. He feels wide open to her now, and this only intensifies every emotion.

He glides his hands down over her curves, and as he reaches her behind, he grips hold and pulls her closer to him. As his rock-hard erection presses into her through his pajama pants, he lets out a loud grown, desperate to feel her.

He runs his hands up to Kristie's shoulders, sweeps her long brunette hair to one side, and trails his kisses along her jawline and down to her neck. He stands back a little, looking down at her body, wrapped in white silk and lace; she's exquisite, so perfect, and so beautiful.

He glides his hand down her chest and continues lower; his fingertips delicately caress the swell of each breast. Kristie rests her hands on the counter behind her, causing her body to arch in the way Enrique finds so sensual. His eyes gaze at her glorious feminine figure, drinking in every drop. Her beautifully erect nipples are pushing through the luxurious white silk of her nightdress, and he finds it so erotic he feels like he's about to explode.

Cupping her firm and now even fuller breasts, he brushes his thumbs over her erect nipples as they protrude through the silk. Kristie lets out a moan as her head tips back; her voluminous brunette hair is cascading behind her. As the carnal pleasure surges through her, Kristie's back arches even more, and her breasts push up closer to Enrique. This only makes her breasts look even more sensuous, and Enrique can't get enough.

His grip tightens, and his fingers dig in, then he pinches each nipple between his thumbs and forefingers, pulling them through the silk. Enrique watches as Kristie's seductive body responds to his every touch, drinking in every delicious move.

He leans across to her full lips and kisses her with fervor as he continues to tease and torment her nipples. His hands slide down her curves to her thighs, and as he reaches the hem of her nightdress, while caressing her legs, he pushes the white silk up at the same time. Kristie lifts herself up so he can glide the nightdress up over her hips.

Enrique's hands slide from her hips and slowly down to the junction of her thighs. With his fingers fanned out over the top of her thighs, he runs his thumb down the smooth skin to her clitoris; she is soaking. He moans with appreciation as his thumb drenches with her arousal, and he massages her clitoris.

Watching her glorious body shimmer before him, he slides first his middle finger, then his forefinger inside of her, as he continues to rub her clitoris.

"So, fucking sexy." He breathes as he watches the erotic show before him.

Her moans get louder as her orgasm builds higher and higher. "Ahhh... Enrique... ahh!" Kristie comes explosively, screaming his name as she does, before crashing into another orgasm; her body is shuddering and shaking as she absorbs every ounce of pleasure Enrique is giving her.

Slowly pulling his fingers out of her, he leans over and kisses her lips. He holds back for a second and slides his fingers into her mouth. Her passion-filled eyes meet his as she sucks her own arousal off of his fingers. Fuck! I'm gonna come any second, Enrique thinks to himself. He pulls his fingers out of her mouth and kisses her with fervor.

"I need you." Kristie pleads. "I need you."

"Oh, baby, I need you, too." He breathes.

And with that, he quickly pulls down his pajama pants, holds his erection in place, and slides it into her, letting out a loud groan as he does. She feels absolutely unbelievable. They hold each other tightly, and Kristie wraps her legs around his waist, and their bodies begin to move as one.

With her face in his neck, Kristie bites down on his shoulder as she tries to absorb the carnal ecstasy that's racing through her while her nails dig into his back. Fuck! All these sensations are so arousing: so carnal. After everything that's happened tonight, all the talking, all the tears, all the emotion, Enrique has been ripped wide open, and every feeling, every sensation, is way more intense than ever before.

For the first time in his life, he's allowed himself to be completely vulnerable, and it feels so good. He's now free. And even after everything that's happened, everything he's told her, Kristie's still here, and he feels like the luckiest man alive. In fact, he is the luckiest man alive.

Kristie's body starts to tense, and her grip is getting tighter. He knows her body well enough to know she's close, and he is too. She bites down harder on his shoulder, and her nails sink deeper into his back as she screams through another orgasm, pulling Enrique to an explosive climax, so powerful and so euphoric he can barely take it; his mind is blown.

He can't stop. His orgasm keeps coming and coming. It's so intense it's almost painful. His legs are weak, and he can barely stand. What the fuck? It's practically unbearable. He's never come like this in his life. Then all of a sudden, tears fill his eyes; he can't control them, and they pour down his handsome face. With his heart racing, he buries his face in Kristie's neck as he holds her tightly, begging silently for the peace she always gives him. She strokes his hair as she holds him to her. He can feel her love for him radiating off of her. He's so overcome with so many emotions; he doesn't know how to handle them. Fuck! What is happening to me, he asks himself. This is too much.

His orgasm finally subsides, but the tears keep pouring down his face. What the hell is going on? Since his father's disappearance, he's become a crying emotional wreck. This is so unlike him. But is this all part of the process? All part of him healing?

"It's OK, babe... it's OK," she whispers, reassuring him. "I love you... I love you."

"I love you, too, baby... more than words can ever describe." He nuzzles tighter into her neck. "Thank you... thank you for being there for me... thank you for being such a beautiful person... I'm so lucky... so lucky to have you."

"And I'm lucky to have you, babe." She whispers, still stroking his hair. "Please don't keep thanking me… I'm here for you… just like you've been there for me… we're there for each other… we always have been." She kisses his cheek. "It's been a pretty intense night… you're just releasing everything you've been burying for all these years… and that's a good thing. It's all coming out… it needs to… and you'll feel better for it. Trust me." She guides his head, so he's facing her and kisses away his tears.

"Ya know, I'll thank God every day for blessing me with you… for having you in my life." He kisses her lips. "I will never take it for granted… how lucky I am… how blessed I am to have you here… especially after everything that's happened… and you're still here." Enrique's voice is shaking through the tears. "Ugh God, I feel like such a wreck… look at me." He allows himself a tiny smile at his own expense as he wipes his tears away. "I never cry… before all of this… I hadn't cried since I was a child… well, actually, that's not entirely true."

Kristie looks at him expectantly. Aside from when she told him about the baby, she has never seen him cry, and to her knowledge, the last time he cried was at his mom's funeral when he was six.

"I cried when you left." He admits.

"You did?" Kristie finds this sad to hear, but she can't help but feel shocked at the same time. When she left, she had the impression that she was the one that was the more emotional about their break up. Although she knew Enrique was upset behind his façade, aside from a couple of occasions, he never really showed it. When they were apart, Kristie would cry herself to sleep most nights, as she was so devastated; she missed Enrique every second they were apart. She knew that he felt the same as her, but he always acted so cool and like he had everything under control. To hear him say he cried when she left, especially knowing what a big deal this is to Enrique, is news to her.

"I did, babe. I cried all night. I knew I was making the biggest mistake of my life... but I couldn't do anything to stop it... it was torture."

"Oh, baby... that makes me feel awful... I always thought you were so... I don't know... had everything so under control."

"You know I'm very good at acting that way." He smiles. "I didn't have anything under control whatsoever. Losing you destroyed me... but like we've said... it had to happen for me to face things... to push me to deal with things."

"I know... I just... it just surprises me, that's all."

"I know… but there you go… I've admitted it." He smiles sweetly. "And now I can't stop." He wipes more tears as they fall. "Ugghhh."

As Kristie listens to what Enrique has to say, she wonders if the night she left was the turning point for him. Perhaps, as painful as it was at the time, it was the start of him opening up. The fact that he cried that night, really does mean something to her. "I think that was the moment… the night I left… I think you were starting to open up… the pain was forcing its way out of you… like it was the turning point for you… for us… it was where your healing began?"

"In a strange way, I think it was. It shocked me; I've gotta be honest… I mean, the tears were uncontrollable… there were floods of them… like now. I think you leaving was definitely the moment when things shifted… when things were getting so agonizing that I had to do something… unfortunately, I still took my time to actually do what I needed to do." He shakes his head with disbelief at his own actions. "It's so crazy… I mean, I'm a go-getter… in life, I see what I want, and I go right after it. If there's a problem… I solve it. Yet, when it comes to my emotions… to my grief… I have no clue how to deal with it and end up running… running as fast as I can… it's quite pathetic, really." He smiles. "Can you imagine if I run my company that way? It wouldn't last five minutes."

"You're not pathetic... emotions are very different from business. With business, you detach your emotions... it's practical... with this... it's anything but practical... it's hard... and I think you're very brave for how far you've come in such a short space of time... and as for all the crying... I know it may sound silly but, I think it's a good thing... it's your body's way of releasing all the hurt, anger, and pressure." She kisses his lips tenderly. "And it's OK... I'm here for you... it's all gonna be OK." Kristie kisses his perfectly toned chest and then runs her hand over his firm muscles, admiring him as she goes. She looks into his eyes full of love. "I love you, Enrique Cruz. I love you more than anything in the world," she says, wiping away his tears and kissing his lips.

"I love you too, Miss Carrington... my gorgeous girl. Look at you. You're so unbelievably beautiful... I just can't get enough of you." Enrique looks at her with complete adoration and kisses her lips tenderly.

"And you're so unbelievably handsome, Mr. Cruz... and I can never get enough of you."

They kiss once more. "I need to make you something to eat," he says, thankful the tears have finally stopped. He lifts her off the counter, and her nightdress slides gracefully down her curvaceous body. As Enrique glances down her glorious figure, he can see her little bump is showing through the silk. He bends down to kiss it before kneeling in front of her and resting the side of his face on the bump. Feeling the closeness with their unborn child, he wraps his arms around her waist, closing his eyes at the same time. Kristie runs her fingers through his unusually messy yet sexy-looking hair and looks down at him, smiling. Enrique turns his head and kisses her bump.

"I love you, little one." He whispers.

"You are so adorable." Kristie smiles.

Gazing up at her with his summery blue eyes, he says sweetly. "And so are you... both of you." He kisses her bump once more, then rises to his feet and kisses her lips. "What would you like for breakfast, my darling?"

"Something Cuban." She smiles.

"Something Cuban, ay?" He smiles back with a sexy glint in his eyes. "Well, Miss Carrington, I can most certainly arrange that."

"Hmmm...." Kristie bites her lower lip as she thinks about what she wants Enrique to do to her.

"Hmmm...." He moans against her lips before kissing her hard, then turning Kristie around, he glides up her nightdress and gives her exactly what she's begging him for.

* * *

"I'll have a small cafécito and some OJ, please, babe," she says, smiling as she helps him cook their breakfast. She can see that Enrique is so nervous inside about going to the authorities, but she can't see any other way of dealing with it. These guys, whoever they are, don't seem to be getting anywhere, and she doesn't like the sound of them, either. As far as she's concerned, the authorities should be dealing with this, not Enrique. God knows what could happen to him or them; it doesn't bear thinking about.

Once they've had breakfast, she will call her client for advice. Jackie is such a dear person; Kristie loves her. She may be sweet and kind, but she also takes no shit and is exceptional at her job. She may work in a man's world, but Jackie always jokes that she can do anything a man could do... but better, and Kristie is well aware that she can, so much so that she knows that Jackie is going to be the person who is going to help them. She is sure of that.

Enrique places the drinks on the breakfast bar and continues to cook their breakfast. Turning the home fries on the skillet, he looks to Kristie and says, "I found Leon the other day." He pauses, shaking his head with sadness.

This stops Kristie in her tracks. She knows what this means. Whenever Enrique says he's found Leon, it means that he's had a relapse. "Baby, no,"

Kristie says as she rushes over to her man and holds him from behind. "I'm so, so sorry." She kisses his tanned naked skin before resting her face on his back. "I'm so, so sorry."

Kristie's heart breaks again. Enrique has been through so much lately, more than most people would go through in ten lifetimes, and the fact that he's still standing just goes to show the inner strength he really does have. He never gives himself credit, especially when it comes to emotional strength.

"Thank you, baby." He whispers, rubbing her arm back and forth as she holds him around his waist. "I found him in Charlton... strung out on heroin, and God knows what else." He turns to look at Kristie as he holds her. "Oh, Krissy, it was so awful to see." Enrique starts to get emotional. It's all been way too much for him to handle lately; so many highs and lows. And now he has to go to the D.E.A. Of course, he knows it's the right thing to do, but it's torturing him inside.

With his emotions still extremely conflicted as far as his father is concerned, Enrique is starting to worry that something will happen to his dad, and if it does, he feels it might as well be him pulling the trigger. He knows he will blame himself for the rest of his life, but he also knows it's another risk he will have to take, just like the risk he took telling Kristie. Luckily that one paid off, and he prays this one will too.

"Oh, babe... I'm so sorry... so much has happened... I can't believe how much you've been put through over these past few days... you must be devastated? He was doing so well... he was working so hard at the gym... helping so many people... plus he was doing so much good for others at the rehab center."

"He was... I don't know... perhaps it wasn't the right thing to do... allowing him to work there? Maybe it was too soon... even if it was only a few hours a week?"

"No, babe... don't blame yourself. Leon has always wanted to work at the center... ever since you opened it... you know that... it was really helping him cope with his own issues... he's been clean for ages."

"I know... but I can't help but think about it. Ugh... I don't know..." He pulls Kristie into a tight embrace. Kissing her hair, he whispers. "You need to eat, babe." He kisses her hair once more. "You've been up all night, and with all the stress and shock... it's not good for you or the baby." He kisses her again. "Go sit down, and I will bring you your breakfast." He looks at her lovingly with a sweet smile.

"OK, Mr. Cruz." She smiles back. She loves the way he looks after her. It's true, she can look after herself, but Enrique is so sweet, and she knows how much he loves to take care of her, and she's happy to let him.

They sit down and begin to eat their breakfast.

"I know you're nervous about meeting with Jackie. But honestly... it's the right thing to do... you've tried everything else. We can't leave it any longer... and I can't think of anybody else better to get this sorted. She's incredible at her job... I trust her implicitly." She rests her hand on Enrique's forearm, looking deeply into his eyes. "We're gonna get José back safely... don't worry," Kristie says confidently.

"Thank you, babe... thank you for everything you've done for me." He smiles through his pain. "I'm just so scared something's going to happen to him... I know I sound confused... that's because I am... the whole situation is so messed up... I don't know what I feel about it from one minute to the next." He lets out a long slow breath. "I mean, I can't stand what he's done... but he's still my father... and I love him... that will never change," Enrique says, finishing his coffee.

"I can understand that, babe... it makes complete sense... that you would feel that way. It must be so confusing... I can't imagine how you must be feeling... but we will get through this... together... and we will get your father back... I promise."

He takes her into his arms and holds her tightly. Kissing the side of her head, he says. "I love you... my perfect girl... I love you so much. Thank you."

"And I love you, my perfect man...."

"Baby girl, I think I'm far from perfect." He says, interrupting her mid-sentence.

"You are perfect... perfect to me" Kristie looks up to him for a second.

He shakes his head, closing his eyes briefly. "Far from it, baby... I have more issues than...."

Kristie places her forefinger on his lips, stopping him from saying any more. "You're perfect to me... everything you did... throughout all of this... this situation... has been out of love... out of thinking you're doing the right thing for your father. And the rest... the grief... you're facing that now... and we will get through this...." She removes her finger and kisses his lips softly, before whispering. "I love you so, so much... with all of my heart."

Enrique smiles as Kristie's words wash over him. "Darling girl." He kisses her again. "What would I do without you?"

"You'll never have to find out." She smiles.

He shakes his head with wonder and smiles back widely before pulling her into another tight embrace and burying his face into her neck once more. "You will never know how much that means to me." He whispers. He can't believe what he's hearing. He's longed to hear those words from Kristie for what has felt like an eternity.

After a short while, he lifts his head to look at her. Sweeping her hair out of her face, he says. "Will you come to Church with me?"

"Of course, baby."

"I want to pray... pray for us all... ask God to guide us through all of this."

"Of course... we both can ask Him... we can pray together."

"Thank you, baby... it means so much to me... it means the world...." He smiles, cupping her beautiful face gently in his hands and kissing her soft full lips.

"Don't thank me... I know how much this will help you... it will help me too... we can both pray... for your father... for Leon... for you...."

"You are so beautiful." He smiles.

"And so are you." She smiles back. "Baby, I totally understand your feelings toward José. It must be so confusing? I mean, I know I'm totally confused,"

"It is so confusing. Like, one minute I hate him... the next I love him so much... I worry myself sick... then I think he deserves everything he gets... but it's like you said... we don't know the facts yet... we don't know the truth... once we get to the bottom of it, then I can figure out how I feel about things for sure, I guess."

"Exactly."

While finishing their breakfast, they decide that Kristie will call Jackie at about 10am to give her a chance to get into work and catch up on what she needs to do. Once they've tidied the dishes away, they head upstairs to get ready.

"If you can get through what you did last night, you can get through this," Kristie says, reassuring Enrique, who is looking at her full of fear and trepidation. She holds him in her arms. "Just think of it as it's going to bring your father home... it's a means to an end. Try to look at it as a positive thing... and I'll be with you every step of the way."

"I know, and I am so grateful you are," Enrique says, then kisses Kristie on the lips.

"I know you are, babe... I love you."

"I love you, too."

Enrique looks suave and sophisticated wearing a mid-blue suit, a crisp white shirt, a white pocket square, and black dress shoes. He has his sunglasses in his inside pocket, ready for when they head out. Kristie is wearing black skinny jeans, a black blazer jacket, a silk blush camisole top, which is the perfect match for her black and blush Valentino heels. She's wearing her hair straight and large gold hoop earrings. Her wrist is glistening with her platinum and diamond, square-faced Cartier watch, which Enrique gave her for their first Christmas together. The entire watch is covered in diamonds, the strap, the face, everything. It is so beautiful, and it's so precious to her, just like all the gifts Enrique has given her, even if she always insists he doesn't.

Kristie wouldn't usually wear jeans to Church, but she's very limited to what she has to wear, as she only has a few days' worth of clothes, which Enrique gathered for her on the day of the break in.

"Are we going to St. Patrick's Church on the beach?" Kristie asks, knowing this is where they always used to go together, plus it's where Enrique has always gone to Church.

"Yes, babe," Enrique replies. "You good to go? Jorge's just text... the car's ready."

"Yes, baby... do I look OK? I'm not so sure about wearing black and jeans to Church."

"You look sensational… so beautiful." He kisses her lips. "So, so beautiful."

"Thanks, babe. I will need to get some clothes soon. I'm running out of them."

"We can go shopping once we know what's happening… and get this sorted out. Maybe go to Palm Court or Bal Harbor Shops? We can do some laundry, too," Enrique says as they head downstairs.

Enrique stops by his office to get the burner phone from his desk drawer. He needs to check it to see if there are any calls or texts; there's nothing. No contact. No news on his father. He takes the phone with him and walks into the kitchen where Kristie is standing. It's now 10am, and Kristie takes her cell from her purse and unlocks it with facial recognition. She looks at Enrique and says, "Ready to do this?"

Enrique takes a deep breath in and then slowly out. "Yes, let's do this. I just want this whole nightmare over… this is the best way," he says, tidying things around the already immaculate kitchen, busying himself. His hands are starting to shake a little, and his chest is feeling tight at the mere thought.

"It will all be OK, babe," Kristie says with reassurance.

"As long as I have you… you and our baby… I will always be OK." He smiles at her through his excruciating anxiety.

Kristie smiles back before looking down at her contacts list on her cell, finds Jackie's number, and hits the call button.

Chapter 26

Kristie has tried to call Jackie a couple of times, but her phone has been engaged for the past hour; this only adds to their anxiety levels. Kristie tries again, and finally, she gets through.

"Hey! Jackie?" Kristie says in an upbeat tone. "It's Kristie. I'm so sorry to bother you...."

As Enrique hears that Kristie has finally got through to Jackie, he stops what he's doing; it's like he's bolted to the floor. He's looking in Kristie's direction, listening to every word. Panic sets in. He can't move. What the fuck are we doing, he asks himself in his mind. He contemplates taking the phone off of Kristie and ending the call. No. Not a good idea. You've got to do this; you've got to see this through. We're doing the right thing. We will tell the D.E.A., and the D.E.A. will take down whoever has my father.

"Yeah... I uhh... I have an issue... and you said to contact you if I ever needed to." Kristie raises a tiny nervous smile. "So... I'm contacting you."

Oh, fuck! Oh, fuck! Oh, fuck, Enrique screams in his mind.

Kristie looks over at Enrique, who is so obviously in a state of panic. She walks over to him, takes his hand, and kisses his lips, letting him know that everything will be alright.

"Yeah, I don't want to discuss it over the phone... can we meet?" Kristie says to Jackie before looking at Enrique and saying, "Is there an empty apartment we can use to meet Jackie?"

"Yeah," Enrique manages. His mouth is so dry, he can barely speak. He clears his throat. "Yes, babe."

"Jackie. Come to Alta Vita... we will meet you in...." Kristie says, looking at Enrique for where best to meet Jackie.

"Apartment 8810," Enrique confirms. Penthouse B would be a slightly better choice due to its private entrance, but he decides against this, as he can't trust that Ziv hasn't left anything behind, like recording devices or cameras.

"Apartment 8810," Kristie says, nodding at Enrique for his approval. He nods back. "No, it's not sold yet... yeah, that's a great idea. OK, Jackie. We'll see you in an hour." Kristie hangs up the phone.

"She's coming over in an hour... she said she'll be in disguise... so nobody will recognize her... she's gonna pose as a potential buyer," Kristie says to a startled-looking Enrique. "She's gonna text to keep me updated."

"OK," Enrique's still struggling to speak. Have I just signed my own father's death warrant, he asks himself silently.

"It will all be OK, baby... you'll see. Jackie is the best person to deal with this... I know she is... trust me." She says with reassurance and takes him into her arms and holding him tightly. "I promise it will all be OK... we'll get your father back."

Enrique nods as he takes in a deep breath, breathing in her scent.

Kristie pulls back a little and says. "Sorry, babe. It doesn't look like we will be going to Church... but I guess it's better to do this sooner rather than later."

"Yes, you're right. We can go later. If not, I can pray at home. I feel it's something I need to do," he says. Enrique has been raised Catholic and attends Church as regularly as he can.

"I know, babe. But I just know how important it is to you." She pauses. "Let's get this meeting with Jackie over with... and then we can figure everything out from there."

Suddenly, the burner phone vibrates on the kitchen counter, where Enrique had left it. They both look at it with eyes wide and in complete shock. "Fuck," Enrique exclaims. "It's either gonna be Ziv or Gutiérrez... oh, God! Do they know we've contacted Jackie?" He starts to freak out.

"I highly doubt it... it's OK. Answer it... let's see what they have to say."

Enrique walks over to the phone and picks it up. "Yeah," he answers, in a tone that is obvious that he has no respect for whoever is on the other end of the line. Then he looks horrified. "NO FUCKING WAY!! NO!! We are not using drugs! Are you fucking kidding me?"

Kristie looks on with concern. This is beginning to get real. Drugs? Her heart starts to race, and she's beginning to panic. Trying to compose herself and stay strong for Enrique, she moves closer to him but gives him space at the same time. She can tell he's angry and that this is way beyond anything he has ever done in his life. He's never even gotten a speeding ticket, let alone handled drugs.

"NO WAY!! DO YOU HEAR ME? I'M NOT HAVING ALL THAT COKE END UP ON OUR STREETS!! You'll have to find another way!!" He says in a threatening tone that shocks Kristie.

She's never seen him like this. She knows how he feels about drugs, especially with everything that's happened with Leon. It would crucify him to know that he's involved in putting cocaine on the streets. Kristie understands Enrique's anger and frustration. At the end of the day, he didn't ask for any of this, and he's basically had this dumped on him through no fault of his own.

"I DON'T GIVE A FUCK!! FIND A WAY!!" Enrique shouts with venom, then slams the flip phone shut and throws it down on the side. He stands leaning with his hands on the kitchen counter, with his head down, trying to calm himself. Then a few moments later, he looks at Kristie with a regretful expression and says, "I'm so sorry you had to see me like that, my darling." He turns to her and sweeps her soft dark hair away from her pretty face, and looks deeply into her eyes. "I shouldn't have acted that way in front of you... I'm so, so sorry." He kisses her.

"It's OK... don't apologize... you're going through a lot... and I know how much you hate drugs... I know how hard this is for you, babe." With concern etched across her face, she asks. "What did they say?"

"They said the meeting has been arranged for early tomorrow morning... 4:30am in the bay at Bear Point. They're bringing in the drugs on a fishing boat... drugs they want me to buy to get my father back." He shakes his head quickly with a dismissive look. "I'm not doing it. They'll have to find a way of using fake drugs or something... as I know what will happen to that coke. It will end up on our streets for people like Leon to use... I can't do it, babe." His face darkens with disgust and anger. "I'm so angry with them."

"I know, babe, I know... it'll be OK... we'll find a way. We can tell Jackie all of this when we see her... and she will help point us in the right direction. It's her job... she'll know what to do, trust me," Kristie says, looking into Enrique's eyes, trying to reassure him.

"We can't tell her anything about José... we just can't," Enrique pauses. He feels bad for saying this, but how can he? "We don't know what's true or false with these morons... I need to hear it from my father before I do anything like that."

"Babe, we need to be honest with Jackie... and the authorities... they need to know all the facts so they can help us. We can't keep anything from them, babe. I feel terrible at the thought of asking Jackie for her help and not giving her all the information," Kristie says, looking worried.

"I know... I do too, but how do I know they're not just spinning me a line? It could ruin my father's reputation... it could ruin everything." He tries to explain, shaking his head. "It's not a risk I'm willing to take at this stage."

"I see what you mean." Kristie nods reluctantly. "But I'm not happy about it though," She knows Enrique's right. If it is lies, there could be no end of trouble. José's reputation will be completely ruined, even if he is proven innocent. People have a way of believing the bad more than the good.

"OK... we'll tell her everything apart from the information about your father. As you said, there's no proof either way... but it should still give the D.E.A. a chance to get the other cartel and confiscate the drugs they have, at least."

"Exactly. Thank you for understanding, baby. I'm so sorry to put you through this." He runs his fingers through her glossy brunette hair and tucks it behind her ear.

"I'm here for you, babe... and we will get through this together." She pauses as she has a thought. "I think we should leave the security situation until after we've spoken to Jackie. We don't want to alert anybody at this stage. What do you think?"

"That's a good point. Hopefully, we can get this sorted sooner rather than later, and the security situation should dissolve naturally. We don't want to start changing things at this stage and make them suspicious."

Kristie's phone vibrates on the kitchen counter. It's Jackie.

I will have long blonde hair.
Name; Sammy Richardson.
See you in ten.

Kristie shows Enrique the message, and he contacts Armando. While Enrique's on the phone with Armando, Kristie calls the spa to let them know she won't be in for the rest of the week, as she's still sick. She tells Colette, her assistant, that she will be on call if anything urgent comes up.

Enrique tells Armando that a lady is coming to view apartment 8810. She's a friend of Kristie's, who's interested in purchasing it. Enrique explains that he's happy to show her around himself, so not to worry about accompanying her.

Once off the phone, they head down to the apartment and await Jackie's arrival. Exiting the elevator, they head to the apartment and step inside. The couple walks across the room past a single L-shaped sofa, and Enrique finds himself standing at the floor-to-ceiling window, looking out at Biscayne Bay. Kristie knows he's drifting, and she knows his thoughts are beginning to make him question their decision to involve the DEA.

She stands behind him and wraps her arms around his waist. "It will all be OK." She whispers. "This is the right thing to do, babe."

He turns to face her; his red bloodshot eyes are beginning to well up with tears. "I can't help but think I'm doing the wrong thing involving the D.E.A... like, what if they find out? I could be signing my own father's death warrant for just talking to them." Pain and torment are written all across his face.

"Baby, you know this is the right thing to do… we have to do this… and nobody is going to find anything out." She looks at him with seriousness. "This is the best way to get José home safely… and you'd never live with yourself if you didn't try to stop these drugs from reaching the streets." She pauses for a second, before saying confidently. "We'll get your father home… I know we will." Kristie stares deeply into his eyes. It's like she can see into his soul, and she always knows the right thing to say.

Suddenly, there's a knock at the door. They both turn quickly, facing toward the entrance. With wide eyes, fear surges through them both, and their hearts begin to race. As they look at Armando and Jackie as they stand in the entryway, Enrique says to himself silently; here goes.

"Miss Carrington. Mr. Cruz." Armando says cheerfully. "Miss Richardson is here to see you both. Can I be of any further assistance?"

"Thanks, Armando… no… we're good… thanks," Enrique replies, and Armando says his goodbyes, then turns and leaves.

"Sammy!" Kristie greets Jackie with a warm hug. "It's so good to see you."

The two ladies embrace each other. "Wow, look at you with blonde hair. It really suits you," Kristie states.

Turning to check that Armando has definitely left, Jackie turns back to her and says. "Thanks, honey... and you look gorgeous as always." The two ladies break away, and Jackie makes her way over to Enrique. "Enrique. Good to see you again. How are you?" she asks, shaking his already extended hand.

"I'm good, thanks, Jackie. How are you?" Enrique asks. Good? He's far from good, but he didn't really know what else to say.

"I'm great, thank you. So, what can I do for you both? There must be something up for you to call me like this?" Jackie says inquisitively. "You know I'll do anything to help you guys."

"I have a situation," Enrique says. "It's kind of crazy."

"OK," Jackie says curiously. "Let's sit down, and we can talk about it."

They sit on the sofa together. Kristie holds Enrique's hand as he starts to do his best to explain what's happened with his father. He leaves out any details about José's alleged cartel dealings, plus anything about Ziv and Gutiérrez, as he and Kristie had previously discussed.

Jackie explains to them that, with the information Enrique's told her, there's more than enough for the D.E.A. to take the cartel down, get José back safely and stop the drugs from getting on the street.

"This is really serious, Enrique," Jackie says, with a tone that borders admonishment. "I can't believe you've been trying to deal with this by yourself. These guys are some of the most dangerous criminals in the world... if you'd have called me sooner, we could've helped you before it even got to this stage. We've been trying to take this cartel down for years."

"I know, I know. I can't believe I took it on by myself, but I was so worried they would kill my father like they said they would," Enrique pleads for her to understand his predicament. "I've only just told Kristie, as I've been trying to protect her from it all too... as soon as I told her, she said we should call you, and here we are."

"I understand that, but you really should've called me sooner. What could have happened to you doesn't bear thinking about." Jackie says, almost scolding him. She can't believe what he's done, but she's going to get him out of this mess, that's for sure.

"I know. I'm so sorry... I guess I just got sucked into it all. It's like I was in quicksand. Once I was in it, I couldn't get out of it. I was just so focused on getting dad home," Enrique explains.

"I know," Jackie says as calmly as she can manage after hearing what Enrique has done. "I will do everything in my power to take them down and get your father back. I need to call my boss first and run this by him... come up with a plan." Jackie says as she stands.

"Before you call your boss," Enrique stops her. "I need you to know what they want. Of course, at first, I hoped that all they wanted was a payoff to return my father... but when they last contacted me, they told me exactly what the ransom was." Enrique turns to Kristie and then looks back at Jackie.

"So, what do they want from you?" Jackie asks curiously.

"Cocaine. They want me to buy them a ton of cocaine," Enrique says.

"Sorry, what? They want you to trade a ton of cocaine for your father?"

"I know. I thought they would want me to pay a ransom for him... I mean, I would have paid anything for his release... but for some reason, they're not interested in money... they just want drugs."

"OK, OK. This changes things a lot... I need to call my boss right now and get him up to speed... then we can see what the next step is," Jackie tells them.

"Do you mind if I just go into another room to call him?"

"Of course." Enrique gestures to the door of one of the rooms in the apartment. "Thank you so much, Jackie," he says gratefully, standing momentarily as she gets up to make the call.

Enrique and Kristie sit and watch as Jackie walks into the next room and closes the door behind her. Enrique puts his head in his hands and takes a deep breath in and then out. Kristie puts her arm around him. "It will be OK, babe... we're nearly there. Jackie and her team will get your father home, I know it."

"Thank you, baby. Thank you for being here with me. It means so much," Enrique wraps his arms around her. "I'm so grateful," he says and then kisses her.

"I'm always here for you... you know that," she says, as they sit on the sofa, holding each other.

Enrique is plagued with nervous energy as thoughts run rampant through his mind. Can they help? Will they help? Was this the right thing to do? Fear grips his chest even tighter than it already is as he faces the fact that he will most probably have to go to the meeting and put his life in danger once again. He feels sick to the stomach as he considers having to leave Kristie and their unborn baby behind to carry out whatever mission he will be required to do.

Staring at the door, he wills it to open, willing Jackie to come back through with all the right answers. Suddenly, he feels the burner phone vibrate in his inside pocket. He stares at Kristie in shock.

"What? What's wrong?" she asks.

Pulling the phone from his inside pocket, he looks at her. "It's them. What should I do? Should I answer it?" Enrique asks her with a whisper.

All Kristie can do is nod her head; words elude her.

Enrique stands, and taking a deep breath, he flips open the phone and answers it. "Yes."

"It's me," Ziv tells him. "The deal is set. But there has been a small change to the plan."

"What do you mean a small change to the plan? Is everything OK? Is my father OK?" Enrique asks, starting to panic.

"Yes, yes, he is fine. The change is to the terms of the deal. We need you to bring $22 million cash to the meeting to buy the merchandise." Ziv talks to him like it's something that everyone just has lying around.

"What the fuck are you talking about? How the hell am I meant to get $22 million in cash by tomorrow morning?" Enrique rages at Ziv.

The door to the other room opens, and Jackie walks back in. Looking first at a pacing and clearly enraged Enrique, she then looks to a worried-looking Kristie for answers. Kristie mouths to her that it's the kidnappers on the phone. Jackie nods and then walks across the room and sits on the sofa.

The conversation with Ziv continues. "The deal changed, Enrique. La Espada contacted his own supplier to get the product for you to buy. They cut Gutiérrez and me out of the deal because they are in such a rush to get hold of the product. We have no other choice than to do this their way. There isn't any way to fake this. Their supplier is fronting them ten tons of cocaine for the down payment of one. This is why the deal has to go down so quickly. I'm en-route to try and intercept the goods from their supplier now to help protect you. But we have to make it look like it's a legitimate exchange still. So, you bring the money. We take the money. We give them the drugs, and they give you your father. This is how it has to go down now. We have no choice!" Ziv explains.

"Fuck! If that's how it has to be! I guess I have no choice." Enrique sounds more agreeable this time. But this is only so he can inform Jackie, so she can advise him on the best course of action to get José back and stop the drugs hitting the streets.

"I will be in touch later to confirm everything with you." Ziv hangs up the phone.

Jackie looks at Enrique and says to him, "I guess things have changed a little since I went into the other room?"

"You could say that yes." Enrique sits back down next to Kristie and takes her hand.

"My boss is on board. Tell me the rest, and we will get this in motion," Jackie tells them both.

"The meeting is set for tomorrow morning... 4:30am. There is a bay at Bear Point. I need to bring $22 million cash to buy the cocaine for them from their supplier. He's giving them ten tons of cocaine for the payment. Once that deal is complete, they will return my father," Enrique tells her.

"That makes a lot of sense," Jackie begins to explain. "I've been authorized to discuss something confidential with you both. We raided one of their stash houses a few weeks ago... up in Tallahassee. We shut down a major supply conduit for them... a large amount of cash and drugs were seized. For them right now, getting the product in and keeping their customers happy is more important than money. That must be why they took your father and initially refused your cash. They have obviously managed to find someone willing to deal with them, and that's why the deal has changed. Suppliers generally give more product upfront to their dealers with down payments and expect the balance paid in full at a later date." She pauses for a second as she considers the task at hand. "This is going to be a difficult operation to put together in such a small amount of time... but I know that my boss and I can get it done." She looks at Enrique with disbelief, even if she does kind of understand his reasons. "I just wish you had come to us earlier... but we can't change that now. I need to go and set the wheels in motion. I'll contact you through Kristie in case they have your phone bugged." Jackie stands up to go.

The couple stands, and Kristie steps toward her friend and gives her a tight hug. "Thank you so much, Jackie. You will never know just how grateful I am for all of this."

Once the two ladies separate, Enrique reaches out his hand and shakes Jackie's, thanking her for her help, and they all move toward the door. Just as Enrique's about to open the door, Jackie stops him. "We'll need time to go over our plan with you tomorrow. With that in mind, I will pick you up at 3am so that we have time to discuss what'll happen. There's no need for you to do anything else now, leave it to us. Also, I'll arrange for some agents to stay with Kristie to ensure her safety… if anything else happens, please let me know ASAP."

"Sure." Enrique agrees. "Thank you again, Jackie, for all your help. If anything changes, I promise I will get in touch." His face is full of disbelief, wondering how the fuck he's going to do this without any questions being asked. "I guess I need to find a way to withdraw a large amount of money very quickly."

"Don't you worry about that… we seized more than enough of their cash in the Tallahassee raid to cover the buy. I'm sure my boss will be more than happy to use their own money to take them all down." Jackie says, smiling at them both. "We will get your father back, and we will take them down. You did the right thing contacting us." She says, full of sincerity before turning and opening the door. She puts on her large black sunglasses, steps out into the corridor. "I'll be in touch if we need any more info, but if not, I will see you in the morning," she says as she closes the door.

Kristie drapes her arms around Enrique's broad, muscular shoulders and looks into his gorgeous blue eyes, which are full of panic and worry. "You did good, babe."

"Thanks, baby." Enrique shakes his head. "It just feels so wrong. I feel like whatever I do, is wrong… whichever way I turn." He pulls Kristie into an embrace.

"I know, babe, I know. But you're not seeing clearly, as you are so caught up in it all. I'm somewhat distanced from it in a way, and all I can see is this is the best thing to do," She says with meaning. They break away for a second. "I take it that was really Ziv on the phone?"

"Yes, babe, it was." Enrique looks down. "He said the other cartel had gotten impatient waiting for them to get the drugs. So, they've arranged for their own deal... which makes sense after what Jackie's just told us. Ziv is trying to intercept the shipment, so hopefully, he and Gutiérrez will bring it in instead. Other than that, everything is as I've already explained."

"Thanks for telling me," Kristie says as she kisses him. She's so proud of her man. She knows this is complete torture for him, but he still did it. "I'm so proud of you, babe. Once tomorrow is over with, we can get on with our lives."

"I can't wait. I really can't," he says, resting his forehead on hers, looking into her eyes. "I'm so proud of you too. Thank you... I can't thank you enough for what you've done for me... not just today but during our entire relationship," he kisses her lips before gazing into her beautiful eyes with pure love and adoration. "Let's go home," he says, taking her hand.

Chapter 27

When they arrive back at the penthouse, it's nearly 5pm. They're both drained and exhausted, plus they're both really hungry.

"Shall we cook some food?" Kristie suggests. "I don't know about you, but I'm starving."

"Good idea," Enrique agrees, struggling to put one foot in front of the other. He's beyond tired—tired of this whole nightmare, but also more on edge than ever; almost jittery.

That's it. He's done it. He's gone to the D.E.A., and now he has to wait until the morning and hope everything will go as planned.

He's absolutely petrified that something will go wrong, not only with his father, but what if something happens to him? The thought of Kristie being left on her own to have their baby and bringing him or her up on her alone is unbearable. With that thought weighing heavily on him, he pulls her into a tight embrace.

"I'm so scared, babe... I'm so, so scared." He whispers with his voice trembling. Tears fill his eyes. "What if this is the wrong thing to do? What if meeting Jackie was a huge mistake?"

"I know, baby, I know. But it is totally the right thing to do. Honestly, you will be with the best of the best tomorrow, trust me," she replies, hugging him back tightly. She completely understands how scary this situation is; there's no denying that. If she's honest with herself, she's just as scared as Enrique, if not more so. But all she can do is be there and be strong for him, and that's exactly what she's going to do. "Come on. I'll cook us some food. Steak?" she suggests cheerfully.

"Yeah, steak sounds good," Enrique replies.

"I'll make some cheesy mashed potatoes, spinach, and your peppercorn sauce... just the way you taught me to make it," Kristie says, knowing the comfort food will help Enrique feel a little better, plus she knows this is one of his favorite meals. Arm in arm, they walk into the kitchen. "Sit," she says playfully while pulling out a white leather stool at the breakfast bar.

"I'll help you, babe."

"No, you won't." She insists. "I won't hear of it. Now, what can I get you to drink, Mr. Cruz?"

"I know what I want, but I said I wouldn't."

"I think after the last twenty-four hours, you deserve one. And I never said I thought you should stop drinking altogether... I just don't like how you drink to excess when things get too much for you," Kristie says, getting two Baccarat tumblers from the cupboard and Enrique's favorite Havana Club rum from the kitchen counter. She places the glasses down on the breakfast bar and gets a sphere of ice out of the freezer and a bottle of Fiji from the refrigerator. She places the ice in one glass, pours some rum on top, and hands it to Enrique. Then she pours herself some Fiji into the other glass. Holding her glass up to his, she says, "Salud." They clink their glasses and take a sip.

Enrique takes a long sip of the rum and breathes out. "What a day," he says to Kristie, who has just started preparing the food.

"It sure has been. We just need to get through tomorrow; then we'll be free of all this. Free to move on with our lives," she says, brimming with positivity as she peels the potatoes. "I'll be right here for you when you come back... I'll be waiting for you, babe... me and our little baby." She smiles and caresses her bump.

"I know, babe... and that's why I love you. You're always there for me... and I'm glad things are different now... even with all of this going on," he says. He's decided not to mention to Kristie about his fears of not coming home. It's not fair on her; she doesn't need ideas like that in her head.

Once Kristie has prepared their meal, they dine out on the balcony and watch the sun as it starts to set. Will this be the last sunset he'll get to watch with Kristie? Enrique can't help but entertain the thought as it runs through his mind. Trying to push it out of his head, he turns to her and says, "Shall we have a bath and get an early night? We have a big day ahead... I'm not sure if I'll manage to get any sleep, but I should try. You should too, baby." He brushes her cheek gently with the back of his fingers. He's concerned about Kristie. She's holding up so well, but he's still worried about what effect this is having on her. "Are you OK, baby? I'm worried about you. You're so strong... but I worry what's going on inside of you."

"I'm OK... I mean, yes, I'm worried about you... but I know you'll be fine. You can more than handle this... and you're in good hands... with the best of the best," Kristie says. She's anxious about what Enrique's about to do, but she knows he's more than capable, plus she trusts Jackie and her team implicitly. "Let's go up... have a hot bath and go to bed."

Once upstairs, Kristie begins to fill the oversized white standalone bathtub. Enrique lights some white candles and places them around the bathroom. They each undress in the closet, and Kristie takes off her make-up in the bathroom. Once the tub is full, they both climb in and relax as best they can.

The twinkly lights of downtown and beyond are their backdrop as they sit in the tub quietly, contemplating what lies ahead. Enrique knows Kristie is nervous: more nervous than she's letting on. He moves up closer to her and puts his arm around her. Breaking their silence, Enrique whispers, "I love you."

"I love you too," Kristie whispers back. She's completely drained.

Enrique gently caresses her shoulder with his fingers. "Sit between my legs, baby."

Kristie shifts and sits between his legs, facing away from him. Enrique takes some massage oil from the stand next to the bath, starts to massage her shoulders, up the back of her neck, and down her back. He kisses her intermittently, on her back and shoulders, as his fingers knead her aching muscles. "Your skin is so beautiful... so soft," Enrique says, feeling Kristie's shoulders relax as he massages them. If only they could just stay in the penthouse, enjoying romantic moments like this forever. He feels at one with the love of his life, having her so close to him, caressing and massaging her.

The view of the city from the tub is spectacular, and the gentle flicker of the candles only adds to the romantic ambiance. It's just the two of them being together, enjoying each other, and that's just the way he likes it. Enrique loves moments like this, and he wants them to last forever.

Then suddenly, thoughts of tomorrow cross his mind. Ugghhh... no... he isn't going to let this happen. He's in the moment with Kristie, and the two of them, and their little baby, are all that matters to him right now. He will deal with tomorrow when it comes.

Kristie turns to face Enrique. "Thank you, babe. That felt so good… you always give the best massages… they're so relaxing." She kisses him on the lips.

"You're so welcome, baby… I love giving you them." Looking at her with eyes glistening with love, he tucks a loose strand of hair behind her ear and says. "You look so beautiful in the candlelight," he kisses her lips, noticing her eyes are heavy; she's tired. "Shall we get ready for bed?"

"Yes… I'm exhausted… I'm sure you are too."

They get out of the bath and dry off. Enrique extinguishes most of the candles in the bathroom and brings the ones that are still lit into the bedroom to help keep a relaxed ambiance. Kristie puts on her short silk nightdress. It's sapphire blue, with black lace edging running across the front and down the sides, with thin straps. Her long brunette hair is flowing over her shoulders and down her back.

"Wow," he says as he pulls on his pajama pants. He walks over and kisses her lips. He stops and looks down at her body. Her pretty face. Her glorious dark brown eyes. Her sensual curves. Her tiny bump. Her silky, tanned skin. Her beautiful full breasts. Her erect nipples. She's intoxicating.

He's instantly aroused. He kisses her again, harder this time. She reciprocates. His erection is pushing through his pajama pants, and as he holds her closer, it presses into her body, through her nightdress. As they continue to kiss, they start to move slowly toward the bed.

Enrique gently lowers her down onto the bed and leans over her on his elbows, still kissing her. He moves to his side and runs his fingers gently down her neck, her throat, her sternum, to her breasts. He softly caresses the swell of each breast through the silk, running his thumbs over each erect nipple, one at a time.

Then he continues down to her stomach, over her tiny bump, and down to her thighs. "I love feeling your skin beneath my fingertips." He breathes, in-between kisses. "I love to watch your body... as it moves... you're so sexy... so seductive." He runs his fingers over her thighs, then up between them, but not touching her *there*, just skimming past, and then back up to her stomach.

He repeats the process, over and over again. Kristie's body is shimmering as all the erotic sensations and feelings wash over her. It's so sensual. Enrique loves caressing Kristie's body and teasing her with his touch. He could do this for hours, and Kristie is more than willing to allow him.

Enrique continues feeling and caressing Kristie's figure, and then finally, he runs his fingers over her clitoris; her breath hitches as her entire body shudders at the contact. She's so ready, so, so ready, and it's beyond arousing. He moves down her body, lifts her tiny, short nightdress, and runs his tongue up her labia to her clitoris, tasting her arousal. He's in heaven.

He licks and sucks, watching her body move, her back arching off the bed in the way he finds so seductive. He slides his tongue inside of her and moves it in and out; then, he glides it back up to her clitoris, relishing every beautiful second. She's so feminine, so beautiful, and the love he feels for her is so pure and so consuming. He will do anything for this lady... anything.

He holds her thighs open as he devours her. Her moans get louder and louder as her orgasm builds. Then suddenly, she tenses, and her upper body lifts off the bed as she comes, flooding into Enrique's mouth as she does, running her fingers through his hair and pulling it as she screams out in ecstasy.

Once her orgasm subsides, Enrique removes his pajama pants, climbs up her body, and kisses her deeply as he slides into her. Breaking their kiss for a second, he stills, wanting to feel her, every inch of her. Gazing into her rich dark brown eyes, he holds her face with his hands and kisses her deeply once more. Her arms are wrapped around his muscular back, and her legs are wrapped around his. With their bodies entwined, they begin to move slowly, savoring every sensual second.

Kristie kisses Enrique's neck, holding him tightly. Her breathing accelerates, as does Enrique's. This is so special and meaningful. Enrique's so scared he might not come home after what he's going to have to endure tomorrow, and he wants to make this the most beautiful and loving memory. He wants Kristie to remember the last night they spent together to be loving and romantic, and he has a feeling, although she'll never admit it, that Kristie has the same fear as him.

"I love you, my darling," Enrique whispers, looking deeply into Kristie's eyes, which are shimmering in the soft glow of the candles.

"I love you too, baby," Kristie replies, then kisses his lips. Opening her eyes, she looks into Enrique's. "I want us to get married," she whispers, sounding so sure of what she's saying.

"You do," Enrique replies with a huge smile. He can't believe what he's hearing.

"Yes... yes, I do. Once everything is sorted out... I want us to get married." She says sweetly. "I love you, Enrique... let's not waste any more time," she says, smiling back at her man, who's looking at her with complete adoration.

"I would love that," he says as tears start to fall from his eyes. "Oh baby, I would love that."

Kristie holds his face with her delicate hands and kisses his lips. "I can't wait to be your wife." She whispers through her own tears.

"Oh, baby," Enrique's voice is trembling through his tears. They hold each other tightly, and he starts to continue his rhythm that was interrupted momentarily by words he thought he could only dream of hearing.

Moving slowly as one, feeling Kristie's heavenly body beneath him, he becomes overwhelmed with emotion. He can't believe how lucky he is. Kristie, the love of his life, the lady of his dreams, the mother of his child, has just agreed to marry him. He holds her tightly, and his pace starts to increase. He begins to move faster, and Kristie follows his lead. They grip each other tighter and tighter, moving faster and faster until they both come loudly and explosively together, calling out each other's names in between cries of love and passion.

They both lay in each other's arms as they float in the heavenly paradise that is the afterglow of their love-making. The love they feel for each other has just intensified; it's now even more stronger and deeper than ever before. They're going to become husband and wife, as well as parents, and they couldn't be happier. Wrapped in each other's arms, bathed in candlelight, they soak in the beautiful moment they're sharing.

Eventually, Enrique manages to lift himself up on his elbows and holds Kristie's face gently with his hand, gazing into her glorious brown eyes.

"I love you. I love you. I love you," he says, kissing her lips. "So beautiful."

"I love you too, and yes, you are," Kristie replies. "And, Mr. Cruz... I meant what I said... I've never been so sure of anything in my entire life."

"Do you know how lucky that makes me feel?" Enrique says, shaking his head with a huge smile on his face. He glides his hand down Kristie's beautiful face. "Do you have any idea... any idea how much this means to me... after everything... everything we've been through... all of this with my father... everything." He kisses her lips softly. "It means the world to me, baby." He kisses her once more, holding her face in his hands. "Oh my God, babe... I thought I could only ever dream of this happening... hearing you say those words." Enrique looks at Kristie with complete love and adoration.

"It means so much to me, too, babe. I've wanted us to get married for so long... I know you have too." She smiles. "I just feel we've already come so far, and I don't want to waste any more time." She looks down for a second before looking back up into his summery blue eyes full of excitement and love. "This situation... with José has made me see things differently. I can see how it's affected you... and I can see how you've opened up to me in such a short space of time. It just feels right. I can't explain it. I don't know... it's like something's clicked everything into place with us." Kristie feels this situation with José has not only put everything into perspective for them both, but it's also changed Enrique; changed him for the better. As strange as it is, and despite it being such a horrific situation, it's made him see things more clearly. It's like it's forced him to face everything that he's been running from and harboring for all these years.

"Thank you, baby... and I sure feel like things have fallen into place with us too... I mean, as difficult as last night was, I think it served a purpose... as excruciating as it was... I'm open... wide open... to you... for the first time in my life, I've been able to talk to you about my grief... my pain... and I feel honored that after everything... you want to be my wife." Enrique says gratefully, rolling onto his side. They rest their hands together on her bump, and he plays with Kristie's platinum Cartier Love bracelet he gifted her not long after they first got together. It means the world to him that she didn't remove it when they broke up; it's still locked into place since the moment he put it on her delicate wrist. He smiles at the memory as they lay together.

"I feel honored that you felt like you could be that vulnerable with me, babe... that you felt you could open up to me that way... I feel closer to you now more than ever. I mean, we've always been super close... we've always had such a strong and powerful connection... but it's way more intense now... it's like you've finally bared your soul to me completely."

"I have, baby, I have." He kisses her lips before reaching down and kissing her bump. "I love you." He whispers to their unborn baby before kissing Kristie's lips again and whispering. "And I love you, too."

"I love you, too... we love you, too." She whispers back with a smile.

As he lies with his girl, he can't believe this is happening. Kristie has just agreed to be his wife, and he's elated. Although he doesn't want to sound ungrateful, he can't believe the same thing's happening to him again. The moment something so special happens with Kristie, he has to deal with something so daunting right afterward; how is this so? But he's willing to take it any way he can. Tomorrow is still ahead of him, but he and Kristie are going to have a baby, and now she's just agreed to marry him, and he's over the moon about it.

In a way, both the baby and now their wedding are beautiful distractions from the horror he's had to face over the past few days. Beautiful distractions that have given him hope and light, which has helped him through it all. Moments like these have been what's kept him going.

"You make me so happy, baby. I'm so grateful to have you." He kisses her lips. Opening his eyes slowly, he whispers. "I can't wait to plan our wedding... and have our little baby... we've got so much to look forward to."

"We sure have." Kristie kisses his lips. "I can't wait to call you my husband."

"And I can't wait to call you my wife." He smiles against her lips. "We can have any kind of wedding you like?"

"A quiet one... I want it to be about us... nobody else."

"Sounds perfect to me." He kisses her again. "I'd be happy just to get the jet and go to Vegas. All I want is you... you and our baby... and many more babies... if you feel you want to," Enrique says, smiling and caressing her bump.

"Many more." She smiles. "And I like the sound of Vegas... but tasteful... or maybe a beach wedding? We can look into it all together."

"Most definitely... and I need to get you a really big diamond." Enrique smiles, holding her hand and lifting it to his lips, then kissing her wedding finger.

"You know I don't need any of that... I'd be happy with just a nice simple wedding band," Kristie says, and she means it too.

"Absolutely not. You're gonna have a nice big rock... something people can see." He winks, then laughs. "You know... keep the boys at bay... make sure they know you're taken," he says, still chuckling, pulling her to him and holding her tightly.

"I don't need a big diamond for that." She giggles with him, wrapping her arms around him and then kissing his cheek. "I love you, Enrique Cruz."

"I love you, Kristie Carrington," he says, kissing her lips. They lay holding each other, enjoying the moment in the soft glow of candlelight and love.

After a short while, somehow, they feel as if they don't have a care in the world, and they drift off to a tranquil sleep together.

Chapter 28

Enrique wakes with Kristie in his arms. He snuggles up to her and inhales her scent, smiling contently as he does.

"I love you, my babies." He whispers as he caresses her bump. "I love you more than anything in the world." He kisses her shoulder as she sleeps peacefully in his arms.

As he absorbs the beautiful moment with the love of his life and their unborn child, suddenly, a feeling of fear and doom sweeps in and tries to steal the precious moment from him. He tries to resist and force it from his mind, but panic takes over before he can do anything to stop it.

He is now wide-awake buzzing with feelings of fear, dread, and panic flying rampantly around his body. Thoughts of what he has been forced to get involved with today rip through his mind, and he's starting to feel nauseous. Can he do this? Will he be safe? Is it the right thing to do? Will he get his father back? Will something happen to José? The noise in his mind is so loud it's deafening.

He looks at Kristie, who is still sleeping peacefully; she looks so beautiful. She calms his racing heart and mind as he watches her float in her sea of dreams. Then he remembers what happened last night; Kristie agreed to become his wife. He smiles widely at the memory. Can he get any luckier?

He watches her sleep for a few more moments and then decides to get up; he needs to prepare for the day ahead. But first, he needs to pray for guidance and strength to get through today and for everyone's safety.

Kissing Kristie's shoulder, he gently pulls away from her and carefully climbs out of bed. As he stands, he checks both phones; still, no news relating to his father. He sighs quietly to himself as he prays that today will be the day he gets him home.

The next thing he notices is, it's 1:05am. He has just under two and a half hours until he has to meet Jackie. He quietly walks out of the bedroom and down the stairs. Kristie needs all the rest she can get, he thinks to himself. Today is a big day for her too.

Once in the living area, he opens the sliding glass doors and steps out onto the balcony. Leaning on the railings with his hands, he looks out over the bay, which is shrouded in darkness and takes in a long deep breath, then breathes out slowly. He repeats this a few times and then sits down on one of the chairs. He leans forward, resting his elbows on his thighs, holds his hands together and prays. He asks God for strength, guidance, and for forgiveness, also for Kristie and their baby's health and happiness, then finally, for the safe return of his father and himself. He gives thanks to God for bringing Kristie back into his life and for the blessing of their unborn child; also, he asks for help to be the best husband and father he can be. He finishes his prayer with the sign of the cross, then sits for a few moments looking back out over the bay.

After a short while, he decides to make some coffee. Heading to the kitchen, he forces himself to distract his mind with happy thoughts, as it seems to help him cope with the extreme anxiety he keeps being overwhelmed with. Thinking of Kristie and the baby is his happy place, and he's more than willing to live in denial for as long as he can and indulge in these thoughts.

While making his coffee, he starts to think about how he's going to officially propose to Kristie. He shakes his head in disbelief at the thought. He can't believe it. She's agreed to marry him. He's going to make it more than special for her, and of course, he's going to get her a big diamond. Why wouldn't he? Then he remembers her telling him that she's always wanted to go to the Maldives. That's it, he thinks to himself. The Maldives! I'm going to take her to the Maldives. We can stay at the Sanchester, the one she mentioned, and we'll get the best overwater suite they have. I'll fill it with Krissy's favorite white candles and scatter white rose petals all over... everywhere. We'll have a romantic meal under the stars, and I'll propose to her. It will be the most romantic moment of our lives. Perfect idea, he thinks to himself.

Maybe we can take the jet, or if we fly commercial, we could use one of the airlines that have residences inside. We could have the privacy of flying private but fly commercial. Hmmm, he thinks to himself. Food for thought.

Enrique has heard about these residences, and they sound awesome. A few people he's done business with have experienced them and said they're fantastic. He's super excited at the thought of planning all of this and surprising Kristie; she will love it.

While they were having lunch on the pool deck, she'd told him how she had seen videos of people swimming with turtles in the ocean and how she would love to do it. Kristie loves anything like that, as long as they aren't in captivity. If they're in their natural habitat, she's happy. They even have a rehabilitation center there to help save marine life. She will absolutely love it. He can't wait to do this for her. He pours his coffee and decides to get a cigar from the humidor, and heads to the balcony.

Lighting his cigar, he inhales the rich, smooth smoke into his mouth, holds it for a few seconds, and then breathes out before taking a slow sip of his coffee. He has a feeling that he's going to need to drink a lot of coffee to get through another long agonizing day, so he brought the whole jug out with him. He's hopeful that he'll get his father back and that this will be the last of these excruciatingly painful days, where he's been pushed beyond his absolute limits; he wants nothing more than to get on with his life.

Keep thinking happy thoughts, he tells himself. He starts to think about what kind of ring he'll get for Kristie. It will have to be Tiffany's; Kristie loves Tiffany's. What kind of wedding will we have, he asks himself while taking another puff of his cigar. Vegas or beach? Hmmmm... this is exciting. He's almost forgotten about the hell he's about to endure in a few hours.

He remembers the email he got from the Sanchester Hotels & Resorts about their property in Bora Bora. That's the honeymoon sorted, he thinks. I'll have to check with Kristie first, of course, but how perfect will it be to propose to the love of my life in the Maldives and then honeymoon in Bora Bora. He smiles at the thought as he sips his cáfecito. Then he has another thought: the baby. Will Kristie be able to fly? If so, how far and up until which month? He'll have to investigate. Maybe he'll get the chance to ask the doctor discreetly when they go for the scan. Taking another puff of his cigar, he sees movement out of the corner of his eye; it's Kristie.

"Hey, babe. I didn't wake you, did I?" he asks, putting his cigar down and standing to walk over to her.

"No, babe. I just woke and found you weren't there, so I came looking for you." Enrique wraps her in his arms. "Are you OK?" she asks, remembering the last time she found him sitting on the balcony. She's worried, especially with what lies ahead today.

"I'm OK, mi amor. Just having some coffee and a cigar," he reassures her. "Shall I get you some tea?" he asks. "Or, I've made some cafécito, if you'd like?"

"I'll have some tea, I think," she says as they walk to the kitchen.

Enrique makes Kristie some tea, then they head back onto the balcony, and he pours himself some more coffee. He extinguishes his cigar and moves the ashtray to another table; he doesn't want to smoke around Kristie as she's pregnant.

She sits on the chair next to him in her blue nightdress and a black silk robe, and they sip their drinks as they sit quietly. Enrique puts his arm over Kristie's shoulders and pulls her to him. He knows she's nervous; they both are, and he knows she's trying to be brave for him, and he loves her for that, but he still wants to reassure her.

"It will all be OK, babe," he whispers calmly. "I know you're nervous... I am, too... but we will get through this. Once this is over, we are going to plan our wedding... get married and then our little baby will be born not long after. We have so much to look forward to." He looks at her with a loving smile. "It will all be OK. I promise." He kisses her cheek.

Kristie climbs on top of him, and as she holds him tightly, she begins to cry. "Please, Enrique... please be careful. I... I... don't know what I would do without you," she sobs, with her head resting on his shoulder. She loves how he knows when she's worried about something. He always picks up on it and comforts her without saying a word, just like he did in the bath last night. He knew she was worried about today, so he gave her a massage to help relax her. She didn't need to say anything; he just knew. "You always know when I'm worrying about something... and you know exactly when I need comfort," she says through her tears. "Thank you, baby."

"Of course, I do... and you do for me too. I'm just glad I can let you be there for me now... I'm glad I'm learning how... and it feels so good." He whispers as he holds her close. "Everything will be OK... I promise. It will all be over in a few hours, and I will be home." He strokes her glossy brunette hair and then kisses her soft full lips.

She moves so she's sitting across him on his lap, and with their arms around each other, they finish their drinks.

"I better go have a shower and get ready, baby," Enrique says, with feelings of dread but doing his best not to show it. It's his turn to be strong now for his girl. He feels safer in the knowledge that the D.E.A. is going to send two agents to the penthouse to look after Kristie during the meet to make sure she's safe, plus she won't be alone.

"OK, babe... I'll come with you," she says, wanting to spend every second with him before he goes. It's just hit her hard that he might not come home. She knows he's going to be meeting up with one of the most barbaric cartels in the world, and she's worried sick, but she needs to do her best to stay calm for the baby and for Enrique.

They head upstairs and get into the shower together.

"I want to wash you," Kristie whispers to him.

He holds her beautiful face in his hands and whispers. "I would love that, baby." He wants to feel her delicate hands all over him; he wants to memorize every touch, every heavenly caress of each of her fingertips.

Kristie lathers some body wash in her hands and glides them over his muscular chest and down to his chiseled abs. His breathing gradually accelerates as she rubs the body wash over him in small soft circles feeling his dark skin. Following the gentle ripple of his muscles, she moves to his back, massaging his tense shoulders and then down to his firm buttocks. She kneels before him as she washes his legs. She absolutely loves doing this; feeling his body, inch by inch, it's so intimate and beautiful.

Once she's washed his feet, she travels up the front of his legs and then stops as she notices his erection. She leans forward and takes it into her mouth, looking up at him at the same time. Enrique looks down at her running his fingers through her wet hair. He moves his hips back and forth, watching as his erection slide in and out of Kristie's mouth; this is so erotic.

Then suddenly, swept away with a carnal need to feel her, he lifts her up to him, and she wraps her legs around his waist and her arms around his broad, muscular shoulders. Holding her up by the back of her thighs, he pushes her against the wall and slides into her, kissing her with fervor as she wraps around him.

With his strong body holding her up against the wall as he moves in and out of her, he puts one arm around her shoulders and grips her right breast with his other hand; his fingers are digging into her flesh as he tightens his grip.

"Ahhh... fuck... ahhh!" Enrique hisses through gritted teeth as he pants for air, struggling to hold back.

"Fuck me... fuck me hard!" Kristie pleads through her moans as they get louder and louder.

Their bodies tense as they push each other to the brink. Suddenly, all their feelings of fear and trepidation surrounding this impossible situation, exchange momentarily for carnal need and scorching desire for each other. Kristie's nails are digging into Enrique's back as his thrust gets more rapid and vigorous, and she takes everything he's giving her; they so desperately need this right now.

"Fuck, you feel so fucking good, babe... so fucking good." He groans. And with that, he can't hold back any longer. His orgasm crashes through his body, immediately taking Kristie with him. He keeps moving, forcing her to come again.

Fuck! That was so intense, he thinks to himself, as he gradually brings Kristie to her feet and tries not to fall in a heap on the floor himself. He kisses her hard. "Fuck! You drive me crazy, Miss Carrington."

"Oh, Mr. Cruz... you drive me crazy too." She replies with a smile.

After losing themselves in their moment of unexpected salacious lust, they catch their breath as they hold each other closely, standing naked under the warm, steady stream of the rain shower above them.

After a short while, Enrique begins to wash Kristie, taking his time over her, just the way she did with him. He memorizes the silky feel of her mocha-colored skin beneath his fingertips, every sweep of her curves, the beauty of her femininity and grace, the delightful feel of her tiny baby bump, and the warmth he feels as his heart swells with love every time he glides his hand over it; he too, will carve the memory of every detail of Kristie's beautiful body, into his mind, just the way she did with him.

Once they have both washed, they reluctantly get out of the shower and get dressed. Kristie chooses blue skinny jeans, a simple white T-shirt, and gold hoop earrings. She applies minimal make-up and is wearing her hair straight, as she'll be staying around the apartment and wants to be comfortable. Enrique is wearing a dark blue suit, white fitted shirt, white pocket square, and tan wingtips shoes. "I'm wearing one of the suits you gave me... for luck." He smiles nervously, walking over to Kristie and draping his arms around her waist.

"It will bring you the best of luck... not that you'll need it. You'll do great... you will get your father back, and you will come home to me and this little one in no time." She smiles, brushing her hand over her bump.

Kristie has an idea. She breaks away from him for a second and heads to the closet; Enrique follows her. Opening his watch drawer, she takes out the platinum watch she gave him for his birthday last year. Handing it to him, she says, "I think this will go perfectly with your outfit."

"It most certainly will." He smiles back at her, taking the watch from her and putting it on his wrist before kissing her softly.

It's now time for him to leave, and Lord knows he doesn't want to, but he has no choice. He looks into her eyes with sadness. "It's time for me to go, baby." He says with a whisper.

Kristie nods, with tears glistening in her eyes, trying so desperately to stay strong for her man.

He cups her pretty face with his hands and whispers. "I'll see you in a few hours?" He has a look of certainty as he says this to her before finding her lips with his and kissing her tenderly.

"See you in a few hours." Tears are filling her eyes; she can't stop them.

"You will," he says with meaning, and then he holds her tightly. Kissing the top of her head, he whispers. "I love you... I love you both."

"I love you... we love you, too."

Enrique looks down at his girl. He can't help but entertain a thought he's having that will most definitely make light of the situation. When Kristie was getting dressed earlier, he couldn't help but notice that she's wearing white lingerie; his favorite, plus it's very similar to the lingerie she wore when they went to brunch a few days ago. He pulls back a little and runs his thumb over the visible bra strap, where her loose T-shirt has started to slip off her shoulder slightly. "I'll be back to take you out of this later." He says flirtatiously with a sexy smile. She smiles back naughtily. "You know how I adore you in white lingerie," he whispers into her ear, sweeping her long dark hair away from her neck and kissing it. "Very sexy... very beautiful." He kisses her neck softly once more. "And... don't forget your Louboutins." He's almost breathless.

Kristie leans into his kiss, and then he moves to her mouth and kisses her lips. He kisses her hard, with his hands in her hair pulling her closer to him. Kristie kisses him back just as passionately, and she doesn't want this to end.

Then they slowly and reluctantly break away. Resting on each other's foreheads, with their eyes closed, they take in this perfect moment of intimacy with Enrique's hand still in her hair and Kristie's arms around his neck. They gradually open their eyes together and look at each other full of love. "I'll see you in a few hours." He whispers. "Then we can start arranging our wedding... yeah?" He means every word. I WILL be back home, and we WILL be arranging our wedding. I'm not going to think any other way. I won't allow myself to, he tells himself.

"Yes. I'll see you in a few… and I can't wait to start arranging our wedding." She smiles through the tears, wiping them away at the same time. She's trying so hard to be brave and strong, but she isn't succeeding today. It's like she's been so strong for Enrique; now she's struggling with it all, he's being strong for her.

Kristie's cell vibrates in the back pocket of her jeans. They both know it's the D.E.A. She pulls her phone out and unlocks it with facial recognition. "They're here, baby." She whispers, full of sadness.

Enrique presses his lips into a hard line as he glides his fingers through her silky hair. Looking deeply into her eyes with concern, he says. "I don't wanna leave you, babe… I hate this."

"I'll be fine, baby… don't worry." Kristie smiles through her pain.

"I do worry… I can't stand that I have to leave you like this, but I…."

"You have to do this… and once this is over… once José is home… we can move on with our lives… I have the agents coming to look after me until you get back… please don't worry, babe."

"I'll always worry about you… it's what I do."

"I know... and I will always worry about you... but remember what I said before... this is a means to an end... we get through this... this difficult time... and then we have so much to look forward to... our baby... our wedding... our future."

"I know, babe, I know." He smiles and kisses her lips. "I love you... I love you to the moon and back."

"And around the entire universe."

"And back again." He smiles as they recite a saying they have said to each other since they first started dating.

They kiss each other once more before taking each other's hands and heading out of the closet, through the bedroom, and down the stairs. As they pass the side table where Enrique's mom's photo is sitting, he stops for a second and whispers, "I love you, mom." Before raising his fingers to his lips and blowing her a kiss. He smiles at her as she smiles back at him, and in his mind, he tells her that he will get José home safely, no matter what it takes. Kristie grips his hand tighter and reaches up to kiss his cheek.

"Your mom's so proud of you, babe... and she loves you so much."

Gripping her hand back tightly, Enrique raises a tiny smile and nods. He turns and kisses her before saying. "Thank you, baby... that's all I've ever wanted... for her to be proud of me."

"I know, babe... and I know for certain that she is... now more than ever."

Standing by the front door to the penthouse, Kristie wraps her arms around Enrique, not wanting to let go. Will this be the last time I hold him? The last time I feel him close to me, telling me he loves me? She holds him tighter and closer to her, trying to carve the memory into her mind, so she will always remember how it feels, just like she was doing in the shower earlier. "I love you... I love you with all my heart... we love you with all our hearts."

"I love you with all my heart too... I love you both... so deeply... so, so much." He whispers. "And don't worry... everything will be OK." He tries to reassure her while holding her tightly, breathing in her scent. He nuzzles his face in her neck as he closes his eyes and breathes in her natural scent, laced with Coco Chanel, once more. It calms him a little, and then a horrific thought crosses his mind. Will this be the last time I do this? He dwells on it for a second and breathes in one more time. He forces himself to snap out of the negative thoughts, lifts his head up, and looks at Kristie full of love and devotion. "I'll see you in a few."

"I'll see you in a few," she replies, trying to hold herself together.

Then the doorbell rings, notifying them that it's time for Enrique to go. They kiss once more, a kiss that is so intimate and full of love, hope, and promise. Then Enrique holds Kristie tightly, kisses the top of her head, and holding back the tears, he whispers, "I love you."

"I love you too." She reciprocates his embrace, and then they walk to the door arm in arm, and Enrique opens it. The D.E.A. agents walk in with Jackie, and they show their identification as Jackie introduces them; it's as real as it ever will be. Enrique is about to do the most frightening thing of his life, and as scared as he is, he's more ready than ever to get it over with.

"Should take around thirty minutes to get there at this time of day," Jackie says to Enrique. Jackie looks at Kristie with a reassuring smile as she notices the look of fear and sadness on her friend's face. "Don't worry, Krissy... he's in safe hands; the best." Her smile widens. "We do this every day... it's OK... this is just another day at the office for us... and Enrique and his father will be back in no time...."

"Thanks, Jackie." Kristie smiles back. "And I know... you and your team are the best of the best... I know that." Kristie says bravely. The two ladies hug, and then Jackie turns to Enrique. "You ready?"

"Let's get this done… let's get my father back,"
Enrique says to Jackie, sounding like he's ready for
this to be over with.

"That's exactly what we're gonna do," Jackie
replies. "We'll give you two a minute." She and the
two agents head out of the penthouse and stand
outside the door.

Enrique holds Kristie tightly again. "I love you."

"I love you too."

He kisses her again, holding her face with his
hands. Sliding his hands down Kristie's arms, he
holds her right hand with one hand and holds her
bump with the other. He kneels down in front of
her, lifts her T-shirt, and tenderly kisses her bump.
"I love you too, little one. Daddy will be home
soon," he says to their baby inside of her. He holds
Kristie around her hips and brings her closer to
him, resting his cheek on her stomach as he savors
the moment.

Kristie runs her fingers through his hair as he rests
on her bump and gazes down at him, brimming
with love for her man and their little baby. She
manages a smile as she finds it so adorable to hear
him call himself "Daddy."

Then, reluctantly he rises to his feet, holds both of
Kristie's hands, and kisses her lips.

"I can't wait to get home to you." He whispers.

"I'll be waiting." She whispers back.

He smiles against her lips as they kiss once more.

Holding hands, they head to the door.

Enrique's heart is breaking, and leaving Kristie and their unborn baby behind is making him feel a pain that's almost physical. But he has to go. He has to do this.

As they reach the door, he kisses her one final time, tells her he loves her and their baby once more, before gently breaking contact with her, and slowly, agonizingly walks out of the penthouse.

Chapter 29

Enrique and Jackie travel down in the service elevator to the service bay. His heart is breaking for Kristie, but he has to try to be strong and get focused so that he can get out of this alive. It's extremely difficult to do, but he has to try and only concentrate on what's at hand; he can't go into this falling to pieces. He has to show them he means business and get the job done.

There's a black SUV waiting for them in the service bay, and Special Agent in Charge Julio Ramírez is waiting for them inside.

"You sit with Ramírez in the back... he'll explain the plan to you on the way," Jackie instructs as she opens the back door for Enrique to get in, he climbs in alongside Julio and closes the door, as Jackie gets into the passenger seat.

The driver pulls the vehicle quickly out of the service area and onto the main street, before a second and third SUV joins the convoy, one at the front and one to the rear. Enrique looks around nervously.

"Don't worry, Señor Cruz... it's standard procedure to travel in convoy... especially when you have $22 million in the trunk," Agent Ramírez explains while gesturing to the rear of the vehicle.

Enrique nods and says nothing; what can he say?

"Let me explain what's going to happen this morning," Ramírez starts. "First, please can you put on this body armor... it needs to go underneath your shirt." He smiles. "I'm glad we have a white one," Ramírez says, noting that Enrique's wearing a white shirt.

Enrique takes the vest from Ramírez. This is starting to become a little like Déjà vu—all we need now is a map, Enrique thinks to himself as this is all too familiar to him after his little jaunt to the marine stadium with Ziv at the weekend.

Starting to undress, he sees Ramírez pulling a map from the pocket behind the driver's seat. And there it is, he thinks to himself, somehow managing a smile. Unfolding the map, Ramírez waits for Enrique to finish redressing.

"So, from the information that you've provided us, we've set up accordingly. We have forty agents already in place throughout the woods to ensure that nobody can escape... plus, we have boats out in the ocean in case anyone tries to flee by sea." Ramírez says like he's memorized every detail of the plan, which he has. "We will have a silent drone in the sky throughout the meeting, with an infrared camera... to keep an eye on things from above... and finally, helicopters are on standby as well. From what you've said, the drugs are coming in by boat... we're assuming that your father will also be brought in this way. But the meeting with

Los Fatalitos will have to go down by the docks. We'll park up here in the woods and wait for them to arrive. Once in place, you will drive us forward and stop twenty feet from the dock. Understand?"

"Got it," Enrique replies.

"JJ and I will be in the rear of the SUV. When you give us the signal, we'll get out and bring the money to you... we're your helpers." He allows himself a tiny smile. "From there, we have to let this play out the way they dictate it to. But the money goes nowhere until you've seen your father, and you're completely satisfied he's alive and well." Ramírez continues. "To them, we're just the hired help... nothing more. When we arrive, I will show you a spot on the ground that I need to ensure you stand on," Ramírez demands of Enrique.

"OK... can I ask why I have to stand in a specific spot?" Enrique asks, not understanding where this is going.

"They're bound to check if we're carrying any weapons... it's very usual for cartels to do this... so, the reason I need you to stand on the spot, I tell you... is because there are guns buried in the dirt in specific places... just in case we need to protect ourselves... I'm sure this won't be the case... but we have to be prepared all the same... does that make sense now?" Ramírez raises his eyebrows at Enrique.

"I get it… it makes sense now." Fear washes over Enrique as he considers the prospect that he may have to defend himself to the point where he may have to kill someone.

Ramírez notices and understands Enrique's concerns. "We intend to arrest as many of them as we can… we don't want to have to use our weapons… they are merely a last resort and for our own protection."

"Sir, I'm not under any illusion that this will be a walk in the park… I'm fully aware of how this situation could end up."

"It's always good to be prepared… but I need you to remain calm…."

"I know… and I will." He says, sounding way more confident in his abilities than he actually feels, but one thing he's very good at is putting on an act when he's falling apart inside. So, he should be able to give off the impression that he's got everything under control for the duration of this mission. What other choice does he have?

"That's good to hear," Ramírez says, feeling sure that Enrique can handle this. "The likelihood is, they'll be heavily armed… we need to be prepared." He pauses for a second, looking at Enrique for approval to continue.

"Go on…."

"When we take them down… bullets may start to fly because I'm sure they won't go down without a fight… if and when this happens… you need to get down low and get to cover quickly." He stops for a second as he tries to read Enrique's expression. He needs him to be prepared, but at the same time, he needs him to be calm. Enrique seems to be handling it OK, so he continues. "You, your father, and my agents' lives are the most important part of this morning's operation… and I have absolutely no intention of losing any of you." Ramírez is deadly serious; his expression says it all.

The driver looks in his rearview to Ramírez. "Boss. We're ten minutes out."

Enrique checks his watch. It's 3:45am. There's still forty-five minutes until the meeting. Ramírez is on his radio talking with the other people in the convoy. As he sits beside him, it's becoming apparent to Enrique that this is most definitely the right thing to do. In less than an hour, Ramírez has given him more faith and confidence in the situation than Ziv or Gutiérrez has given him all week. Forty agents, boats, helicopters, and drones, as well as a plan that actually makes sense; how can he feel anything other than confident?

"Everyone pull over to the side." Ramírez is talking into the radio again.

The convoy pulls to the side of the road. The driver exits the SUV, heads toward the first SUV, and climbs into it.

"Are you ready, Señor Cruz?" Ramírez asks.

"I'm ready," Enrique replies confidently, but truthfully he's nervous as hell inside. He tries to keep telling himself it's just like any other meeting. Over the years, he has had to do things in business that he's been nervous about. For those situations, he has a game face reserved. He can be scared as hell on the inside but cool, calm, and confident on the outside. This is a technique he has developed over the years, which has got him through so many difficult situations in business. In his personal life, on the other hand, he isn't quite so successful with handling things; but that's now changing.

"You need to drive now, Señor Cruz," Ramírez says.

"Please... call me Enrique."

"Enrique... there's a side road in three hundred feet... make a right once you reach it, and then follow it down to the dock. JJ, you're in the back with me now," Ramírez instructs before he's back on the radio again.

Enrique and JJ change their seats, and the two other SUVs start to pull away. As Enrique sits in the driver's seat, he watches as the taillights disappear into the distance. He pulls out slowly until he sees the side road turning on the right. He turns into the side road and drives the mile-long bumpy track before they reach the bay.

Driving through an open gate, he pulls up near the dock and stops the SUV. "Where is it you want me to stand, Agent Ramírez," Enrique asks.

"Is the area still clear?" Ramírez asks over the radio. "Very good." He turns to Enrique and JJ and says, "Jump out, and I'll show you both."

The three of them exit the SUV and move around to the front, standing in the beams of the headlights.

Ramírez explains the rest of the operation to Enrique. "The spot I need you to stand on is this patch of grass right here... we've tried to make it as obvious for you as possible while keeping it discreet... our guns are located four feet behind to the left and right. JJ, you got this too?" Ramírez asks.

JJ and Enrique both nod their response.

He gestures for them to get back into the SUV.

"OK. For now, what I need you to do is reverse the vehicle up that track there." He points in the direction of the track, before looking back at Enrique. "We need to be far enough along so they can't see us... to make it look like you have just arrived."

Enrique reverses the vehicle using the rear parking camera and drives slowly back up the track. As the dock disappears out of view, he stops. "Agent Ramírez, is this far enough for you?"

"Perfect. Give me a few minutes now," Ramírez responds.

Enrique shuts off the lights but leaves the engine running. Ramírez is on the radio talking with the other teams, ensuring that everything's in place; he's leaving nothing to chance. Seeing how meticulous he is with his plans, helps top up the confidence Enrique has already built since they met this morning. This gives him hope that this morning will go well; he's going to get his father back safely, plus he's going to return home to Kristie and their baby safely too.

Chapter 30

It's been one of the most surreal twenty-four hours Enrique has ever had to endure in his entire life. He spent most of the previous night baring his soul to Kristie, not only about the grief he's been suppressing but also about the horrifying situation with his father.

That long agonizing, yet liberating conversation, was followed by a meeting with Jackie, a D.E.A. agent, where he told her about his father's kidnap, as well as his clandestine meeting at the marine stadium. And in the midst of all this craziness, Kristie has just agreed to marry him, which of course, he's delighted about.

He's had phone calls with Ziv about what the abductors want in exchange for his father, and he has the weight of not revealing the full details about José to the D.E.A. on his mind, as well as the fact that he's also lying to Ziv and Gutiérrez. And to top it all off, he's just had to leave the love of his life, who is pregnant with their baby, to carry out whatever is expected of him, with one of the most dangerous cartels in the world. To say he's overwhelmed by the situation is the biggest understatement of the year.

Desperate for reassurance, he reminds himself that everything is now a means to an end; he needs to get his father back, and everyone needs to be safe. Ziv and Gutiérrez have pushed him way too far. They've been trying to involve him in things that are way too risky, like drug deals and early morning meetings, which resulted in a mass-murdering blood bath; this is not the way to deal with things. He has to do it the right way, just like Kristie said.

Involving the D.E.A. is the only way this can go now. It's the best chance he's got of getting José back safely, plus he can't allow that amount of drugs to be put onto the streets, let alone be affiliated with it, even if it is to bring his father home. Anxiety floods his body as he thinks about everything. Yes, he does feel uncomfortable with the fact that he hasn't given the D.E.A. the full story, but he doesn't know if his father's involvement in the drug world is true; in fact, he doesn't know anything anymore. All he has is their word: the words of criminals. Until he's heard the truth from his father, he will have to give him the benefit of the doubt.

"Enrique. Enrique. Can you hear me?" Special Agent Jackie Jones pulls him from his daze. "Are you ready?"

"Sorry... eh yes... I'm with you, JJ," Enrique replies, trying to get his words out. "I'm just, well... are you sure this is going to work?" Nerves have well and truly set in, causing him to start questioning the D.E.A.'s plan to get his father back. But before JJ can respond to him, Enrique hears Special Agent in

Charge Julio Ramírez speak to him from the back of the SUV.

"Enrique, you have to trust us... we've done this many times, and it will go as we've planned. My agents are some of the best in the country, and I have absolute faith in them and their abilities."

Enrique turns to look at him. "I don't doubt that... but this is my father we're talking about... it's just...." Suddenly, he feels somebody's hand on his shoulder; he almost jumps at the contact. He turns quickly and is relieved to see it's Jackie.

"Enrique, this will work... just have faith in us, please." She says softly.

Letting out a long breath he's been holding in for what seems like an eternity, Enrique has to agree; the plan does seem pretty watertight. They have everything covered. He's just having a bit of a moment of insecurity, but now he's ready to do this.

Ramírez is running through all the eventualities again with Enrique, as well as talking on the radio with his other teams, and then suddenly they hear. "Movement! We've got movement!

"Everyone on standby. Wait for my signal. I want all of the players on this one. Nobody is to get away." Ramírez orders. Turning back to JJ and Enrique, he says, "We let this play out. Wait for them to set up... then move forward. Remember, park twenty feet from the dock and then get out. We all stick to the plan. Got it?" He instructs.

Both JJ and Enrique nod in agreement. Three black SUVs pull up next to the dock, and people start to climb out. Enrique can feel himself begin to shake as he watches what's unfolding before him; this is so far out of his league, he doesn't know if he can pull this off. Even from this distance, he can see that they're all carrying automatic weapons. His hands are cold and clammy as he observes what's happening in front of him with wide eyes. There are so many variables to this situation, so many different ways this could go wrong; it doesn't even bear thinking about. Nothing could have prepared him for this; nothing.

A pat on his shoulder from Ramírez is his signal. Turning on the lights of the SUV, Enrique slips the vehicle into drive and begins to move the vehicle forward. He does a quick count in the beams of the headlights, and from what he can see, there are approximately twelve to fourteen of them in total.

As he drives closer, he's greeted by a wall of gun barrels as all of the men point their weapons in his direction. Enrique's heart is racing, and he's beginning to get palpitations; this isn't a good time for a panic attack, he thinks to himself. Fuck! When is it ever a good time for a panic attack?

He stops the SUV where Ramírez instructed, twenty feet from the dock. He looks in the rearview mirror, nodding to JJ and Ramírez for approval to get out; they nod back. With that, Enrique reaches for the door handle, takes a deep breath, squares his shoulders, and puts on his game face. You've got this, he tells himself in his mind; you've got this.

He pushes the car door open and steps from the air-conditioned vehicle into the hot and humid, early morning atmosphere. The smell of the sea air always has a calming effect on his mind and body, and thankfully, today is no exception. It's go time!

Swinging the car door shut, he holds his arms out wide and begins to walk toward the heavily armed men.

"Stop right there!" one of the men shouts in Spanish as he holds his hand up to direct Enrique.

Glancing at the floor, Enrique notices the spot Ramírez told him to stand on; it's three feet further to his left. He puts his hands up as if to block the light shining in his eyes, pretending the headlights are blinding him. Trying to cover up his deliberate move, he takes a few stumbling steps to his left and stops as he reaches the grassy patch Ramírez pointed out earlier.

"I said don't move!" comes a booming voice from beside one of the SUVs in front of him. The same man then waves one of the other guys over to him. "Check him for weapons!" He demands of the man.

The man passes his rifle to the guy next to him before removing his pistol from its holster and pointing it in Enrique's direction. He takes a metal detector from the man that issued the order and walks cautiously but with purpose toward Enrique.

Once in front of him, the man waves the wand across Enrique's body. He turns back to the guy that appears to be somewhat in charge and confirms that he's clean before heading back to the rest of the group.

"Where's the money?" the man asks.

"Where's your boss?" Enrique demands. The conversation continues in Spanish. "None of this is going down until he shows up." Enrique is pleased his technique is working so far. He sounds extremely confident, although inside, he's a nervous wreck.

The man turns, slaps his hand twice on the SUV, and the rear door opens, and out steps a man dressed in a white suit. The door is shut for him from the inside as he begins to hobble with a cane toward Enrique.

Suddenly, one of his men removes something from the trunk of the SUV and rushes around to the front of the vehicle with what seems to be a stool. Placing it down, he helps the man in white sit down. Enrique looks on in shock at the frail state of the man in front of him. Can this really be La Espada?

"Enrique is it?" he asks in Spanish.

"That's correct... and you are?"

"Most people know me by the name La Espada... but I am in no mood to exchange pleasantries. Let's get on with this, as I have no time to waste!"

Stories about this man's brutality are commonplace throughout Miami. The news regularly reports gangland violence, but when they're talking about this man, it turns Enrique's blood cold. The level of brutality that he subjects his victims to is barbaric; people have been skinned alive for just looking at him the wrong way. Enrique can't comprehend that this little old man is capable of or behind such brutal violence.

Enrique looks directly at him. "Let's get this done!" Enrique says matter of factly. "Where are the men with the drugs you need me to buy for you?"

La Espada signals for one of his men. "Tuto, call them in now."

Tuto nods and pulls a radio from his belt. "We are all clear. Come in now."

La Espada turns back to Enrique. "You have the money?"

Enrique nods. Lifting his right arm, he beckons for JJ and Ramírez to join him. As the two open their car doors, La Espada's men all turn and cock their weapons.

"Hey! Hang on. They're with me!" Enrique shouts, putting his hand up, looking sternly at the heavily armed men. "Do you know how much $22 million in cash weighs? I'm not carrying that myself or driving around alone with it either."

La Espada begins to laugh.

This makes Enrique nervous. Why's he laughing? Then, suddenly, La Espada appeases his concerns.

"A man after my own heart!" He laughs some more. "Why do something yourself when you can get others to do it for you." He turns to his men and orders. "It's OK... but check them for weapons."

JJ and Ramírez move around to the back of the SUV, and open the trunk, and remove the four diver bags. Each bag weighs roughly fifty-five kilos and holds just over $5.5 million in $100 bills. Lifting one onto each shoulder, they make their way back around the driver's side of the SUV and toward Enrique. As they reach him, they separate and stand just behind him, in the spots where Ramírez directed them earlier. They drop the bags down at their feet as JJ stands to Enrique's left and Ramírez to his right. The man with the metal detector steps forward again and directs them to hold out their arms before checking each of them out. Turning back to his boss, he confirms that they're clean.

Suddenly, the sound of a boat engine fills the bay, forcing them to turn in its direction. It's difficult to see who or how many people are on board the fishing trawler as it enters the bay, but Enrique feels it's safe to assume that at least Ziv and maybe Gutiérrez are on board. As they watch the boat move closer to them, it slows to a crawl, then the engines are cut, and the forward anchor is released. The next thing they see is an inflatable dinghy being lowered from the side of the boat, and the sound of its small outboard engine cuts through the silence.

Turning to La Espada, Enrique says to him, "I have the money. They have the drugs. Now, where's my father? This money isn't leaving my side until I see him."

Turning to Tuto again, he signals for him to contact someone else. Tuto talks into the radio again. He turns back to La Espada and nods his response.

"Your father is on the way. A deal is a deal, and I am a man of my word. The deal was the drugs for your father. You have kept your side of the bargain, and I will keep mine," La Espada tells him.

The dinghy reaches the dock, and a man in a balaclava ties it to the post. He steps onto the dock and heads toward them all. Once he reaches them, he looks around. "Who has my money?" he demands.

Enrique turns to him and points to the bags behind him. "I have your money. Feel free to check the bags, but they're going nowhere until this man keeps his side of the deal."

The masked man shrugs; he steps toward the bags and begins to pull them open. He pulls out bundles of cash and starts to flick through some of them in the car's headlights. Then he moves from bag to bag to ensure that the bundles are correct and he isn't being ripped off.

The sound of another boat entering the bay makes the men turn again and look out to sea. A sport fishing boat pulls in and begins to lower its anchor, maybe thirty feet from the other fishing vessel and fifty feet from the shoreline.

La Espada clicks his fingers, and Tuto hands him a night vision scope. He then turns and gives it to Enrique. Pointing to the fishing boat, he says, "Your father is on the boat... take a look."

Enrique eagerly takes the scope, looks through it, and he sees the sport fishing boat. The night vision still makes it difficult to see who he's looking at entirely, but he can see a man being brought out onto the deck. As he watches on, he sees the man being turned to face toward the dock. The first man looks a lot like Manolo, but it's difficult to be absolutely sure. Squinting into the scope, he takes a long hard look and notices the other man has a bag over his head.

Suddenly, the guy that looks like Manolo pulls the bag free. Staring hard at the man as his face is revealed, Enrique tries to focus the scope so he can be sure it's José. He gets a clearer look, and yes, yes, it's his father, and to Enrique's relief, he looks OK and unharmed.

Enrique can't believe he's barely fifty feet from him, and at last, this nightmare is finally coming to an end. Turning slightly, he looks out at the trawler that's docked in the bay, trying to get a look at who's on board. At the rail of the boat stands a large, muscle-bound figure. While he has his back turned to Enrique, it seems it's likely to be Ziv.

"Are you satisfied?" La Espada asks Enrique.

"Yes." Enrique replies to him. "Let's just get this over and done with."

La Espada turns to Tuto, "Take the bags of money to the boat and check the coke... let me know if everything is as it should be."

Enrique looks toward the masked man. "Are you satisfied?" he asks him.

"Everything looks good." He replies, lifting a bag onto each of his shoulders while Tuto picks up the other two bags. They walk together down to the dock and then throw the bags into the dinghy before climbing onboard. The masked man starts the engine, and they head out to the fishing trawler.

Enrique looks from JJ to Ramírez and back again. JJ winks at him in a gesture to try and calm his nerves and let him know it's all going to plan. Suddenly, everyone turns again as a high-powered boat speeds into the bay. It turns sharply and pulls alongside the trawler. The early morning light is beginning to make things easier to see, and Enrique can sense that everyone's becoming more on edge the lighter it gets.

"What the fuck is that?" exclaims La Espada. He snatches the radio from the man standing next to him. "Tuto, what the fuck is going on out there?"

"Jefe... everything is good. The coke is at least ninety-five percent pure," Tuto responds back to him.

La Espada's fury is obvious as he replies, "What the fuck is with the powerboat? What's going on over there?" He snipes as he shifts on his seat so he can face out into the bay; anger and rage are evident across his face.

Enrique faces Ramírez and mouths. "What do we do?"

Ramírez gently waves his hand to say it's all-OK. He's been made fully aware of what's going on in the bay, thanks to a drone in the sky above; a play-by-play account of the events has been quietly detailed to him through his earpiece since they arrived at the meet.

Tuto comes back over the radio and says. "It's for the dealers. They say that the trawler is part of the deal. Everything is as it should be out here."

"Tuto, take the boat." La Espada commands. "You know where to go."

"Yes, Jefe."

"Gentlemen... and Lady," La Espada winks at JJ as he gives the beautiful brunette a flirtatious smile; this makes her feel nauseous, but she goes along with it, just like she always does. It's all part of the job, as well as her cover; she can take down these guys herself if she wanted to. "It seems that our business here is complete. I have my drugs, they have their money, and your father is free to go,

Enrique." He presses the button on the radio again before saying. "You can release Señor Cruz now. Bring him to shore, and let's get out of here."

"Yes, Jefe." A man responds over the radio.

Then out of nowhere, a roar of the powerboat engines fills the bay, followed closely by the sound of birds scared from their nightly resting spots. The dawn is fast approaching, and the powerboat isn't hanging around to see what daylight will bring.

Enrique can only assume that Ziv and Gutiérrez are onboard, and he can't believe they're getting away with $22 million, but he has his father back, and that's all that really matters. Looking through the night scope, he can see two men on deck of the boat, and it looks like his father is being untied; a third man is lowering a small boat from its rear into the water.

"It is time for me to go now. It has been a pleasure doing business with you, Enrique." La Espada laughs. "You rich people... make this all too simple for men like me to take advantage of you... you all think that you're untouchable. Taking your father has meant that we are now back in business, without having to spend a dime of our own money... and I now have ten tons of cocaine to flood the streets." La Espada looks more than happy with himself for pulling this off so easily.

Enrique's confused. Does La Espada not know that my father's El Espectro? This makes no sense. Manolo was so adamant he knew who my father was. How can La Espada not know?

As La Espada starts to rise from his seat, a massive explosion rocks the bay, sending everyone flying off their feet. Lying on the ground, Enrique holds his hands over his ears as a constant ringing sound screeches through them. He lifts his head and glances around. He sees that everyone's lying on the floor, and then he looks out at the bay in horror, as he watches the remains of the trawler slowly sink below the waterline.

"Move in! Everybody move in! NOW!!" Ramírez is screaming into his wrist mic.

"D.E.A.! Nobody move!" Ramírez's team shouts their demands as they appear from the tree line.

La Espada is lying on the floor and yelling to his men. "Kill them all! Kill everyone!" Picking up a gun that's fallen next to him, he points it at Enrique. "You fucking double-crossing son of a bitch." His face is dark and evil. "You and your father are dead," he says before flicking off the safety. Enrique closes his eyes. Thoughts of Kristie and their baby flood through his mind, leaving scorching agony in their wake. I'm never going to see my girl, the love of my life, ever again. I'll never get to meet our baby. I'll never see my family again, nor my friends, Sánchez and García. What about Leon? Will he recover after his relapse? Oh God, Krissy will have to bring up our baby alone, oh God. Tears begin to escape his eyes that are screwed tightly shut, and then suddenly, the sound of a single gunshot erupts.

After a few seconds, Enrique slowly opens his eyes. Am I still alive, he asks himself.

He looks at his surroundings. JJ is lying just behind him with a gun in her hand. He quickly turns back to La Espada. He's shocked to the core as he sees a small trickle of blood is pouring from the entry wound in the center of his forehead.

Then suddenly, the brief moment of silence is disrupted by gunfire as it erupts around them. D.E.A. agents are coming in from the tree line returning fire on La Espada's men. Even with their boss' death, they're unwilling to go down without a fight.

JJ and Ramírez are now on their feet, with their pistols in hand. Enrique turns and looks out into the bay. The dust is beginning to settle from the trawler's explosion. He looks across to the sports fishing boat, and he can just about see two men still on the deck. Thankful that he can still see movement, he finds the strength to climb to his feet. Maybe his father is still OK? And then suddenly, he's grabbed from behind.

"Are you trying to get shot?" Ramírez drags him down behind one of the SUVs.

"I was looking for my dad… I… I didn't think!" Enrique replies, looking back out to the bay, as his eyes refuse to give up on trying to find his father. On the ground, he sees the night scope. Picking it up as JJ and Ramírez return fire on La Espada's men, Enrique lifts it to his eye to try and check again for José. Before he can even look, a second explosion rips through the bay.

"NOOOOOOOOOOO!!!!!!!!" Enrique screams at the top of his lungs. Scrambling to his feet, he charges down toward the dock. Just as he's about to dive into the water, JJ tackles him from behind and pins him to the ground, resisting his every effort to shake her off.

"Enrique, please stop! There isn't anything you can do," JJ begs him.

"Get off me! I have to help him! Get the fuck off me!" Enrique rages at her.

"He's gone, Enrique. He's gone. I'm so sorry." JJ rolls off of him.

Enrique lays on his front, staring out into the bay, as tears fall freely from his eyes. What the fuck has just happened? After all of this. After everything, everything that he's gone through to get to this point, his father has just been killed right before his eyes.

Chapter 31

Kneeling on the ground, Enrique stares blankly at the burning wreckage of the sports fishing boat. Chaos is all around him. D.E.A. agents have La Espada's men in cuffs or covered with sheets.

JJ's talking to Enrique, but the shock of the situation has left him zoned out to his surroundings, meaning he can't hear what she's saying to him; he can't even speak. He's completely numb.

The magnitude of the situation is too much for him to bear; one of his worst nightmares has just played out right in front of him. Thoughts of Kristie and the baby are giving him just enough strength to stand to his feet. Emotion overwhelms him again as he realizes he will never be able to tell José he's going to be a grandfather.

JJ stands in front of him and places her hands on his face, pulling his eye line down to her and away from the wreckage. She tries to talk to him again. "Enrique, come with me, please... Enrique, please," she begs him. She puts her arm around his waist and takes his hand, helping him walk back toward the SUV. His legs are nearly buckling underneath him. As they approach the vehicle, another agent looks at him solemnly as they open the rear door for them and help him up and inside.

"Enrique, I can take you home... Agent Ramírez has given you clearance to go. We can wrap the paperwork up later." JJ says, but she's unsure if he's taking it in or not.

Everything's a daze. His mind is running out of control, unable to fully comprehend the extent of what's just happened in front of his own eyes. Looking up, he tries to focus on JJ. "Does she know?" Enrique whispers; his words are barely audible.

"Does who know what, Enrique?" JJ replies with a gentle tone to her voice.

He clears his throat before saying. "Does Kristie know... about my father? Does she know what's happened?" His voice is a little louder this time.

"We haven't told her anything. The agents with her have been briefed not to give her any details without your permission... I'll take you back to her now," JJ says as she pulls away from the dock and heads toward the main road.

"I want to go to Star Island... for now... I... I need to figure out how to tell Kristie about what's happened." Right now, he's struggling even to speak, let alone be able to explain to Kristie what's just happened. He's in a complete state of shock, and he feels that maybe going to his father's house might help him somehow, perhaps give him some sort of comfort. To be honest, he has no clue what to do.

"OK... no problem. I'll take you there." She glides her hand through the air as she drives the SUV back to Miami. "You've gotta do what you've gotta do," She says sympathetically. "I understand this must be so difficult for you to process... but you did everything you could, Enrique."

Enrique replies with a nod. He can't say anything right now. All he can do is stare out of the window. He wants nothing more than to go home to Kristie and wrap his arms around her: to be close to her, but he's so messed up by everything that's just happened he needs a little time. He needs to find the strength and words to tell her, and he wants to be able to be there for her and comfort her.

As his mind flows through thoughts of how Kristie will take the horrific news about José, he's fully aware that he knows her too well, and he knows that she will most probably blame herself somehow. He knows he not only needs the strength to comfort her but to help her see that none of this is her fault. Kristie taking responsibility for any of this is something he will not allow, as he honestly doesn't blame her at all.

"Is there a way of finding out how Krissy's doing... without making it obvious?" Enrique manages to ask JJ eventually. He's concerned about how she's coping but doesn't want to worry her just yet with anything else.

"I've just checked in with the agents at your apartment," JJ says. "They said Kristie's doing OK. She's been keeping busy, and she's cooked for them," Jackie smiles. "They said she cooked them the biggest, most delicious breakfast of their lives."

"That sounds like my girl... she's always looking after people." Enrique smiles at the thought. "I just need to pull myself together a little... then I'll head home." He misses Kristie so, so much, and he can't wait to see her, but he's absolutely dreading telling her. She adores José.

The drive takes a little longer as the traffic's started to build. Enrique just wants the journey to be over with now. He wants to be alone for a while, alone in his dad's house, around things that remind him of the happy memories they shared. He decides he will only remember him for all the good. As for the so-called "Drug Kingpin"? That will be something he will never get to find out one way or the other. Enrique shakes his head at the thought. It's something he's glad he will never know.

Chapter 32

Once they arrive at José's house, Enrique unsteadily climbs out of the SUV, thanks JJ, and stumbles into the grand Mediterranean-style mansion. As he enters his father's house, he looks around in a state of shock and disbelief. It was only about ten days ago when he and José were on the dock, enjoying a drink and shooting the breeze, just like they had so many times over the years.

He then casts his mind back to just under a week ago, when he learned the news about his father being kidnapped, and he was trying to find clues of his whereabouts. Now he's here, alone, and his father is dead, blown up right in front of him. He shakes his head with agonizing devastation. How the hell is he supposed to come to terms with this? And more to the point, will he ever come to terms with it?

Enrique walks through the empty house, as he had given all the staff paid leave, while he dealt with his father's kidnapping. Uggghhh, I have to tell them all too; they'll all be completely heartbroken, Enrique thinks to himself.

In the living area, he stops to look at a photo of his mom and dad on their wedding day. Gina looks so beautiful and graceful dressed in white, and José is looking equally as elegant in a custom-made suit and tie. Enrique picks up the platinum framed photo and gazes at it with tear-filled eyes. "You're together now." He whispers. "That's all you ever wanted... to be together again... and now you are."

Tears flood relentlessly from his eyes as he contemplates his parents being reunited, just like José has longed for ever since the day Gina passed; finally, they can be with each other again and be at peace. "I love you, mom." He whispers to the photo. "I love you, dad... now you can be together again... now you can hold each other, and your pain will disappear... you will never have to feel that agony ever again... you can finally live happily ever after... in harmony... and as much as I want you both here... with me... to meet your grandchild... I'm happy you're both together... just like you should be... I love you both so, so much."

He tries to wipe his tears, but it's hopeless; they don't stop falling. As crippled by grief as he is, he desperately tries to take on the pain and look at it as a sacrifice so his parents can finally rest in peace together.

A while later, he finds himself slumped in his father's favorite chair, staring down at the dock where José had been pacing less than a week ago. For the last hour, he's been replaying the events of the previous six days. Could he have done something differently? Was this his fault? He was the one who contacted the D.E.A., and he was the one that agreed to their ideas. "Fuck!" Enrique exclaims, bringing his hand to his chest. It's like his heart is being ripped out of his body. He's never felt a pain like this in his life. He tries to breathe through it, as he had before when he had the panic attack on his balcony the other night.

This morning he has been filled with a mixture of fear and hope. Fear for very obvious reasons, and hope that he was getting his father back and would be able to give him the exciting news that he too was going to be a father. This is something José will never know now. He will never know that his only child is going to be giving him his first grandchild.

"I need to be with Kristie. I need to see her now," Enrique says to himself as he considers driving one of his dad's cars home, then he realizes he's in no fit state to drive. Calling Emilio his driver is out of the question, as he can't face anyone right now.

Not thinking straight, he decides to call Kristie and ask her to come to Star Island. He will wait for her to get there before he tells her anything, as there's no way this conversation is going to happen over the phone. If necessary, they can stay at his father's house tonight.

Reaching into his pocket, he pulls out his cell. He unlocks it and dials Kristie's number.

Kristie answers within one ring. Enrique tries to speak; the words won't come out.

"Enrique… baby, are you there? Is everything OK?" Kristie starts to panic as she hears nothing but silence at the end of the phone. She doesn't know where Enrique is, or even if it's him on the other end of the line.

"He's gone," Enrique says with a whisper; his words are barely audible.

"What do you mean, babe?" Kristie asks softly. Her voice is beginning to tremble as the meaning of what he's just said begins to register.

"He's dead," Enrique manages with a whisper. His words just pour out before he can stop them.

"Oh my God… Enrique… NO!" Kristie cries. "Where are you? Tell me where you are?"

"I'm at dad's house," Enrique says, a little clearer this time.

"I'm on my way," she says urgently.

"No. No. No," Enrique says, sitting up in his chair. "You're not driving." This pulls him out of his melancholic state a little.

"I'll be OK."

"No." His tone is firm. "I should never have told you over the phone… I meant to tell you when you got here." Enrique tries his best to make sense to her, as he's all over the place. What was he thinking to call Kristie? She would know there was something wrong just by hearing his voice. He can't have her drive now, not after what he's just told her. "I'll contact Emilio. He'll drive you," Enrique says almost sternly. He means it. He doesn't want her driving. She's upset, and he needs her to be safe, both her and their baby. Not only is he in complete emotional torture, but he's also now extremely frustrated with himself. What the hell was he thinking calling her that way? I should have just got Emilio to take me back to Alta Vita in the first place.

"It's OK, baby... it'll take too much time," Kristie says with reassurance.

"No, Kristie. I mean it. You're not driving." Enrique is now being extremely firm with her and is suddenly more alert than ever. There is no way he's letting her drive, even if it means calling Jorge and telling him not to bring her any of the cars. He'll never forgive himself if something happened to her and the baby, even more so today.

As he's talking to Kristie, he hears the sound of a high-performance boat coming from behind the tree line. As the boat draws closer, it pulls up to José's dock. This brings him to his feet immediately. Then he sees Ziv.

"What the fuck?" Enrique exclaims.

"Sorry?" Kristie says with surprise. Enrique rarely swears at her, even when they argue. But then again, this is an extreme situation; he has just lost his father.

"Sorry, baby... that wasn't meant for you... uhh... a boat's just turned up at the dock." He pauses. "It's Ziv?" Enrique says with confusion. "I need to talk to him... I need to find out what he knows!" He feels anger swelling inside of him. This guy has some nerve showing his face here after what's just happened.

"You go and talk to him... I'll see you as soon as I get there," Kristie replies.

"Please, Krissy... don't drive," Enrique begs as he walks toward the boat.

"Don't worry, babe." Kristie isn't waiting for his driver; she's already at the valet and waiting for his Ferrari. She needs to get to José's house right this second to be with Enrique. Besides, she feels perfectly OK to drive; if she didn't, she'd never get behind the wheel in the first place. Enrique knows this, but he's just being over-cautious.

As Enrique approaches the dock, rage is boiling inside of him. Glaring at Ziv, he can see that the asshole is all smiles, and is laughing and joking with someone else on the boat. This only drives the anger to get the better of him. Even though he knows he has little or no chance against this guy, right now, all he wants to do is kill him.

Suddenly, all of the wind exits his body instantly, as he sees what's before him. The person Ziv's laughing and joking with is Manolo. He's been set up. Rage erupts within him. He sees red.

"YOU!" He seethes at Ziv. Enrique's face is clouded with darkness and fury. "YOU... YOU SET MY FATHER UP... YOU SET ME UP! YOU WERE IN ON THIS ALL ALONG!!" He yells down the dock at Ziv and Manolo; he's losing control.

Ziv holds his hands up to Enrique, trying to get him to calm down, pleading with him that it's all OK. Well, it's not OK, Enrique thinks to himself. He can see Ziv's mouth moving, plus Manolo chimes in too, but Enrique's rage is so wild that he can't hear a word they're saying.

"YOU FUCKING KILLED HIM!!!! YOU KILLED MY FATHER, YOU FUCKING PIECES OF SHIT!!!! THIS WAS ALL A FUCKING SET UP!!!" Enrique bellows, his voice is so threatening; he sounds evil. He's never been so angry in his entire life. "I'LL FUCKING KILL YOU... I'LL KILL BOTH OF YOU MOTHERFUCKERS!" He snaps, charging down the dock toward the men; boiling with rage, he's ready to murder the pair of them.

Manolo backs away a little and stays on the boat. Ziv, on the other hand, is up and onto the dock in a few quick strides. Enrique continues to charge toward him, lost in the red mist that's descended across him. He lunges wildly for Ziv. One good punch, and I'll have the upper hand, Enrique quickly tells himself. How wrong can he be?

Ziv deflects the punch with one swift move, and using Enrique's own momentum against him, he has him in a rear-naked choke in one single motion. Enrique begins to flail about wildly, grabbing for anything he can get hold of. But Ziv's too strong, and he knows what he's doing.

Suddenly, Enrique can feel everything starting to fade, and he has very little control. He knows there's nothing that he can do. Is this the end? As he begins to blackout, he sees a figure appear in front of him. Is that...? No. It's impossible. It can't be... can it?

Just as he's about to fade into darkness, Ziv releases his grip, and Enrique collapses to the floor on his knees. He desperately tries to inhale, and thankfully oxygen fills his lungs and rushes around his body. As his blurred vision slowly starts to clear, he lifts his head slowly, and as his eyes begin to focus, he sees two pairs of feet.

Lifting his head up higher, he first sees Gutiérrez. "You fucking asshole! You're part of this too?" Enrique rasps at him.

"There was no set up, Enrique," Gutiérrez says calmly. "Let me explain."

Enrique's face is full of confusion. "What the fuck is going on then?" He snaps.

"In fairness, Enrique, it would have been a lot easier if you hadn't involved the D.E.A. You should have just followed my instructions," Gutiérrez's tone is beyond patronizing.

Enrique's head drops back to the ground. "Maybe it would have been easier for you... but you gave me no choice. I told you I wouldn't be part of a drug deal, and you weren't making any real progress." Enrique takes a breath. "You fuckers only made things worse."

"Enrique. It's all OK... everything has worked out for the best in the end."

What the hell? That voice. It can't be. Enrique lifts his head a little quicker than he should. Looking in the direction of the voice, the bright sunshine is glaring directly in his face. As his eyes adjust, he can vaguely make out another person. Then the blurry figure moves to the side to shade him from the sun.

"Come on." Says a caring and familiar voice.

The man reaches his hand to Enrique, and as his eyes adjust further, he notices a scar that runs along the palm. No fucking way. This isn't happening, Enrique thinks to himself. Am I dreaming?

Chapter 33

Squinting his eyes against the sun, Enrique reaches out and grabs the outstretched hand. As he's pulled to his feet, he recognizes the man as he comes face to face with him. To his complete disbelief, the man helping him to his feet is his father.

Lifting his hands, he cups José's face and then pulls him in close, hugging the man that he thought was dead. How? Does he really care? Of course, he does, but right now, he just wants to hold his father, a man he loves so dearly; a man he's always been so grateful to have in his life. He holds José so tightly that he has to ask Enrique to let him go so he can breathe.

"How?" Enrique asks as he releases his father from his tight embrace. "How are you alive? I literally watched you get blown up?" He can't contain all the questions that flood up from deep inside of him.

"Come on... let's go inside, and we can explain everything to you!" José says, looking his usual suave and sophisticated self.

All five men turn to head up to the house, and Ziv stands there smiling at him. "No hard feelings, ahh, Enrique? I'm sorry for what I had to do to you!" Ziv holds out his hand. Enrique ignores him and heads toward the house with his father.

Ziv shrugs then turns to follow them. They all walk along the side of the sun-drenched pool, through the glass doors, and into the great room. Once in the grand living area, José gestures for them all to sit. "Where's all the staff, Enrique?" José asks.

"I sent them all home... gave them a paid vacation... I uh... didn't know what else to do." He says, full of sadness and tear-filled eyes. "You were gone... and I didn't want them all asking questions and worrying about you," he explains before getting straight to the point. "I have so many questions... and I need you to be honest with me with all of them. After everything that's happened this week... today...." he looks across sternly at Ziv, Gutiérrez, and Manolo for a second, before looking back at his father. "It's the least I deserve, don't you think?" He raises his eyebrows at José with a look of admonishment.

"You do, yes," José says matter of factly, turning his hand in an upward motion. "Ask me anything you want." He sits down facing Enrique.

Ziv, Gutiérrez, and Manolo all take a seat. Enrique looks around at them all. Manolo has two black eyes and a broken nose, plus he's covered in fresh scars. "Why are you here?" Enrique asks Manolo, full of confusion. "I can't imagine you'd want to be anywhere near these two assholes?" he snipes, pointing at Gutiérrez and Ziv.

Manolo looks at José for permission to answer Enrique truthfully. José nods and gestures for him to continue.

"I work for your father," Manolo explains. "I have done for years... Ziv was the only one that knew... Gutiérrez didn't know anything." He looks at Gutiérrez. "I doubt he would have believed it even if I told him."

"Even when José was telling me... I didn't quite believe that it was true." Gutiérrez admits.

"Hang on. Hang on. Let's start from the beginning." Enrique interjects. He looks at his father and asks with trepidation. "Are you or are you not El Espectro?"

Staring down at his feet, José replies quietly. "The short answer is yes... yes, I am." He looks back up at his son, desperate for his understanding, but Enrique is anything but understanding; how can he be?

"You fucking what?" Disgust and fury make his handsome face look dark and menacing; he cannot believe what he's hearing. His world has just come crashing down around him, and he's about to go orbital, but somehow, he manages to hold his counsel.

"Enrique... it's complicated... way more complicated than you can imagine."

"Oh, really?" Enrique raises his hands in an upward motion. "It's complicated." He's mocking his father's pathetic way of trying to give him an explanation.

"It is." José protests.

"Really?" Enrique seethes. "Complicated how?" His eyes are wide and full of accusation; he can't believe what he's hearing. "So, you lie to me... my whole life... because it's complicated...." his eyes narrow. "You lied to mom...."

"Enrique, please...." José looks at him full of regret.

"Enrique, please... what?" His blood is boiling. Right now, his feelings of wanting to kill his father are way more profound than ever. How dare he do this to him... to his mom?

"I have obligations... to people far more powerful and dangerous than you could possibly imagine."

"Oh really?"

"Yes, really." José leans forward, looking at his son, who he knows is about to explode any second. "Please... will you let me try to explain?

"Explain away." Enrique waves his hand through the air, gesturing for José to tell him his story. He sits back in his chair, suddenly numbed with complete disbelief; he feels like he's living in the twilight zone. "Go ahead... please...."

"I tried to walk away from it all before you were born... but they threatened everything... and everyone that I loved. In the end... I did what I felt was best for everyone. I stepped far enough away to be able to protect you and your mother... but stayed in just enough to keep them happy."

"Oh, that's so nice of you." Enrique's tone is oozing with ridicule; he doesn't believe the words that are coming from his father's mouth. "How sweet."

"Enrique... please."

"I'm just sitting here trying to make sure I've got things straight." He tilts his head to the side. "So, you never left the drug world... you lied to mom... you lied to me... to everybody... and now you're sitting here telling me I have to understand that it wasn't your fault... and you did it all for the good of mom, me and our family?"

"In a way, yes," José says calmly.

"Wow!" Enrique raises his eyebrows, nodding his head at the same time, sounding way more calm than he actually is. In fact, he's gone past angry; right now, he's enraged. "So, if that's the case... and you were keeping them all happy, why the fuck were you kidnapped?"

"I was never kidnapped! I just had to make it look like I had been, to you and Gutiérrez." José replies.

"What the fuck! Why the hell would you have to do that?" Enrique sits up in his chair, getting ready to stand and rip his father's head off. How the fuck could he do this to him?

"Enrique, let me explain everything to you from the beginning." José starts. "Please...."

"Go on then." Enrique just about manages to stay in his seat. "It better be a fucking good explanation for all the shit that I've been through this last week."

Shifting awkwardly in the chair, José composes himself. "It's all been going on since your mother died... your grandparents never forgave me for what happened to her... they blamed me, and as you know, I blamed myself." He pauses as he swallows the agonizing grief that's trying to choke him. "I swore to myself that no matter what... I would find those responsible for her death."

"But you've always told me that it was an accident... whenever I've mentioned my suspicions about what happened, you've always stood by the fact that it was an accident." Enrique states. He's beginning to soften a little toward José. At the end of the day, they both share their grief for Gina, and it's something that has always made them so close; it's given them an unbreakable bond.

"If it was an accident, then why was there barely any investigation... why was nobody ever found and prosecuted for it?" José shakes his head as his pain sears through his heart. "It was no accident." His voice is full of certainty. "I just didn't want to confirm your suspicions to you... I didn't want you to feel any worse about the situation... and I have to be honest with you... your grandfather knew it was because of me... and deep down, so did I." He pauses once more and takes in a deep breath, trying to ease his internal torture. "After all, she was driving my car on the night that it happened." Tears begin to fill José's eyes; the love he still feels for Enrique's mom is as strong as ever. "They were clearly after me... it was a warning... I had to get to the bottom of it... in some ways I felt like I owed it to her... how could I just leave it alone?" He looks down as he tries desperately to hold back his tears. "Your mom is my world... she always will be... I've never been able to move on with anyone else since Gina... I could never bring myself to... I never will. She was the love of my life... she still is, and nobody could ever take her place."

"I know that... but if it wasn't an accident and you knew that, why not talk to the police about it?"

"I did so many times... but nobody would ever listen... to them, the case was closed. The trouble was, in those days, a lot of the authorities were so easily paid off." He looks at Enrique, begging for his understanding. "I mean, I had an idea who

381

could have been behind it all." He tries to push through the pain of reliving a part of his history that he can never forget. "The night before the accident... I had been at The Bounty in Coconut Grove with friends. I uh... I'd gotten into an argument with a man over a table... it was so stupid... he said it was his, but we were already seated and had no intention of moving; nobody was telling me to get up and move tables." He explains. "We had no idea who each other were... we just got on with our nights, or so I thought, and my friends and I left a few hours later in my car and thought no more of it." He takes a second as he prepares himself to tell the rest of the excruciating story. "The next day, your mom took my car as hers was in the shop. This man obviously took great offense to our disagreement and went way too far in retaliation." José says with deep sadness as he replays the events in his mind.

"WHAT?" Enrique can't believe what he's hearing. "So, mom died over an argument about a fucking table?" He erupts.

"You have to understand Enrique... these were very different times. People would get shot for a pack of smokes back then." José tries to reason with his son. "I needed to get proof, and that was something I couldn't get alone. That is where Manolo came in." José looks to his battered friend and manages a smile. "I owe this man so much for giving me closure. He went into Los Fatalitos ten years ago, and he found out recently what I needed to know. He found out that the man I argued with was La Espada... and just as I thought... he had ordered the hit on me. Not knowing who I truly was... he accepted the death of Gina as justice in his eyes. Once Manolo came to me with the information, I just had to find a way to lure him out."

"Why? Why lure them out? Why not just go to the police with the new information and let them deal with it for you? How many people have had to die this week just for your revenge?" Enrique tries to control his rage but barely succeeds.

"It was Manolo's word against La Espada's. There was no way the police would do anything to help us... besides, people in my world don't go to the cops," José continues.

"People in your world? You should listen to yourself." Enrique shakes his head in disgust. "So, you thought you'd just drag me along for the ride." He stands and moves away from his chair before he does something he may or may not regret; he hasn't quite figured it out yet. He looks back at José. "So, explain to me why the fuck I had to be dragged into this?"

"That would be my fault," Gutiérrez says.

"How the fuck is it your fault?" Enrique snaps, swiftly switching his glance to Gutiérrez.

"For years, your father has been telling me it wasn't an accident. He's wanted to go after La Espada and make him pay for what he believed he had done. I wouldn't allow us to go to war over his assumptions." Gutiérrez reveals.

"Oh, wonderful!" Enrique says in a high-pitched tone of mockery. "Mr. Psycho, here is the reason that my father didn't go on a murdering rampage across Miami. Fucking hell, does this get any better? Do you guys hear yourselves? This isn't fucking normal behavior!" Enrique rages, tapping his forefinger on his head, implying that they're all crazy. Throwing his hands in the air, he shouts. "Come on then!! Out with the rest of it!!"

José continues, "The kidnapping was faked along with the clues that I left you… like the texts and the note. These were all designed to get you to involve Gutiérrez. I knew if you contacted him, he would know that something was seriously wrong… I needed him to come in and believe that it was real, and the only way I could sell that was for you to be the one telling him." He explains. "He knew that you had nothing to do with this life… so when you contacted him, it was easier for Gutiérrez to believe. When you were in the Monastery, Ziv informed me that you were about to leave… that you weren't believing what Gutiérrez was telling you about me… about my… uh… business… so I sent you the texts… the texts about the meet at the marine stadium… I'm sorry I had to do that to you… but I had to make sure you didn't contact the police."

Gutiérrez sits back in his chair and nods his head in agreement as Enrique listens on in horror.

"Once he was involved, it was up to Manolo to play his part. The meeting at the stadium was set up months ago between us, and thankfully it all played out to plan." José smiles at Manolo. Manolo clasps his hands together and nods his approval at José.

"FUCK ME!" Enrique yells at his father. "All went to plan?? I watched two men have their brains blown out and five more shot up like Swiss cheese!!! That's your fucking idea of a plan?!!" Enrique is unable to control his temper any longer. Picking up a crystal vase from a side table, he hurls it at the opposite wall; shards of glass crackle and clink as they cascade down to the dark wood floor. He's red with rage. "HOW THE FUCK IS THAT TO PLAN?!"

"Enrique, calm down… please… I'm trying to explain?" José attempts to be the voice of reason.

"NO!! I WILL NOT CALM THE FUCK DOWN!!" He rages at his father. Then he points at Manolo, "I drove this poor guy out to Stiltsville for these two fuckers to beat the shit out of him." He points back and forth between Gutiérrez and Ziv.

Manolo turns to Enrique. "It's OK... it was for the greater good," he says, trying to pacify the situation.

"NO!! No, it wasn't for the greater good! Fuck's sake! How can you rationalize what's happened to you as being acceptable? Nobody deserves to have that happen to them." He turns sharply to his father. "Who the fuck are you, dad? This isn't the act of a sane and rational man... the man that I call my father." Enrique looks at José with complete disgust.

"I am still your father," José manages with his voice trembling.

"Really?" Enrique can't control himself. He's never spoken to his dad this way ever, but this really isn't the man he knew as his father. He just wants this over so he can get the fuck out of there. "Just get on with it... tell me the rest of your fucked up, disgusting story," Enrique exclaims, brushing the dust off his suit from the meeting that turned into a warzone at the bay earlier. He has no idea why he's remotely worried about how he looks at this moment in time, but he keeps doing it anyway.

"Ziv had to take out anyone that was there so that nobody knew my true identity. Once Manolo had told you who I was in front of his men, he had signed their death warrants. Until that point, they only knew me as José Cruz... a man with money, money they needed. Manolo took his beating like the man that he is... he waited until the right time to pretend that he would turn on La Espada. He had already explained to his wife and kids what may happen to them because of everything, and for that, they have all been well-compensated," José explains.

Enrique stops him in his tracks and looks in disbelief at José. "Fuck me... how can you act like this is just normal? Seven men dead just to keep your identity a secret? People's families kidnapped? You're fucking insane!" he snaps, shaking his head.

"No one could be left alive knowing my true identity that I couldn't trust. Manolo returned back to La Espada to explain that he'd kidnapped me... but I'd put up a fight... this explained the state he was in... and he also informed him that you wanted to make a deal." José pauses for a second. "The D.E.A. busted their warehouse in Tallahassee, and La Espada was desperate for product but short of cash to make the purchase. So, on your behalf, Gutiérrez attempted to broker a deal. Little did we know just how desperate La Espada was and that he had no intention of working out a negotiation with Gutiérrez. He decided to use me to leverage money out of you for a buy from his own supplier... the supplier offered him a deal that was too good to pass up, but he still needed the funds to be able to purchase the cocaine."

Enrique listens to his father, struggling to believe what he's done.

"La Espada's greed was his undoing. He used my kidnapping to get the funds from you to make the buy. But his arrogance forced him to be there in person... he wanted to make it look like he was the mastermind behind all of this... plus his ego would never allow someone else to take the acclaim... I knew all of this already... I know that piece of shit better than he knows himself... and he played right into my hands." José can't help but allow a smug smile to spread across his face. "That gave us the opportunity for me to get my revenge." José seems so confident in his reasoning that this all makes sense. "La Espada contacted his supplier and managed to arrange a shipment earlier than we'd expected. This made things a little more complicated... but the plan was adapted. Manolo and I set about arranging a new course of action," José says, looking across the room at Manolo before looking back to Enrique. "Things were playing out perfectly until you called the D.E.A. and got them involved with everything. I had hoped you would have trusted Gutiérrez and Ziv to deal with this." José's tone has turned a little; he's beginning to sound disappointed with how Enrique handled himself.

"Oh, well, excuse me for fucking up your crazy plan for revenge." Enrique snaps back at his father. "I was at a loss for what to do. As a law-abiding citizen... to me, it made perfect sense to go to the

D.E.A. about it all. But you wouldn't know about that, would you?" Enrique snipes back at them. He points at Gutiérrez and Ziv. "Everything these two lunatics kept doing was getting people beaten up or killed. That is not my life, the way I want to live or what I want to be involved in," Enrique scolds back at his father. "I went along with their way until Kristie's apartment was ransacked, and someone left a message threatening her and our baby!"

José's face drops. Kristie is like the daughter that he's never had, even when she and Enrique broke up. He turns to Gutiérrez, Manolo, and Ziv with a look of agonizing disgust. "You never told me about any of this... the break in... that they had threatened her life?"

"That was me." Manolo pipes up. "I did it to keep her away from her apartment... she was safer with Enrique, so I had to think fast... I wanted to make it bad enough that she would leave and go back to the penthouse... so we could keep her safe... keep them in one place... so I made it look like her apartment had been broken into...."

Before José can say anything else, Enrique steps in. "It isn't their fault. This is your fault! Are you crazy?" He's glad to notice that José hasn't reacted to the baby news. He obviously didn't hear everything he said; the break in must've thrown him off. "Don't go blaming them when you're the reason all of this happened in the first place! Don't go deflecting your shit on to them! You know this is all your doing!" He snipes. "I contacted the D.E.A. because it was all spiraling out of control. I trusted their way, and it was getting us nowhere." He points at Ziv and Gutiérrez again. "I had to go to the D.E.A. when they threatened the love of my life! You were lucky I didn't tell them about your alleged involvement in drugs... the reason I didn't was because I couldn't believe that it was true." Enrique stops himself from mentioning the baby again. He tells himself, right now, I don't even know if I want José in my life, let alone having him in my baby's life.

"I really am sorry about Kristie...." José begins; his face is full of regret.

"I don't want your fucking apologies." Enrique interjects, cutting his father off mid-sentence.

José looks back at his son with a downcast expression, before continuing to explain the rest of what happened. "Luckily, we know a few people in the D.E.A., and they reached out to me via Ziv. In some respects, it worked in our favor. It was them that took out La Espada, not me. To his people, that would be an acceptable loss of life. Whereas if we'd have done it... it would have been all-out war." José can't help but raise a smile at the thought of La Espada's demise.

"No, no, no no! FUCK NO!" Enrique rages. "They shot him! Right in fucking front of me! If they hadn't been there, he would have killed me! He thought that I had double-crossed him when the first boat blew up! None of this is acceptable! I don't understand how you can think otherwise! How can putting my life at risk be acceptable to you? I could never do that to someone I love... or to anybody... and what you have put Kristie through is inexcusable! If anything had happened to her, they might as well have killed me too!"

"Your life was never at risk," José states, sounding a little arrogant.

"For fuck's sake, dad! What part of this are you not understanding? None of this is okay with me. I don't get how you're reasoning that this is all acceptable?" Enrique starts looking around as his rage is filling him again; his urge to lash out is getting all too much for him to control. As he looks around, he sees a photo with him and his mom, which is sitting on a side table not far from the photo of his parent's wedding day, which he was looking at just a few hours ago. Momentarily he feels foolish for feeling the way he did when he looked at the photo earlier when he first came back to the house. He can't help but feel relieved that his mom never got to see who José really is and never had to live through this nightmare. He's also grateful that she's been spared from the torturous heartache he is feeling; he knows she would have been devastated. Suddenly, he feels a sense of calm wash over him; she's always been a calming feature in his life.

"Just explain to me then. What happened in the bay? I mean, I saw it... I watched you get blown up!" Enrique wants this over with more than ever and has to get the fuck out of there. He just feels like he needs to know the details for closure, but he's beginning to feel nauseous, as the reality of who his father truly is, sickens him.

"That was the easy part, really." José unintentionally lets out a quiet chuckle. In his mind, he's dismissing Enrique's rage, like he's a child having a tantrum. "Once I'd discovered that you'd spoken to the D.E.A. I called Gutiérrez and explained everything that had happened to that point... then we went about undermining the agency's operation... we took control of the drug boat and sent in an empty replacement loaded with C4. Manolo was nice enough to let La Espada believe he had me on the sport fishing boat. When in fact, the people on the boat were some of my own men that had betrayed me."

"Hang on a second," Enrique interjects. "This is something that has confused me since the meeting. La Espada didn't seem to know exactly who you were?"

"That would be my doing also," Manolo answers. Enrique turns to face him. "I never told him your father was El Espectro, only that he was José Cruz. I suggested to La Espada that we could use your father to make you pay a hefty ransom... that way, we could buy our product and get back in business, and your father's life would be less at risk. I knew that whatever happened, your father would cover any financial loss to you. It was La Espada that decided to make you purchase the product for him, as he was too impatient and had commitments he needed to meet quickly."

"Oh well, as long as you had my finances protected, it must be OK," Enrique says sarcastically. He can't believe this guy. "It was never about the money... all I wanted was my father back alive." He shakes his head in disbelief. "So, during all of this, nobody actually knew my father's true identity... only that you had kidnapped a wealthy businessman?"

"That's correct," José states. Enrique turns back to face his father as he continues talking. "The men that betrayed me were paid to bring the sport fishing boat into the harbor. One wore a mask to look like me, and both acted out the required roles. Ziv then brought in the trawler with his own man. When Tuto came to check the drugs, we forced him at gunpoint to lie to La Espada that everything was OK. Then Ziv and his friend made a quick escape on his powerboat."

"Whoa whoa whoa! You killed two innocent men when you blew up the decoy boat you were allegedly on! You blew up Tuto on the fishing trawler! Does this insanity have no end to it?!" Enrique shouts, staring in shock at his father.

José shrugs his shoulders at Enrique. "Tuto was a casualty of war... he wasn't innocent by any stretch of the imagination... and the other two got what they deserved for betraying me. Ziv made off with the D.E.A.'s money, and we also still have La Espada's cocaine." José laughs at his own genius. "Gutiérrez came to pick up Manolo and me from my friend's yacht." He can't help but look pleased with himself; the gangster that he truly is, is rising to the surface. "Once the first boat exploded, it set the D.E.A. off against the cartel members... the second explosion meant that there would be no questions about me."

"Seriously, dad... how the hell are you going to explain to the D.E.A. that you're still alive? When as far as they're concerned, I watched you get blown up?" Enrique looks dumbfounded at his father.

José stands, looks around the room, and then back to Enrique. "I've decided it's time for me to retire from this life. So now, as far as the world is concerned, I am dead. I have already changed my identity and have purchased a new property in the Bahamas." He smiles. "You're always welcome to bring the boat over... bring Krissy along with you," he states with a smile like he actually believes it's a possibility.

"You crazy motherfucker!" Enrique's heard enough. "How the fuck do I explain to Kristie that my dead father's alive and well, sunning himself in the Bahamas under an assumed name? Oh, and we are welcome to visit anytime!" Enrique rages sarcastically at a shocked-looking José. "I'm done! Done with all of this!" He turns and heads toward the front door. Just about containing his rage, he turns back to his father and says with venom. "Consider me dead, José! Because to you, now I am!" He seethes, meaning every word. "I am disgusted with you and who you are! The man that I thought was my father doesn't exist in reality! He never did!" He screws his face up with revulsion. "Mom would be disgusted with who you are!"

The stinging pain of Enrique's scorching words is evident on his face; José can't believe what his son's saying to him.

"Don't fucking look at me like that." Enrique looks José up and down with repulsion. "You know I'm fucking right... no matter how much you try to justify any of this, you're wrong." His voice is low, but the venom is still oozing from his every word. "Mom's death was YOUR fault. I can see that now." His eyes narrow with repugnance. "YOU killed her. YOU are the reason she lost out on being a mother to me... to share happy moments... moments of joy... to enjoy the life she had ahead of her... YOU took it all away from her... from me... but at least she was spared from this... from seeing who you really are, you sick piece of shit!" He points. "What you failed to hear earlier was that I'm going to be a father."

José's face lights up a little through the searing agony he's feeling. "Enrique," he manages.

Enrique ignores him as he continues; his voice is still low. "The difference between you and me, José, is that I'm going to be a real father to my child... not a pretend father like I had growing up." His face is clouded with darkness and hatred for the man in front of him. "You will never be a part of my child's life... not ever. All of this has proved to me that you are no better than the man you say killed my mom. I want nothing to do with you ever again. You're a cold, heartless, and uncaring man who deserves to be alone. Don't ever contact me... don't ever contact Kristie... and stay away from me and my family. You're dead to me!" Enrique's disgust toward his father is pouring out of his every word; disgust combined with anger and bitter disappointment. And dare he even think it? Against everything he believes: he now hates him.

José stands staring at his son as tears begin to stream down his face. Gutiérrez, Ziv, and Manolo don't know where to look. They've never witnessed anyone talk to José like this, but they know Enrique would be the only person who would ever get away with it.

For José, reality is beginning to set in. He's pushed Enrique too far, pushed him away in his quest for revenge, and now he's lost his son and grandchild in the process.

"Enrique... please forgive me for what I have done," he crumples to his knees. "Please... please forgive me. I am so sorry. I can't lose you!"

"You lost me when you lied about your disgusting sordid secret life. If you had just walked away from everything... this would never have happened... if you'd hadn't been so full of yourself in that club that night and handled things better... mom would still be alive... we could all be here as a normal family... celebrating our new addition to our family... enjoying what should be a beautiful moment. But instead, you did what you did, and this is where it's gotten you... look at where it's gotten us. Your actions have robbed mom of her life and me of having her around. She would still be alive if it weren't for you! You make me fucking sick!" Enrique turns and heads to the front door. José gets up to go after him, pleading for his son to stop.

As Enrique approaches the front door, he hears a car pulling up outside. Opening the door, he sees Kristie stepping out of his blue Ferrari. His anger starts to fizzle away at the mere sight of her, but he shakes his head in disbelief. "Baby, I told you not to drive," he says to her, a little annoyed but so pleased to see her all the same.

She looks absolutely gorgeous, with her long, straight brunette hair flowing over her shoulders and down her back. She may be casually dressed, but she looks so beautifully graceful in a loose white t-shirt, skinny blue jeans, black Louboutin heels, large gold hoop earrings, and oversized black Wayfarers.

"Baby, I'm OK to drive... I wouldn't drive if I weren't, you know that," she says with reassurance. Enrique looks terrible. His custom-made blue suit is covered in dust and marks, and his eyes are red from crying. Just as Kristie's about to close the car door and begin to walk over to him and hold him in her arms, she's stopped entirely in her tracks; her jaw drops.

Just as Enrique's about to reply to Kristie, he notices the look of complete shock cross her face. Enrique turns to see José standing in the doorway. He doesn't stop walking; he keeps heading toward the car.

"He's alive, Enrique," Kristie says, full of relief but stunned by what she's seeing. "Enrique! Your father's alive!"

"I wish he were dead," Enrique mutters.

"Sorry... what did you say?" She didn't quite catch what he said.

"He's lied to me my whole life. He makes me sick. Please... can we just go?" Enrique says to her quietly, with complete sadness and disappointment, as he climbs into the passenger seat. He needs to get away from his father before he does something he'll regret. Although he's unhappy with Kristie driving at the moment, he sure as hell knows he's in no fit state to drive himself. He looks up through the open roof of the Ferrari, pleading with his girl, who is understandably dumbfounded by what's unfolding in front of her. "Please, baby... just get me out of here."

"Enrique, what's wrong? Talk to me... what's going on?" Kristie asks, seriously concerned for Enrique. His father's alive, and she thought he'd be happy. But then it dawns on her; if he's saying José's lied to him the whole time... he must be who they feared he was. Oh no! This is heartbreaking, Kristie thinks to herself. After everything he's gone through.

"Baby, just get me out of here... please... I'll explain everything when we get home," Enrique begs of her again.

"OK, babe," Kristie says, still in shock. She can see how upset he is. Getting back into the Ferrari, she puts it into reverse and backs it up so she can head out of the driveway. Putting the car into drive, she begins to accelerate away. Looking in the rearview mirror, she can see José chasing the car down the driveway; he looks distraught. "Enrique... your father." She stumbles over her words. "He's alive... what's going on?" she asks once they're through the gates and driving down Star Island Drive. She looks at Enrique, desperate for answers. As he turns to her, she can see the devastation on his face.

Tears fill his eyes as he says. "My father... the one I knew... the one I thought I knew?" He pauses for a second. "He's dead to me now."

Kristie looks at Enrique in absolute shock and disbelief; she's speechless. She's figured out the basics of what's happened, from what he's just told her; this is something she prayed would not become a reality.

Not being able to find her words, she takes Enrique's hand and holds it tightly, letting him know she's there for him.

"You and our little baby are all I care about now," Enrique says, squeezing her hand back. He knows this is a lot for her to take in, and he will explain everything once they get back to Alta Vita.

Kristie manages to acknowledge what Enrique has just said with a tiny smile and a nod. She feels devastated for him. But she knows that together, they will get through anything life will throw at them. Glancing in the rearview mirror again, Kristie can see José still running toward them down the road. She looks back to Enrique; he's seen José too. "Keep going," he says.

And with that, she doesn't say another word and accelerates off the island, onto the causeway, and out of José's life forever.

Epilogue

Sitting poolside at their secluded island home in tranquil Manatee Bay, Enrique feels eternally blessed for how things in his life have changed in the last twelve months or so. Less than a week after what happened with his father and with the D.E.A.'s clearance, Enrique whisked Kristie off to the Maldives on their private jet and proposed to her. It was everything he had imagined and more.

They stayed at the Sanchester private island, and it was spectacular. On the evening of the proposal, Enrique took Kristie to one of the hotel bars at the main resort while the house was being prepared for the special moment. When they returned, Enrique walked Kristie along a pathway made of white rose petals, which was lined with white candles. The path led to the pool deck, which was also covered in rose petals and candles. Kristie's face was full of delight, as she had no idea he was going to propose; she thought they were there on a much-needed vacation.

On the deck, they had the most delicious meal under the stars; it was so romantic. After dinner, Enrique got down on one knee and proposed to Kristie, and of course, she said yes. The ring was from Tiffany's, and the diamond was flawless. The evening was full of tears of happiness, love, and excitement for the future.

The following month they got married; they wanted to get married as soon as possible. It was what they both wanted, and Kristie didn't want to be showing too much of a bump in her wedding dress. They decided on an intimate sunset beach wedding, and it was just perfect.

The doctor was still happy for Kristie to fly, so they flew to Bora Bora, got married, and honeymooned in a private villa estate at the Sanchester hotel. Kristie's parents were so happy for them, and they were more than willing to give their blessing and offered to arrange the most glorious celebration for them upon their return; of course, Kristie and Enrique agreed.

The wedding was simple and elegant. There was no fuss, no dancers, no over-the-top decorations, they even asked if the marriage Officiant could wear just a white shirt and pants, and he gladly agreed. Even Enrique didn't wear a suit! It was just the two of them, on the beach making their promises to each other, under the colorful painted sky at sunset, just the way they wanted it. They both wore white, Kristie's dress was by Vera Wang, and of course, she looked a dream.

It was pure bliss. They enjoyed delicious food, soaked up the sun, swam with the fantastic marine life, and made love over and over again. They felt so lucky and grateful that they got to travel to such incredible places, especially in the space of just under two months.

Bouncing his baby boy Alex on his knee, Enrique smiles with pure happiness. He feels so blessed; it's like he's living in a dream. The couple has decided to take a year off from work and away from the city. Kristie promoted her assistant at the spa to manager, and as part of the package, Colette is living in Kristie's South Beach condo.

What Enrique did with Cruz Construction Inc. was similar, but he still does a little work from his office at home. Guillermo has a family and wanted to stay living where he was, so Enrique gave him a significant pay rise to compensate for the extra workload, plus a little more to show Guillermo his gratitude. This has turned out well as he now realizes it's good to keep the penthouse, so when he and Kristie go to the city, they have somewhere central to stay.

He watches Gabriela and Leon play in the pool with her four children and starts talking to his son. "Who knew this would be how my life would turn out," he says to Alex, who is sitting on his knee giggling and gurgling. "Your daddy feels so lucky... so lucky to have you...." he smiles at his baby boy and kisses the top of his head.

Kristie approaches them from behind and leans down to kiss Enrique on the cheek. Moving around to face them, she kisses Alex's head. "My gorgeous boys," she smiles, stroking Alex's hair. "Babe, please can you hold Sofía while I finish up?" She asks sweetly.

"Of course, babe."

"How's my beautiful girl?" He asks Sofía, kissing his baby daughter, as he takes her from Kristie.

"Thanks, babe," Kristie says, kissing Enrique on the lips before heading back to the kitchen. Enrique's eyes follow Kristie as she walks back inside. She's so incredibly beautiful, even more so after she gave birth to their precious twins. The love he feels for Kristie and their babies grows more and more each day. He never knew it was possible to love this way. He would do anything for them. They're his world; his family.

He still has thoughts from time to time about his father, and he can't understand how he could do what he did to his wife and son. It's unimaginable to Enrique, especially now that he's a father himself.

In the eyes of the world, José Cruz had died in the explosion. After the conversation they had together at his home, Enrique hasn't heard from him since. He's spoken at length with the D.E.A. during follow-up interviews, outlining his father's involvement in the Los Fantasmas Cartel and his role as El Espectro. Although there's no evidence to go on, Enrique felt it necessary to be completely honest with the D.E.A. about what he knew. He explained to them that his father was still alive and relayed the conversation that they had together at José's mansion.

It's true, he does feel remorse for notifying the authorities about José, even if it was the right thing to do; he's still his father at the end of the day, but he had no choice. He had to protect himself and his family from any repercussions. He would never live with himself if anything came back to haunt them; plus, he needed to be honest with the authorities so they could move on properly as a family.

Thankfully, although Enrique had bought Cruz Construction Inc. from his father nearly ten years ago, it had been exonerated from any cartel involvement when in José's name. As it would appear after a deep check by the D.E.A., José had at least made the company the success it was, through hard work and determination, rather than by laundering drug money through the business.

To this day, José has never been found, and his participation in the cartel remains unproven, but he's still a Person of Interest to the authorities, and the search for him continues.

While time is said to be a great healer, Enrique still feels a great deal of pain and betrayal for what his father put him through. One day, maybe he will forgive him, but for now, life is good, and he doesn't want to dwell on the pain of the past.

Looking at Leon playing in the pool, he feels blessed that his dear friend is clean after spending six months in rehab. He now lives in a condo near Kristie and Enrique's house in Manatee Bay. Enrique rented the condo for him as he feels it will be good for him to get away from the city for a while. He's about to start studying to become a professional drug and addiction therapist, taking his part-time job at Enrique's center to a more serious level.

In the past, Leon had met Gabriela a few times at the penthouse; they always liked each other and got on really well. Then one evening, at one of Kristie and Enrique's BBQs, they got together and have been dating ever since. They're so good together, and her kids love him, too. Leon finally has a sense of family, and it's working wonders for him.

Gabriela was cautious because of Leon's addiction issues, especially with the kids, but Leon is doing great. It's like the family environment is good for him; it's exactly what he was missing. This makes Enrique so proud and happy for him. Leon's such a great guy with a massive heart, but unfortunately, that heart had been broken many times, but he's slowly put it back together again and is moving on with his life.

The doorbell chimes.

"I've got it," Kristie hollers from the kitchen.

"Thank you, baby," Enrique replies as he holds the twins.

"Where is he? Where's the birthday boy?" Enrique can hear Sánchez bellowing from the front of the house. "Damn, bro, she's got you well trained!" Sánchez teases his friend laughing loudly as he steps out onto the pool deck.

"Hey man, I love this," Enrique says enthusiastically with a smile, getting up to greet his friends. Kristie and Enrique decided not to have a nanny; they're more than happy to experience everything that comes with having the babies. When they go on date nights, which isn't often, Kristie's parents look after the twins, and they love it; they absolutely adore spending as much time as they can with their grandbabies.

"Come here, Alex... come to your Uncle Rico!" Sánchez scoops Alex from Enrique's arms.

"Happy birthday, bro!" García says to Enrique, smiling at the twins and pulling funny faces at them. They smile back and giggle.

The three men shake hands before Enrique carefully passes Sofía to Carlos. Sánchez is making silly noises to Alex and telling him how cute he is while rocking him from side to side.

"You be careful with my babies... I know what you two are like," Enrique playfully warns.

They roll their eyes at the overprotective father that is their best friend and laugh.

Gabriela and Leon are drying the kids by the pool. "I'm just going to help Kristie," Gabriela says to Leon.

"Gabriela, it's your day off... please... relax and enjoy yourself. I'll go help her," Enrique says sweetly before he walks toward the house. He wants to help his wife, who's putting the finishing touches on the food they prepared together earlier. They're having a small party to celebrate Enrique's birthday today, before a much larger gathering tomorrow at Enrique's grandparents' restaurant where all his family and friends will attend.

Enrique walks into the kitchen and sneaks up behind Kristie, wrapping his arms around her waist. She giggles as she feels his arms around her. "Hmmm... that giggle still gets me every time." He teases as he kisses her cheek, "What can I do to help, babe?"

Kristie turns around and faces Enrique, draping her arms around his neck, and says. "Aww, thanks, babe," she kisses him on the lips softly. "The food on those plates is ready to be put on the grill," she says, gesturing over to the kitchen island.

The house interior isn't dissimilar to the penthouse. The house itself is a white modern design, with an art deco flair, which overlooks the tropical waters. The large rectangular pool has pale blue mosaic tiles which glisten in the sun, and the garden is full of luscious exotic plants and palm trees. At night it looks so beautiful when it's lit up, just like the pool deck at the penthouse. And Kristie and Enrique make use of it the same way they do at Alta Vita.

Although they have twins, things are still hotter than ever between them. They still can't get enough of each other, just like always, but now, although they didn't think it was possible, they love each other even more, and things are getting better and better between them. Right now, they're closer than they have ever been.

Just as Enrique goes to pick up the plates to take outside, the doorbell rings again, and Kristie goes to answer it.

"Oh my God, babe! You look amazing!" Lisa squeals with excitement as she sees Kristie, then gives her a hug.

"So, do you, babe... I love your dress," Kristie replies, hugging her friend back. "It's so good to see you."

"It's so good to see you too." They break away from their embrace. "Where are they? Where are those precious babies?" Lisa asks, jumping up and down with even more excitement. She's arrived with Mario and Gustavo, who are both impeccably dressed as always. They also greet Kristie with hugs as they shower her with compliments; Kristie and her friends are always so positive and uplifting with each other.

"They're out on the pool deck with Carlos and Rico." Kristie smiles as they all head through the house and outside. As her friends are greeting the others and swooning over the twins, Kristie looks over at Enrique, who is grilling the food on the barbeque. She loves him so much, and he's the best husband and father she could ever ask for.

They have already decided to try for another baby next year, and they can't wait to welcome another child into their family. Her thoughts bring a smile to her face. Enrique's come so far. He's been going to therapy regularly, but it's more to deal with what happened with his father, to try to be at peace with it all. Ever since that night when he told her everything, he's been wide open to her, and she can't be more grateful for the way things have turned out. He has a few moments where he seems alone with his thoughts, but that's to be expected; he's been through so much.

Looking down at her wedding and engagement rings, she smiles at the memory of two of the best days of her life, another being the birth of their twins. Enrique had planned the most perfect proposal, and their wedding was so intimate and romantic. The day their twins were born was so special and full of love and happiness, and Enrique was so attentive throughout the whole pregnancy and the birth; he looked after her every step of the way, she couldn't have asked for more.

As Enrique cooks the food on the grill, he stops for a moment and looks around at his beautiful wife, their gorgeous babies, and all of their friends. He finds himself smiling widely, feeling so blessed and grateful all over again. Turning back to the grill, he checks on the food before looking up to the sky.

"I love you, mom." He whispers. "I promise to always make you proud... I just wish you were here to enjoy times like this with us."

And almost like she's read his mind, Kristie puts her arms around his waist and reaches up to kiss his cheek tenderly before whispering, "Babe... your mom, is always with you... in your heart... and she's so, so proud of you."

Made in the USA
Middletown, DE
10 March 2023

26505724R00230